Everything about him spoke working cowboy.

From the frayed cuffs of the denim jacket to the scuffed, slant-heeled cowboy boots, crossed indolently over each other.

Sheryl's mind raced, trying to place him. He was obviously new in town. He pushed his hat back and looked her way. His eyes held her—steel grey and piercing. She couldn't seem to look away and she didn't even realize he had moved until he was almost in front of her.

"Are you Sheryl Kyle?" he asked.

"Yes," she replied hesitantly. "What do you want?"

"I'm here to bring you home."

CAROLYNE AARSEN

has been writing stories almost as long as she has been reading them, and has wanted to write a book for most of her life. When she could finally write "The End" on her first, she realized, to her dismay, that it wasn't. Three rewrites later turned it into a book that was finally marketable. What she learned along the way was to write a story that was true to what she believed and was the kind of book she liked to read.

Her writing stems from her life's experiences. Living in a tiny cabin with five children in remote British Columbia, opening their home to numerous foster children, helping her husband build the house they now live in, working with their cattle on their ranch in northern Alberta—all become fodder for yet more stories to come.

Carolyne hopes her writing will show that our Christian life is a growing, changing relationship with God and a constant fight with our own weakness. Thankfully, God keeps taking us back.

Homecoming
Carolyne Aarsen

Published by Steeple Hill Books™

STEEPLE HILL BOOKS

Steeple
Hill™

ISBN 0-373-87024-8

HOMECOMING

Even the sparrow has found a home, and the swallow a nest for herself...a place near your altar, Oh Lord Almighty....

—Psalm 84:3

To Richard;
my husband, my critic,
my inspiration, my friend.

Chapter One

Mark tugged on the brim of his hat, and shoved open the dented metal door.

Noise poured out like a wave, pulsating, raucous, the air heavily laced with the smell of smoke. He stepped inside squinting in the dim light as the door shut behind him. Not for the first time that day he wished he could head back to Sweet Creek and tell Ed he simply couldn't find her.

Then he remembered the feel of Ed's fingers clutching his and the entreaty in his eyes. Mark was too close to quit. With a glance around the semidarkness, he worked his way through the crowded room to an empty table and dropped into the chair, scanning the crowd.

Half an hour ago, he had tracked Sheryl's address down to a dingy apartment block, three miles from here. No one was home but the policeman parked across the road had recognized the picture Mark had shown him and sent him here.

A slim-figured girl approached the bar, carrying an empty tray. A long swath of blond hair hung down her back almost to the waistband of a tight, short skirt. Mark peered through the haze trying to get a better look at her.

"What'll you have?" Another waitress stood in front of him, tray tucked under one arm, her hand shoving her frizzy red hair out of her face.

The question took him by surprise. He only wanted to ask a few questions but he would probably be less conspicuous if he looked like a customer.

"I'll have a beer."

She quirked a bored eyebrow up. "Really?"

"That one," Mark amended, pointing to a name that flashed blue and white behind the bar. It *had* been a while since he'd been in a bar.

The red-haired waitress returned quickly and set a frosted bottle and glass on the table, then waited to be paid.

"Does Sheryl Kyle work here?" Mark asked pulling out his wallet.

The girl eyed him with distrust. "Why?" she asked handing him his change.

Mark pulled out a worn picture, seeking to allay her suspicions. "I'm from Sweet Creek, B.C. She used to live there with Ed Krickson, her stepfather."

The waitress glanced at the picture. "I'll see if I can find her," she said with a shrug.

Mark sat back. *Please, Lord, let this work,* he thought, the irony of praying in a bar making him smile.

But he needed all the prayers he could send out. He needed to get back to the ranch and he knew if he came without Sheryl, Ed would lose all will to live.

"Two pilsners and two ale."

Sheryl gave her order to the bartender and leaned on the bar. She eased her aching feet out of her two-inch-high heels. Dave, her boss, thought they made his waitresses look alluring.

Sheryl wiggled her toes, relishing the soothing coolness of the hard cement floor, hoping the guys she had shouldered past to put in her order wouldn't step on her feet with their heavy work boots.

She wished she could relieve the pounding in her head that was keeping time with the resonant bass of the jukebox, pouring out its unintelligible tales of heartache and woe. The habitual haze of cigarette smoke hung in a grayblue pall over the rowdy patrons competing with the music.

Friday and payday for the municipal workers had customers lined two-deep at the bar, flirting, making noise and wasting time.

The bartender pushed the frosted bottles toward her, Sheryl slipped the beers onto the tray. With a tired sigh, she wriggled her swelling feet back into her shoes, and turned almost bumping into Tory.

"Sheryl, you're a brat," the other waitress said, her tray making a metallic clatter as she dropped it on the wet bar.

"You're the one that just about dumped my order," Sheryl groused, ignoring the complaints from the men beside her as she balanced her tray.

"You've been holding out on me," Tory continued, hanging well over the bar to take a quick drag off a cigarette that lay smoldering in an ashtray out of their boss's sight. She tossed Sheryl a sidelong glance.

"What do you mean?" Sheryl looked around, hoping Dave didn't notice either her lingering or Tory's smoking.

"There's this absolute hunk of a guy asking for you." Tory fluttered her eyelashes.

"By name?"

"He asked for a Sheryl Kyle." Tory took another quick puff and stubbed her cigarette out. "He knows everything…" Tory grinned at Sheryl's shocked look. "Just kidding. Said you used to live in Sweet Creek, British Columbia. Showed me a picture." Tory lifted one plucked eyebrow expectantly.

"What did he want?" Sheryl ignored Tory's obvious

curiosity, stifling a rising clutch of panic. Sweet Creek hadn't been a part of her life for seven years. "Is anyone with him?"

"Drinking alone." Tory pouted at Sheryl's reticence, her lipstick faded away to a thin, red outline. "Actually sitting alone. He hasn't popped the top off the beer yet. Asked if you could talk to him."

"Where is he?"

Tory raised a hand to point, and Sheryl grabbed it.

"Don't do that," she said. "I want a better look at him first. Just tell me where he's sitting."

"By the west wall, toward the back exit. Can't miss the honey. He's the only one with a cowboy hat." Tory leveled a serious glance at her. "You in trouble?"

"I'm just being careful."

"So what are you going to do?"

"Nothing until I scope him out."

Sheryl lifted the tray of drinks and, working her way through the jumble of tables, managed an occasional glance over her shoulder. A cowboy hat shouldn't be too hard to spot amongst all the baseball caps and bare heads.

By the time she delivered the drinks, her customers were growling. She flashed them her best smile and took a few moments to laugh with them. She managed to sidestep one customer's hand and pocket his cash in one fluid movement, smiling all the while. No easy feat considering the snug fit of her skirt.

As she looked up, she saw him.

All that showed beneath the brim of the battered cowboy hat were the narrow line of his lips, the clean sweep of his jaw. Dark brown hair hung well over the collar of a faded denim jacket that sat easily on broad shoulders.

Everything about him spoke of working cowboy. From the frayed cuffs of the denim jacket to the jeans that sculpted his long, lean legs stretched out in front of him and the scuffed, slant-heeled cowboy boots, crossed indolently over each other.

He was nursing a beer, not really drinking, just holding it and looking as out of place in this bar as a horse would in the parking lot outside.

Sheryl's mind raced, trying to place him. Definitely not one of Jason Kyle's buddies or a cop. He was too relaxed to be either.

He pushed his hat back and looked her way. Dark brows ran in a straight line across his forehead, not quite meeting over the bridge of a long, narrow nose. But it was his eyes that held her—steel gray and piercing.

She swallowed and took a step backward.

"Kyle!" Dave's all-too-familiar voice bellowed from behind her. "Get moving or you're history, babe."

Sheryl gritted her teeth at her boss's comments, pitched, as usual, three decibels higher than the jukebox.

He stood beside her now, heavyset and domineering, his cologne overpowering the smell of cigarette smoke and liquor. Sheryl could tell by the set of his bulldog jaw he felt edgy. "I've got thirsty customers and you're just standing there holding that tray like it was a rosary," he growled. "One more slipup and you're gone."

"Sorry, Dave." She eased away from him, knowing she was treading on thin ice. She knew it would take only one more infinitesimal misjudgment on her part and she would be out of a job. Much as she hated the work, it paid the rent and covered the costs of her classes.

"I asked to talk to Sheryl. That's why she wasn't serving anyone." Now holding his hat, the stranger stood in front of them, a hint of contempt in his deep voice.

"Who are you?" Dave turned on the cowboy. "I didn't know there was a rodeo in town."

"Neither did I." The man smiled, set his hat on a nearby table and pulled out his wallet. "I just need a few moments of Sheryl's time." He handed Dave a folded bill.

Dave glanced at it, then with a leer chucked Sheryl under the chin. "Five minutes, Kyle." He shoved the money in his pocket.

Unconsciously Sheryl wiped her face, then turned on the cowboy, feeling cheap and humiliated. "Who do you think you are, paying him for my time?"

"I wanted him out of the way for a while," the dark stranger interrupted. "I figured he would understand a nice crisp bill."

"I don't need to talk to you." She turned to go.

"It's about your stepfather, Ed."

Sheryl stopped, feeling like he had just doused her with ice water.

"Are you coming?" he continued, retrieving his hat. "Your boss is checking his watch."

"I don't even know who you are." Sheryl found her voice again, shock making her movements automatic. She followed him to his table. He didn't look like anyone she'd ever met in the eight years she'd lived in Sweet Creek, British Columbia.

"Sorry." He glanced around at the seedy bar, laying his hat on the table beside his beer. "I didn't think formal introductions would be necessary. I'm Mark Andrews, partner and brother-in-law of your stepbrother, Nate. Your stepfather sent me because he didn't think you'd talk to Nate." He pulled out a letter, unfolded it and handed it to her.

Sheryl took it, her hands trembling. Though the spidery handwriting wandered across the unlined page, it was unmistakably Ed's.

Swallowing, she slowly sat down, laying the creased paper on the table. What did he want, after all this time? And why send a personal messenger after so many silent years? "How did you manage to find me?" she asked finally.

Mark sat down across from her and laid a photograph on the table beside the letter. "Ed gave me this old picture of you. I knew you lived in Edmonton, and I had a few prayers on my side.'' Mark leaned forward, spinning the beer bottle between his fingers, his eyes on her. ''I found your place by eliminating all the other Kyles. The policeman parked across from your apartment was very helpful. I guess he comes here once in a while.''

''So what do you want?''

He toyed with the bottle some more. ''Do you and your husband have any children?''

''Why?''

''I was wondering if you were able to travel.''

''Why do I need to do that?''

''Do you answer all questions with another question?'' he asked, his voice tight.

''Depends who's asking.'' Sheryl glanced pointedly at her watch. ''Look, I really hate this place, and I really hate this job, but I don't want to lose it. I'd appreciate it if you would tell me what Ed wants.''

Mark looked up at her, his gaze level. A thin thread of fear spiraled through her when she met his steely eyes.

''Would your husband mind if you went away for a while?''

''Jason's dead.'' Sheryl twisted her watch around her wrist. The harshness of those two clipped words jolted her again. The sorrow she'd felt at Jason's death had been eclipsed by relief as she walked away from his grave.

''What about children?''

''No kids,'' she answered shortly. ''Now could you please tell me what you really came all this way for?''

Mark hesitated, pushed his beer around his hat and, just when Sheryl was about to get up, he spoke. ''Ed's been hospitalized for a stroke. He's been asking for you constantly.''

The mighty Ed Krickson felled by a stroke?

Sheryl blinked, staring past him, dredging up her last memory of Ed. He had stood on the porch as Jason had thrown her suitcase in the back of his battered old pickup.

Ed's arms had been crossed tightly over his broad chest, eyes narrowed, saying nothing. What else could have been added to the yelling that had reverberated through the house every time Sheryl had stepped out of the door, every time she'd dressed up, every time she'd ignored him and his dire imprecations of spiritual ruin for the previous eight years?

Sheryl had only glanced once at him as she'd gotten in beside Jason, then turned her head resolutely ahead as they'd driven away. Nothing held her in Sweet Creek anymore. Her mother lay in a grave. The prospect of living with Ed and the constant judgment of a God so different from her natural father's teachings had sent her on a one-way trip with the only person brave enough to stand up to Ed—Jason Kyle, the valley's wild child.

And now his partner said Ed had been asking for her. She had thought she'd been cut out of the Krickson family, possibly even erased out of the family Bible.

"Kyle," Dave's nasal voice pierced her memories. "Time's up."

Sheryl pulled her thoughts to the present. "Look, I'm really touched he still remembers who I am." Sheryl stood, taking her tray with her. "But somehow between then and now, I don't really care what Ed Krickson needs or wants anymore."

"I said time's up, missy." Dave stood beside her, his narrow eyes almost impaling her.

"I'm coming already," she snapped.

"Ed is dying, Sheryl." Mark's deep voice didn't go up a single decibel, but as his words registered they fairly roared in Sheryl's ears.

She turned to face this long, tall, stranger, her tray hanging at her side, questions tumbling through her mind.

"Kyle, if you don't get a move on, you've had it."

She whirled on Dave, her voice tight with mixed emotions and confusion. "Just lay off for a bit."

"I wouldn't use that tone with me, missy." Dave leaned

closer pressing a nicotine-stained finger against her forehead.

Sheryl slapped his hand away. Dave's face registered shock, his hand flew back, and instinctively Sheryl flinched, her tray clattering to the floor, her arm raised.

As soon as she did, she felt foolish. Dave wouldn't dare hit her in front of his customers.

She dropped her arm in time to see Mark put his hand on Dave's shoulder. "Leave her alone," he said quietly. Dave spun around, his face twisted with anger.

"Get out, jerk." Dave pushed Mark away.

Sheryl didn't know what happened next. She saw Dave stumble, take a step back, then fall heavily to the floor.

Fight she thought, seeing anger on Mark's face.

Sheryl straightened, self-preservation kicking in. At the rear of the building an exit sign's red glow caught her eye. Sheryl ran, reached the door, whacked her hands against the metal bar and slipped out into the cool night air. She fell against the brick wall, eyes closed, adrenaline still coursing through her. Her breath came in quick gasps as her anger grew.

It was a sure bet she would be hitting the unemployment office again, she thought, clenching her fists, banging them once against the hard edges of the brick wall. She wished she could use them on any guy that happened within five feet of her right.

The door opened again, the uproar of voices inside the bar pouring out, getting cut off as the metal door slammed shut.

She got her wish. It was Mark Andrews.

"You okay?" His voice registered concern.

"What do you care?" She glared at him. "Thanks to you I just lost the last job in Edmonton. You're such a guy." She shoved her hands in her pocket. She still had the crumpled bills and odd change from her last three orders. Her purse inside held slightly more.

Mark stood in front of her, his stance easy but wary. The light from the street lamp cast his angular features into shadow. "He was going to hit you."

"Are you kidding? Dave prefers more serious threats, like firing me." Sheryl shivered, her satin shirt offering scant warmth in the cool of the evening.

Sheryl pushed herself away from the wall. "Thanks to you I don't even dare go back inside to get my purse and coat."

"I'll get them for you."

"I wouldn't recommend it. The lion's den would be tame compared to what Dave will be like if he sees you again. You embarrassed him." Sheryl dragged a hand over her face. She didn't want to think about the implications of losing her job and her purse with her last few dollars still inside.

The door opened again and Sheryl jumped. Mark, she noticed lifted his hands slightly, as if ready.

Tory slipped through the narrow opening, carrying a coat.

"I heard Dave muttering as he walked over that this was it, he was canning you. I thought I would cover for you and grabbed your things." Tory handed Sheryl her coat, purse and running shoes, glancing over her shoulder as the door closed behind her. "He's pretty ticked. I wouldn't go back in there if I were you." She turned to Mark and winked at him. "Why didn't you deck him?"

"I don't waste my time with guys like him," Mark said.

Sheryl frowned. He didn't fight with Dave? That was a first. "Don't blame you. He'd probably sue."

Tory snorted. She turned to Sheryl, her face suddenly melancholy. "And you, hon, what are you going to do?"

Sheryl shrugged, not wanting to voice her own fears. Instead she bent over, yanked off the high heels and slipped her feet into her old, comfortable running shoes. "Hit the employment office again."

"It's payday today, I'll get your cheque and mail it to you."

"If Dave lets you." Sheryl picked up the offending shoes and, with a crooked grin, wound up and threw them as far as she could. A moment of silence, then they clattered against a metal Dumpster. Sheryl turned back to Tory, ignoring Mark's surprised look.

Tory laid a hand on Sheryl's arm. Sheryl instinctively pulled back, and Tory gave her a sad smile. "I would love to see a sparkle in those pretty green eyes someday."

"I'll be okay." Sheryl felt a rush of thankfulness for her friend, feeling sorry at her reaction to Tory's touch, and then forced herself to lean over to give her friend a hug. "Thanks for being around. There aren't many like you."

Tory clasped her hands between hers and from the expression on her face, Sheryl could see that she had caught her off guard.

"You're full of surprises, Sheryl Kyle." She smiled and squeezed her hands. "If you need a place…"

"I paid my rent for two months, so I'm okay for a while." Sheryl bit her lip, trying to quell the unexpected tears that threatened. Tory was rough, hard edged but generous to a fault. "You better get back."

Tory stretched up and pulled a card out of her pocket. "My man Mike was talking to one of his customers in the garage, a lawyer. He was complaining that his secretary's quitting in two weeks." Tory handed the card to Sheryl with a shrug. "You said you worked in an office before, so I thought it would be worth a try."

Sheryl took the grease-stained business card. She didn't know if she could wait a couple of weeks, but tucked the card in her purse anyway.

"Well. I better get back. I can't afford to lose this job, either, at least not until we got our down payment for Mike's business together." Tory hesitated, then caught

Sheryl in a hug. "I have a good feeling about this hunk," she murmured in Sheryl's ear. "Be nice to him."

Tory pulled away, grinned at Mark, then slipped back inside.

Avoiding his eyes, Sheryl put on her coat and drew her purse over her shoulder.

"I've been pushing my luck already," she said to Mark, glancing behind her. "I'd better get going."

She turned and walked away.

Mark caught up easily, his hands shoved in the pockets of his jean jacket.

"I hate to state the obvious, but what are you going to do now?" he asked.

"That isn't your concern," she replied curtly.

Ignoring him, Sheryl paused at the end of the alley, habit making her glance both ways down the sidewalk bordering the busy street that fronted the bar. A steady stream of semis, full and empty, lumbered past them interspersed with cars and light trucks.

The sun still hovered over what she could see of the horizon, and Sheryl steeled herself for the long walk home. She couldn't afford to waste her tip money on a bus ride tonight.

Mark still stood beside her, the slight evening breeze lifting his hair from the neck of his coat. She shot him a sideways glance, wishing he would leave.

"Sheryl," his deep voice was quiet. "What about Ed?"

All she wanted was her apartment, a hot bath and a nap. She didn't want to think about Ed, or her past.

He's dying.

The thought caught her up short. If Mark spoke the truth, then she needed to face Ed before that happened. She had too many questions that needed answers.

There's nothing for you here, her thoughts mocked her. She clutched her purse tighter, trying to think, to plan. But she was too tired. With a sigh that came from her aching heels, she slowly nodded her head.

"How long will I be gone?"

Mark lifted one broad shoulder. "That's up to you. Nate has a small cabin back of his place you can stay in if you want privacy."

Sheryl squinted at the traffic, not replying. Overhead a plane, engines screaming, dropped down, heading toward the airport across the road. Threaded through that sound was the screech of trains from the rail yard behind them. From the nether reaches of her mind came the picture of azure hills giving way to rugged mountains, the tantalizing image of deep woods, silent and waiting.

It hurt. She knew it would. That's why she kept those memories buried deep. At the mention of the cabin they had slowly spiraled to the surface.

It was to that cabin she used to retreat when she needed space and privacy. It was her private domain, and no one bothered her there. Ed had fixed it up for her, and Nate had helped. That was in the beginning, when things were still easy between them.

"I can pick you up first thing in the morning," Mark said, his voice a quiet sound that registered through the commotion of the city. "I've brought my truck."

Sheryl looked him over again. Tall, broad-shouldered, arrestingly attractive.

Unknown.

Would she be crazy to spend a day cooped up in a vehicle with him?

With a fatalistic shrug she nodded. What would be, would be. In her youth she believed in a God that watched over her, but experience had taught her differently. God had been conspicuously absent in her life in the past years. Dependence created instability. She had to make decisions for herself and live with the consequences.

"I'll be ready. Do you know where I live?"

He nodded. "Is six o'clock okay?"

"Sure." Sheryl kept her eyes averted, her long hair slipping loose from her ponytail, hiding her face. Then she turned with a fatalistic shrug.

"Sheryl, wait. I'll give you a ride," Mark called after her.

She didn't feel like spending any more time with him. Her stomach knotted up at the thought of seeing her stepfather, and she still shook after that business with Dave. But she faced an hour of walking before she was home, and if she was going to be spending the whole day with him tomorrow, a ten-minute drive could hardly be more dangerous. She stopped, shoved her hands in her pockets and followed him back to his truck.

He stood by a dusty, silver Ford, and when she came near he went ahead of her to the passenger door and opened it. Shooting him an oblique glance she shrugged and threw her purse in.

Mark sauntered around the front of the truck his fingers trailing on the hood.

One quick step onto the running board and a jump got her into the front seat before Mark opened his door. She tugged on her skirt trying to at least get it back over her thighs. As soon as she was home this particular piece of clothing was heading for the garbage bin.

She watched Mark as he got in the truck. As if aware of her scrutiny he returned her gaze. His gray eyes met hers, and a gentle smile hovered on his well-shaped mouth. He was entirely too handsome and too much of a puzzle.

She looked ahead as he turned the truck on and reversed, wondering again what she was getting tangled in. It had taken her three months after the accident to find another job, and it was only in the past few weeks that she felt as if her life was getting under her own control.

I shouldn't go, she thought, a shiver of apprehension skittering down her neck. It was as if life had caught her and dragged her back into its current. She felt propelled along a course, clinging to whatever happened to come by.

Drawing in a deep breath, she settled back. When she got back to the apartment, she'd run a bath, go over her assignment…and that was as far as her plans were going for now.

"Sufficient unto the day is the trouble thereof." The quote from the Bible would just have to hold her for now.

Mark pulled up in front of her apartment building, and for a moment she saw it through a stranger's eyes. Built after World War II, it squatted back from the street, square and ugly. Patches of stucco had fallen off, exposing the wires beneath. For two years Sheryl and Jason had called a basement suite in this dull, squat building home.

She should have moved right out after Jason died, but it was the cheapest apartment block she could find close enough to her work and school. The money she saved would pay for two more courses next year.

"Thanks for the ride," she said, turning to Mark.

"Hey, I'm really sorry about your job." He pushed his hat back on his head, sighing lightly. "And your husband."

Sheryl bit back a retort. "Don't lie awake about either. I won't." She glanced at him, surprised to see real remorse on his face. "Dave was just waiting for an excuse to fire me."

"Why is that?"

"It doesn't matter," she answered shortly. Mark didn't need to know any more than the bare details of her life. He was just a blip.

She stepped out of the truck and walked up to her apartment. As she unlocked the front door, she glanced over her shoulder.

He waited, watching her, and when she stepped into the dank lobby, she heard the truck start up, and he left.

She leaned against the locked door, drawing a deep

breath. *Enough girl,* she reprimanded herself, *Tomorrow, think about it then.*

Mark hit the remote button, and the picture on the TV screen shrank and faded away. He dropped the remote and clasped his hands behind his head as he leaned back against the headboard, trying to meld his first impression of Sheryl with the stories he'd heard. The short skirt, the satin shirt and high heels all fit with what Nate and Ed said the few times they talked of her.

Mark picked up the photograph that lay beside him on the bed. Sheryl looked about fifteen, her hair swirling around her face, her mouth twisted in a wry smile. It resembled her enough for identification, but didn't adequately portray the delicate line of her features, the elusive color of her long hair. Sheryl was taller than he had imagined, slender, with an easy grace in her movements—a direct contrast to the hardened edge of her manner.

He remembered again the sight of her clutching her head, and another wave of anger coursed through him. She said Dave wouldn't have hit her, and in retrospect he knew she was right. Dave looked like he worked on intimidation and threats. So what had caused her quick response?

He dropped the picture on the bed.

With a frustrated sigh, he pulled the phone toward him and dialed.

"I found her," Mark said when Nate answered.

"So how was my sister?" Nate's voice held anger that Mark knew had as much to do with his worry over his father as his long history with Sheryl.

"Broke, out of a job, scared."

"Sheryl, scared? I can't imagine that. How's the husband?"

Mark sighed as he leaned back, pinching the bridge of his nose. "He's dead."

"What?" Nate's voice exploded in his ear. "Since when?"

"I don't know. We didn't really exchange much in the way of polite chitchat. I'm surprised you didn't know. Didn't Jason have family in Sweet Creek?"

"He only had his mother, and she moved to Toronto right after they left." Nate sounded flustered. "Why didn't she tell us?"

"I get the feeling from her that she thought no one cared."

Nate fell quiet and Mark, sensing guilt, waited. "How did you manage to talk her into coming?" Nate asked after a lengthy pause.

"She didn't have much choice. Thanks to me she lost her job."

"How's that?"

"I tangled with her boss."

A pause at the other end of the line told Mark that Nate was absorbing his second shock of the night.

"Whatever happened to turning the other cheek, Mark?"

"It wasn't *my* cheek I thought he was going to hit," Mark replied, his mouth set in grim lines. "Anyhow," Mark continued, wanting to forget the debacle, "she agreed to come with me. If we leave on time in the morning I'll probably head straight to the hospital." He didn't speak of his reason for haste, but it hung between them.

"If all goes well, Dad will be discharged in a couple of days," Nate said. "The doctor says he can't live at his own place anymore, so he'll come and stay with us."

"That's going to make things busy for you and Elise." Mark frowned. Elise had enough to do with three little kids. He wondered about the wisdom of bringing Ed there, as well.

"Speaking of busy," Nate said, ignoring his comment, "I checked the hay today. It's ready to bale."

"Did you manage to get hold of a baling crew?"

"Yah, Rob and Conrad. I rented an extra baler. So all that's left is to pray for good weather."

"That's all we can do anyway, Nate." Mark stifled a yawn. "You got any ideas of what I can talk to Sheryl about? Twelve hours is a lot of time to be cooped up in a vehicle with someone you've never met before."

"Ask her what she's been doing the past eight years. We sure don't have a clue." Nate's voice was abrupt, and Mark let that matter drop.

"Okay. Then, I'll see you tomorrow." Mark hung up, staring at the phone, feeling an unexpected pang of sympathy for Sheryl.

Her face came back to him: delicate features, soft green eyes framed with lightly arched brows, and hair that went on forever, tempting a man to run his fingers through it. He had seen many beautiful girls, but somehow she held a certain fascination for him, and when she smiled...

Mark laughed shortly. He was acting like a kid himself instead of an experienced man of thirty-four. He'd had girl-friends enough, just never the right one. The life he had lived didn't lend itself to finding a girl willing to share his life, his faith in God, the isolation of his ranch and the hard work that came with it. Living on the ranch kept him too busy to go looking. And after Tanya, he didn't have much inclination.

He got up, restlessness sending him to the window. Lately the old feeling seemed to come upon him more often.

Nate and Elise already had three children, and Elise, his baby sister, was five years younger than him. As for himself...no one.

He shrugged, attributing his restlessness to spending most of the day driving around busy streets trying to find the bar Sheryl worked. The city always gave him that claustrophobic feeling, and each time he went there for business or visits he couldn't wait until he was back in the open hills riding his horse into the wind.

Mark dropped his shoulder against the cool window of his air-conditioned room, hands shoved in his jeans pockets, frowning at the cars below wishing he was back on the ranch.

He thought again of Sheryl, trying to imagine her on a horse. Nate said she used to ride every chance she got. He couldn't visualize it, not after seeing her this evening, serving drinks in a smoky, noisy bar wearing that narrow short skirt.

He pushed himself away from the window with a sigh and dropped on the bed, tugging his cowboy boots off. He pulled his Bible out of his suitcase, and lay back, paging through the Psalms, looking for inspiration, comfort... wisdom.

With a wry grin he flipped to Proverbs. Between Nate, Sheryl and Ed, he would need the wisdom of Solomon to understand them and all the undercurrents that swirled around their lives.

For now he was only the messenger. Once he brought Sheryl to Sweet Creek, his job would be over and he could get back to the business of keeping his beloved ranch afloat.

Chapter Two

Even though warm sunshine slanted into the cab of the truck, Mark shivered as he turned onto Sheryl's street. He wasn't looking forward to spending the long drive with this self-contained girl. Besides, the work he'd left behind at the ranch lay heavy on his mind. Knowing the hay was ready to bale made him fidgety.

He glanced down the street toward Sheryl's apartment, wondering if she had changed her mind. But as he drew closer to her building, he saw her waiting, a small suitcase on the sidewalk beside her, a backpack slung over one shoulder.

He pulled to a stop in front of her, and she tossed her suitcase in the truck's box and opened the door, flipping her backpack into the cab before he could get out to help.

"Good morning, Sheryl," he said instead, settling back into the seat.

She only nodded at him, climbing easily into the truck. This morning she wore blue jeans and a loose-fitting track coat over a soft pink T-shirt. Mark was disappointed to see that her hair hung in a neat braid down her back.

"Do you want breakfast?" he asked, hoping her lack of

greeting wasn't an indication of what the next twelve hours would be like.

"I ate already. Thanks."

"Okay." Great conversation starter, Mark, he thought as he spun the truck in a tight U-turn. No wonder he was always such a hit with the ladies.

He sped down the street and turned onto the Yellowhead, glad to put this district of Edmonton behind him, restless to see the city skyline in his rearview mirror.

The hum of the tires and the occasional muted swish of a vehicle passing them were the only sounds in the cab of the truck—a cab that seemed to grow smaller with each passing block.

It was going to be a long drive.

Finally they hit the last traffic lights on the freeway until the town of Edson, more than a two-hour drive away. Mark stepped down on the accelerator and Sheryl turned, looking over her shoulder at the city they left behind.

"Second thoughts?" Mark asked.

She turned to him, her face expressionless. "That's a waste of time," she replied her voice terse.

The tone of her voice didn't exactly encourage conversation, but Mark persisted. "How long did you live in Edmonton?"

"Five years."

"Where were you before that?"

"Prince George."

Well things were going great guns, he thought ruefully. At this rate the trip would crawl by.

Mark took his cue from the resolute set of her jaw and turned on the radio. "Do you have any preferences?"

"I don't listen to the radio much."

Mark couldn't imagine that. Driving anywhere back in the valley took time and the only thing that broke the monotony was the radio. Market reports, weather, news, music. Didn't matter much. It was noise and company, and the way things were going he would need both.

Sheryl turned away again.

With a sigh Mark leaned forward, resting his forearms on the steering wheel as he watched the road flow past. One part of his mind on the work that waited back home.

He and Nate had cut the hay before he'd left. If it didn't rain today it would be ready to bale. He was glad Nate had managed to get hold of a haying crew. They were going to need all the hands they could get. Square bales were labor intensive, but the price had gone through the roof for good hay. The buyer from the lower mainland wanted only hay baled in manageable square bales. The money would help nudge the ranch out of the hole it had been languishing in since the drop in cattle prices.

The interchange for Westlock flew past, then Spruce Grove then Stony Plain. The speed limit increased and Mark leaned back.

"Do you have to drive so fast?"

Mark jumped at the sound of Sheryl's voice. He assumed she had fallen asleep. Instead she sat rigid, arms clasped across her stomach, face pale.

"This isn't fast." He glanced at the speedometer—110 kilometers per hour. "I'm going close to the speed limit."

"I'm not comfortable with speed."

"Well we've got over 1,000 kilometers ahead of us and the only way we're going to get anywhere is to step on it."

Mark waited for a response, but she only bit her lip and settled back, rubbing her palms over the legs of her jeans.

"You'll just have to trust my driving."

"I can't." She pressed her hands between her knees.

She didn't look like she could, either, thought Mark. Her pale face and white lips showed him clearly how uncomfortable she was. Biting back an impatient sigh, Mark slowed down and set the cruise at 105. Dropping the speed would add an extra sixty minutes of scintillating silence to an already long trip.

They drove over the interchange for Peace River an hour later, and Mark switched the radio off.

"Are you warm enough?" he asked Sheryl, taking another stab at conversation.

"I'm fine."

He decided to press on. It felt unnatural to share a vehicle with someone without even commenting on the scenery.

"How long has it been since you were in the valley?"

"I left eight years ago."

"With Jason?"

Sheryl only nodded.

Five words. Three more than the last sentence. At this rate she might be up to a paragraph by Little Fort.

He hadn't perfected the outright nosiness of his mother and sister but he was persistent. One way or another he meant to find out something about this enigmatic girl even if all he got was yes and no answers.

"How long ago did Jason die?" He glanced her way, trying to gauge her reaction.

"Eight months." She blinked but continued staring out the window.

"I'm sorry to hear that."

Sheryl shot him a glance and then looked straight ahead again, not replying.

Mark tapped his fingers on the steering wheel. Nate always complained that Sheryl would talk his ear off with her constant chatter. He hoped he was taking the right person back.

"What happened?" he finally asked.

"Car accident."

Well that explained her dislike of speed.

"And you've been on your own since then?"

"If you mean living on my own, yes. If you mean boyfriends, you're right as well."

Two sentences. Disdainful sentences but at least things were picking up. "So what do you plan to do once you're back in Edmonton?"

"I don't plan that far ahead." Sheryl leaned over, unbuckled her backpack and pulled out a book.

Mark glanced at the cover. *Paradise Lost.*

"Don't tell me you're reading that for pleasure?" he asked, ignoring her signal. He kept his tone light, hoping she would warm up to his irresistible charm.

"Actually it's for a course I'm taking."

"College or university?"

"I wish." She opened the book but didn't look at it. "Correspondence course."

"That's pretty impressive."

She frowned at him as if she sensed ridicule.

"Seriously," he protested. "I spent four years getting my MBA, and got away from classes as soon as possible. I couldn't imagine the discipline required to struggle through Milton on your own."

"I like learning."

"What's the course for?"

She shrugged, riffling the corners of the pages with her thumb. "Bachelor of Education." Her voice held a note of deprecation.

"Any specialty?"

"High school English."

"Then you have my prayers. Anyone wanting to try to instill in teenagers an appreciation for Shakespeare and poetry will need them," Mark said with a grin.

"You can save your breath. Prayers are a waste of time." Sheryl paused, a hint of pain crossing her face, then she bent her head to the book, eyes narrowed as if concentrating.

That brief look of vulnerability caught Mark by surprise. He glanced at her again, his eyes following the clean line of her features, the smooth curve of her neck. He had seen pictures of her as a young girl, but most of them were amateur and blurred. None of them had even begun to capture her good looks.

Mark jerked his head back to the road, staring out the window with determination.

They also didn't give a hint of how cold and self-possessed she could be.

Sheryl twisted her head around, trying to ease the crook in her neck. From Edson to Jasper, she had alternately dozed and read and from Little Fort to 100 Mile House she merely stared out the window, trying to keep her mind off what waited for her at the end of the journey. The basic fact of the here and now was that she was in a truck with a man who looked like he preferred to be anywhere else.

After his few attempts at conversation, the ride had been painfully quiet. Sheryl found it difficult to ignore him, however. He exuded a quiet strength that made his presence known with no effort on his part.

By the time they reached Valemount, halfway on the trip, she felt tense and saw how rude she'd been. It wasn't Mark's fault that Ed had felt sudden remorse or whatever emotion it was that had sent Mark across British Columbia and half of Alberta. So she swallowed her pride, her antagonism to men in general, and asked a few questions herself.

Mark told her about Ed and his stroke—how, during the course of the tests, they had found the fatal aneurysm. It was inoperable and now only a matter of time.

She also discovered that Nate had met Elise, Mark's sister, a few months after Sheryl and Jason had left. Mark's parents had bought the Simpson ranch five miles down the road from the Krickson place. Three years later Mark sold his real estate business in Vancouver and joined up with Nate and Ed.

The conversation had wound down after that, and they were back to the radio and strained silence.

Sheryl found it difficult to maintain a polite interest in her stepfather and stepbrother's life, and after discovering that Nate and Elise also had three children, she didn't want to talk anymore.

Sheryl had opened her book again, trying to follow the unfamiliar cadence of words and phrases from another time. But they dealt with the justice of a God she neither trusted nor wholly believed in. If it hadn't been required reading for the course, she would have thrown it out months ago.

The words on the page blurred, and she drifted back in time, remembering life in the valley, recalling working on the ranch, fighting with Ed and Nate. Whenever she pulled herself back to the present and the book on her lap, Milton's words echoed her life too closely, its laments of brokenness struck too near her pain.

Giving up, she straightened, glancing at Mark as she did so.

He lounged against the seat, steering one-handed, his fingers resting on the bottom of the wheel. He looked tired and bored, his finely shaped mouth pulled down at the corners, his thickly lashed eyes, heavy-lidded as he stared with disinterest at the road ahead of him. His hair was long, flowing well past his collar, hanging almost in his eyes. He had pulled off his jacket halfway through the trip and rolled up the sleeves of his denim shirt, revealing muscular forearms. He was a very attractive man, she gave him that. He carried himself with a quiet strength that she wouldn't want to have to face down.

She was glad he hadn't pushed her harder, inquired any further into her own life. She meant nothing to him, he nothing to her.

They were approaching Williams Lake now, and Sheryl sat up, struck by an unexpected jolt of familiarity at the smooth summer brown hills laced with dark green pine ridges.

They rounded a corner, and the lake came into view below them, its waters sparkling in the late-afternoon sun. The hills were staggered against each other, and tapered down toward the lake, surrounding it protectively. It looked like home.

Sheryl bit her lip as she shook that particular feeling off. There was no home waiting for her. God and home were a small part of other memories better left buried.

"We'll be there pretty soon now," Mark said. "Do you want to go straight to the hospital, or did you want to head to your brother's place first?"

"May as well get this part of the trip over and done with," she said with a sigh. She felt a nervous clenching of her stomach at the thought of finally facing Ed after all the silent years.

Against her will she relived the weeks after she sent her letter five years ago. She had set aside her stubborn pride and written, pleading for sanctuary. She had no other place to go. Each time she picked up the mail it was with shaking fingers and fear that Jason would find out. Then the one and only time Jason picked up the mail, the letter came.

Only it was her own—resealed and marked "Return to Sender." She never wrote another one and heard nothing from Ed since.

They pulled into the parking lot of the Cariboo Memorial Hospital and Mark shut off the truck's engine. He leaned back, pulling his hands over his face, blowing out his breath. He looked tired, Sheryl thought, feeling a faint pull of attraction. Understandably. His even features and thickly lashed eyes had made women's heads turn each place they'd stopped.

Sheryl shook her head, angry with herself for even acknowledging his good looks. Men were nothing but trouble and heartache. She should know that by now.

"So, ready to go in?" Mark asked, slowly opening his door.

Sheryl shrugged in reply, slipping her book into the knapsack and buckling it shut. She opened her door just as Mark came around the front of the truck.

He frowned at her as she stepped out, slamming the door behind her. "I was going to open it for you," he said.

"Are you kidding?" Sheryl almost laughed. "That went out with feathered helmets and armor."

"No it didn't," was his quiet response.

Sheryl raised her eyebrows at him as she stepped away from the truck, and without a backward glance, she walked down the sidewalk, effectively cutting off the conversation.

A few strides of his long legs put him ahead of her and, reaching around her, he opened the hospital door. "You're going to make me hustle to prove my point, aren't you?"

"What point?" Sheryl squinted up at him against the bright sun.

"That some mothers still raise their sons to be gentlemen." Mark smiled down at her, his one hand shoved in the pocket of his coat, the other still holding the door.

"Trust me, mister, the words *gentle* and *men* do not belong together," Sheryl replied, a mocking tone in her voice.

"My name is Mark."

His voice was quiet, but Sheryl sensed the light note of rebuke in it.

He may be a man but he had done nothing to deserve being addressed so impersonally. She paused. "I'm sorry...Mark." Their eyes met, and it was as if a tenuous connection had been created by her using his name.

He only nodded, his expression suddenly serious.

Sheryl looked away, took a breath and stepped into the hospital. All thoughts of gentlemen and chivalry were abruptly cut off as the nauseatingly familiar smells of the hospital wafted over her.

The hallways were hushed, the aroma of disinfectant

stronger now. Sheryl fought the urge to turn and run, to forget about Ed. But Mark strode inexorably on, boot heels ringing out on the polished floor. Sheryl followed him.

Mark paused at the doorway to a darkened hospital room, knocked lightly on the open door and walked in. Sheryl wiped her damp palms on the legs of her denim jeans, took a steadying breath and followed him inside.

She didn't recognize the figure lying on the bed. The sheets outlined a body that had hollows instead of muscles. The once-black hair was peppered with gray and visibly thinning. His eyes were closed, the lids shot with broken blood vessels.

His skin had an unhealthy grayish pallor and one side of his face was pulled down in a perpetual frown. Tubes and lines snaked out from his body, connected to an IV and monitors that bleeped from a shelf above his head.

Mark bent over and shook Ed's shoulder lightly. One eye opened fully, the other drooped. Even with Mark's warnings, Sheryl still felt shocked at how his stroke had felled this proud man.

"I've brought Sheryl, Ed." Mark's voice broke the silence of the hushed darkness of the room.

Ed blinked and stared past Mark, squinting with his good eye. Then he struggled to sit up, using only one arm, the other falling uselessly to one side, bandaged and connected to an intravenous machine.

"Sheryl? You brought her?" One corner of his mouth lifted in a parody of a smile, the other stayed resolutely where it was. "Come closer." His slurred speech made him sound drunk, a condition scrupulously foreign to Ed Krickson.

Sheryl unclenched her rigid jaw, struggled to still the erratic beating of her heart. Anger, guilt, frustration, sorrow all warred within her, each trying to make a claim.

Blindly she took a step past Mark, almost tripping over the base of the IV stand.

Mark caught her, his hands warm through the thin material of her jacket. Sheryl flinched and pulled away. She took a steadying breath, her iron control over her emotions slipping.

"Hello, Ed," was all she could manage to say as she faced her stepfather.

"Sheryl." Ed reached out to catch her hand, but she drew back. "You...came. Need to see you...to talk to you."

His halting expression of concern was in total opposition to the Ed she remembered. She had been prepared to face a strong adversary, but this man was not the Ed Krickson she had yelled at and fought with as a willful teenager.

"I've been...feeling...vulnerable," he continued, not noticing her silence. "How...are...you?" He took a breath, swallowed. "Are you...happy?"

What should she say? she thought, clasping her waist with her arms. Did he want to hear about the past eight years, would it vindicate everything he had ever told her? Could she tell this broken man about her pain? Did she want to give him that kind of ammunition?

She settled for the superficial, the inane.

"I'm fine."

"Are...you?" His one eye, as blue as the Chilcotin skies, seemed to pierce her, to bore into her very soul.

Unnerved, she took a step back almost bumping into Mark in the close quarters of the hospital room.

Ed lifted a hand to his head as if it pained him. "Sheryl...I've had...burden for you...needed to...see you." The words came out slowly, tortured, and for a moment Sheryl felt pity for him. Until he spoke again.

"I...do...love you...I need to tell..."

Sheryl swayed, his words echoing in her ears. He couldn't mean it. Did someone who loved you push you and force you to become someone you weren't? Did someone who loved you ignore a cry for help?

His words created a hunger for something that had been missing so long from her life—family and a family's love. A home.

His paltry offering was too little too late.

The ceiling pressed down to meet a floor tilting beneath her feet. The echoing became a roar, and she took a halting step away from the bed. Only a few minutes had elapsed since she stepped into this room, but she felt as if she had lived through a lifetime of emotions. She couldn't stay.

"I'm sorry," she mumbled, turning. "I've got to go." Surprisingly Mark stepped back, giving her room, and without looking back, she stumbled out.

Once out in the hallway, she turned, not sure of her direction but aware of a need to escape, to leave behind Ed's empty words spoken from some need to fix what could never be repaired.

The double doors loomed ahead, and she pushed them open, slipping between them. Forcing down a rising wave of panic, she slowed her steps and walked through the entrance and out into the blessed fresh air and warmth of the parking lot.

She found Mark's truck easily and leaned against it, soaking up the warmth it had absorbed from the sun, trying to dispel the chill deep within her.

Slowly the emptiness became smaller, more manageable. Sheryl inhaled. Vulnerability was weakness. She could depend on no one. Love was a word, only a word, she repeated to herself like a litany.

"I'm sorry Nate isn't here. He had to go up to Lac La Hache today to pick up a bull," Elise, Nate's wife, apologized as she led Sheryl down an overgrown path to the cabin tucked away behind the ranch-style home.

Sheryl was relieved. To face Nate so soon after her visit with Ed would have been too hard on emotions still raw from that afternoon.

When Mark had driven up the driveway to the house, Sheryl experienced a sense of déjà vu. She was again fifteen years old, coming home from another day at school in Nate's truck, looking forward to a quick ride on her horse before chores needed to be done.

The house standing so solidly amongst the fir trees, exuded a sense of permanence. Placed against the rootless years she had spent with Jason, it was another painful reminder of might-have-beens.

Even now, as she followed a pathway narrowed by shrubs and ferns and darkened by towering fir trees, she felt as if all the intervening years had slipped away, and once again she was retreating to her sanctuary.

"The girls and I cleaned out the cabin." Elise grinned at Sheryl over her shoulder as she opened the door. "Now there's room to move around."

Sheryl followed Elise into the cabin. The wave of nostalgia was unexpected, and for the second time in as many days she felt the unwelcome prick of tears. Eight years of hard-won self-control were brushed away as easily as the cobwebs Elise must have cleaned out of this cabin.

She quickly turned away from Elise, concentrating on the room instead. The old metal bed, bought at an auction sale, sat in the same place against the wall, the quilt her mother had made out of her old clothes still covered the mattress. Opposite the bed was a walled-in area that held the toilet and shower, and tucked in the corner between that wall and the cabin wall stood a chest of drawers, an old scarf of her mother's hiding the scarred and gouged top that no amount of sanding could erase.

Sunlight, muted and crosshatched by the limbs of the fir trees, fell through the window and across the old wooden desk that had been the command post of the dreams and adventures of a young girl who longed to be anywhere but here.

Sheryl was drawn to it, and as her fingers unconsciously

traced the initials she had labored over, she glanced out the window to the swaying trees and the creek that tumbled over the rocks at their base. How many dreams hadn't she spun, staring out this speckled glass, chin on her hand, elbow on the desk?

Sheryl shook her head to dispel the insidious memories, turning back to Elise, who stood just inside the door.

"Sorry." Sheryl smiled, a sad twisting of her lips. "It feels like I never left."

"I'm glad it looks the same. Nate didn't have time to help, so the girls and I relied on instinct." Elise shoved her hands in the back pocket of her jeans, and in that movement Sheryl recognized one of the similarities between her and Mark. There were others. Both shared thickly lashed eyes, high cheekbones, strong jaws, but where Mark's dark hair flowed past his collar, Elise's was cut short. However, she looked as feminine with her short hair as he looked masculine in spite of the length of his.

"Nate tells me you used to stay in the cabin quite a bit," Elise continued.

"My stays here started out as a punishment, and soon the cabin became a retreat." She smiled at Elise to ease the bitter note that had crept into her voice. "I probably spent more time here than I should have."

"The girls went riffling through the desk once, looking for paper for airplanes. I'm afraid they took some away. I took the rest and put them in a box under the bed. I'm sorry about that." Elise rocked back on the heels of her runners, looking apologetic.

"Doesn't matter," Sheryl reassured her. "They were just old stories and poems. I'm surprised you kept them."

"They were part of your past, and everyone should have something to remember their childhood by."

"Probably," she replied.

"I'm even sorrier to hear about your husband...."

Sheryl only nodded, letting an awkward silence drift between them.

"Well," Elise said as she brushed nonexistent dirt off her pants, that single hesitant word signaling the end of their conversation. "I've got to get the urchins cleaned up and in bed. You're welcome to come by the house once you've rested."

Sheryl knew she wouldn't. "I'd like to thank you for having me here," she said finally. "I know it must be inconvenient for you, knowing how Nate feels about me..." Sheryl let the last part of the sentence drift away.

"Nate is a good man, a caring husband, but he has his Krickson moments of righteous indignation. Between him and Ed I've learned that I'm better off to draw my own conclusions about people." Elise tilted her head to one side, as if studying Sheryl, her gray eyes soft. "I'll get to know you on my own terms." She lifted a hand in farewell. "See you tomorrow."

Elise carefully closed the door, her footsteps fading quickly away, leaving Sheryl feeling both bemused and warmed by Elise's words. Elise had a quiet strength about her, much like her brother Mark.

With a short laugh Sheryl picked her suitcase up from beside the door. Her impressions of these people didn't matter much. She was only staying long enough to give Ed the peace of mind he seemed to crave, and then she was off, back to Edmonton, back to...

She clutched a shirt she had just unpacked to her stomach, looking over her shoulder at the window and the play of sunlight through the trees. The hushed sounds of the brook filtered through the walls, laying down a gentle counterpoint to the wind sifting through the trees.

Shaking her head, she turned resolutely back to her clothes, hanging them up with rigid determination.

Don't even think about it, she warned herself. There's nothing, not one thing here for you, no life, no friends, no welcome. You made your choice when you ran away from here with Jason.

She heard a soft knock on the door. Elise must have forgotten something, she thought, dropping her clothes on the bed to open the door.

Two girls stood on the shadowed deck, each clutching a handful of wildflowers—lupins, daisies and paintbrush. Each wore dirty T-shirts, and bare feet poked out from the frayed hems of blue jeans. Sheryl guessed their ages to be five and six. These must be the "urchins" Elise set out looking for. Nate's little girls, her nieces. Stepnieces, she corrected herself.

The oldest smiled, hesitantly, showing a mouth bereft of front teeth, and thrust her flowers forward.

"These are for you," she lisped, grinning.

"Thank you." Sheryl took the flowers, unable to keep from smiling.

"And I have some, too," the second girl, a dark copy of her blond sister, pushed her bouquet toward Sheryl, as well.

"My name is Crystal, this is Marla," the older girl said. "And we helped my mom clean the cabin for you." She peered past Sheryl into the cabin. "Pretty clean huh?"

"Very clean," Sheryl agreed, sniffing the flowers. "And these flowers will be just the thing it needs to make it look like a home." Sheryl hesitated, watching the two girls, suddenly jealous of Nate.

Elise's distant voice drifted up to them.

"Oh, brother, there's my mom. She probably wants us to have a bath." Crystal turned to Sheryl. "Will we see you tomorrow?"

Sheryl nodded uncertainly, still holding the flowers. With another grin, they both turned and skipped down the path toward the house, arms outstretched, giggles trailing behind them.

Nate's family. Nate's place. Nate's home.

Sheryl stopped herself. She was getting maudlin.

She glanced down at the bouquet of flowers in her hand, touching them with a forefinger. It was funny. In all the years she had lived here, this was the most welcome she had ever felt.

Chapter Three

As Mark approached Nate and Elise's driveway the next day, he hesitated, then touched the brake, slowing the truck down. Elise had told him she and Nate would visit Ed before church, so he'd left his own home earlier in the hopes of catching them.

He came to a complete halt just before the turnoff and tapped his thumbs on the steering wheel. Would it be obvious if he stopped in? Would he look too much like a nosy Andrews?

Ever since he'd found Sheryl in the hospital parking lot, huddled against his truck, she had been on his mind. Ed and Nate's part of the story he knew by rote. Now, suddenly it had another side.

On the way back from the hospital, she had sat across the seat from him, arms clasped tightly across her stomach, her face averted.

Thankfully Nate was gone when he dropped her off, but Mark knew she would have to meet him today. Would their meeting have the same emotional undercurrents that Sheryl's and Ed's had? Nate had never spoken kindly of Sheryl.

Mark hesitated, then spun the wheel and stepped on the gas before he changed his mind. Dust billowed behind him as the truck flew up the hill. Cresting it, he slowed, then coasted down the other side, stopping behind Nate and Elise's minivan.

Crystal and Marla sat on the verandah, chins on hands, elbows planted on knees, and ruffled skirts brushing the tops of black patent leather shoes.

They jumped up, tripping down the stairs. "Uncle Mark, Uncle Mark," they both shouted, running toward him.

Mark slammed the door behind him and, bending over, scooped up little Marla in his arms and swung her around. He retained his hold on her and pulled Crystal against him. As always, their unabashed welcome warmed him, filling the empty spots of his life.

"We didn't see you for a long time, Uncle Mark," Marla admonished, leaning back as if to make sure he was still the same favorite uncle.

"I was only gone a few days, punky." Mark squeezed both girls. "How do you like what I brought back for you all the way from Edmonton?"

"Mommy told me she used to sleep in my room," Marla hooked a slender arm around Mark's neck. "And I think she's pretty."

"Did you see her hair, Uncle Mark? I bet she can almost sit on it." Crystal tugged at the fine wisps of hair that Mark knew Elise had spent twenty minutes curling. "I wish I had hair like that, then I'd be pretty."

"Don't let Grandma hear you say that," Mark chuckled.

"I know what she would say," Marla interrupted. "She'll say that 'grace is defeatful and beauty is a pain, but...'" She frowned, chewing on her lip. Then with a shrug, dismissed the mangled quote.

"'But a woman that fears the Lord, she shall be praised.'" Mark kissed his youngest niece, stifling his own laughter, and set her on the ground.

"Mom said she probably won't come to church with us. I want her to come because Mr. Hankinson said we should bring a visitor to church, but we never have any visitors," Crystal complained.

Mark stroked Crystal's crisp, sun-warmed hair. "I don't think Sheryl is used to coming to church, Crissie."

"Then she should come for sure, shouldn't she, Marla?"

Marla nodded seriously, twisting the hem of her ruffled skirt around her fingers.

"Can't you ask her, Uncle Mark?"

"I don't think it will help if I ask her." Besides he was unsure of his own reception after what had happened yesterday.

"Of course it will matter," Crystal said, interrupting his thoughts. "Mommy says that all the girls think you're a hunk." Crystal's eyes sparkled.

"You don't need to use words like that, Crissie."

"Like what? Hunk? It's not a swear is it?"

Mark shook his head as he felt a rush of love for these two precious lives. Nate leaned toward a stern upbringing, and it was difficult not to intervene. And as children would, they got very adept at knowing which adult they could cajole and which one would not be led.

"Could you ask her to come?" Marla's voice was soft, her expression wistful. Crystal leaned against him, sighing.

Mark knew they were playing him along, yet he already felt himself softening.

"It would be good for her to go to church," Marla continued.

Marla grabbed his one hand, Crystal the other, and they tugged, pulling him down the path toward the cabin.

"C'mon girls, I don't think she's even awake." *Aren't you the firm uncle*, he thought wryly, unable to resist the encouraging smiles they were throwing his way.

Crystal ran up the steps, Marla behind her, each disregarding her long skirt. Mark hung back as Crystal knocked confidently on the door. The speed with which the door opened was as much of a surprise as the smile on Sheryl's face at the sight of the two girls.

"Well, hello again." She hunkered down, the hair that Crystal so admired falling to one side like a golden, shimmering curtain. "Did you girls bring me that delicious breakfast?"

Her face was animated, her green eyes sparkling, and Mark felt an unexplained tug of attraction.

"We tried not to wake you up," Marla offered.

Crystal stepped forward. "Do you want to come to church with us?"

Mark almost groaned. Crystal's approach was pure Krickson. Full speed ahead, ignore all comers.

The smile on Sheryl's face faded, and slowly she straightened, catching sight of Mark. She paused, their eyes meeting and holding. Mark had to stop himself from taking a step toward her. She looked away, breaking the connection. "I'm not dressed for church."

"That doesn't matter, Auntie Sheryl, we can wait."

"Please come," Marla added her voice to Crystal's. "We never have a visitor, and Daddy said you're only staying a couple of days." Marla turned to Mark, ready to plead her cause, but he saw Sheryl's discomfort.

"We had a long drive yesterday, and Sheryl's probably tired." Mark kept his voice firm, wishing, not for the first time, that his nieces were sweet, shy and tractable.

"I think God wants you to come, Auntie Sheryl." Crystal caught Sheryl's hand and turned her own soft blue eyes up to Sheryl's green ones. A look of pain flitted across her face, so momentary that Mark thought he imagined it.

"Maybe He does, sweetheart." Sheryl smiled down at Crystal, a tight movement of her lips. "Do I have time to change?"

Crystal clenched one fist and jerked it down toward a lifted knee in a childish parody of a hockey player's victory dance. Mark made a note to tell Nate that Crystal was possibly watching a little too much television.

Sheryl grinned, and as she looked up she met Mark's eyes again.

"We'd like it if you came," he said.

"Okay." She lifted her hands up as if in surrender. "I'll be real quick."

Mark caught Crystal's hand and gave it a tug. "We'll wait for you by my truck."

Sheryl appeared around the corner of the house two minutes later, dressed in a loose, flowing skirt and brown T-shirt that set off to perfection the gold of her hair.

The girls ran up to meet her just as Nate and Elise came down the steps of the verandah.

Nate was the first to see her. He paused, his son balanced on one arm, his face suddenly cold, hard, and Mark knew they hadn't seen each other yet.

"Hello, Sheryl." Nate's voice had a tight edge to it.

Sheryl's step faltered, her smile faded.

"Hey, Mom and Dad, Auntie Sheryl is coming to church." Crystal skipped up to her dad, hands flapping in excitement.

The tension between Sheryl and Nate was palpable, but somehow she overcame her obvious reluctance and walked over to Nate, her hand outstretched.

Nate hesitated, and for a moment Mark thought he was going to ignore her. Instead he shifted the baby to his other arm and caught Sheryl's hand in his.

"Thanks for letting me stay in the cabin," she said quietly. "It's like old times again."

Nate nodded, releasing her hand, clasping his son closer.

"Is this the baby?" Sheryl asked, her voice and manner hesitant, totally at odds with the tight, controlled woman Mark had spent the past two days with.

"Yes. His name is Benjamin."

Mark could almost feel the yearning in her as she reached out and touched Benjamin's chubby hand.

Nate didn't even look at her, instead concentrated on his son. Sheryl stroked Benjamin's arm then her hand fell to her side.

Mark wondered how Nate could pretend indifference to Sheryl as she stood before him, her face betraying her inner struggle?

Mark could take no more.

"Why don't you ride with me, Sheryl," he offered. "And Marla can ride on the way up, Crystal on the way home," he quickly added as both girls clamored to be the third passenger.

Sheryl bit her lip, her hands clutching her elbows. She looked like she was caught between two evils, and he remembered.

"I'll drive slowly," he added softly.

Her shoulders seemed to sag in relief, and without a backward glance she walked over to Mark's truck.

A few quick steps got him to the passenger door in time to open it for her. She shot him an oblique glance and got in behind Marla.

Mark closed the door, watching her as he rounded the hood of the truck, still trying to absorb who the real Sheryl was, the self-controlled, secretive woman he spent an entire day with yesterday, or the vulnerable girl she became around Nate and Ed?

Marla chattered to Sheryl as he got in on his side of the truck. "I don't like buckling up."

"It's safer if you do." Sheryl ignored Marla's protests and clicked the belt over her stomach, pulling it snug. She looked up at Mark as he clipped his own seat belt. "Thanks for the ride, Mark." Her voice was soft, husky, and hearing her say his name gave his heart a nudge.

He only nodded in acknowledgment and started the

truck, fully aware of her on the other side of the cab, wondering himself what created these unexpected feelings.

As he pulled away from the house, he glanced at her. The sun coming through the windshield caught her hair making it shine and glimmer. Her soft green eyes were downcast, shaded by a sweep of sable lashes. As she spoke to Marla, she smiled, a gentle movement of soft, full lips.

The girls were wrong. She was more than pretty. Now, with her barriers pulled down, she was stunning.

The rustle of papers and coughs of people subsided like a wave as the minister raised his hands for the blessing.

Sheryl clutched the pew in front of her. It had been years since she had attended a church service.

Her natural father had given her a youthful and carefree trust in God that had managed to withstand the rigors of Ed's interpretation of parents and duty. But it hadn't been able to withstand the reality of being Jason's wife. Broken promises and unanswered prayers had worn her faith down until it had become only a part of her past, like her father's name.

But Crystal and Marla showed such exuberance and so easily had overridden her objections. Had she known that it would include a visit with Ed, she would have been more firm. Thankfully Ed didn't pay much attention to her, and during the visit she stayed in the background, netting yet another disapproving look from Nate.

As the organ played the familiar introduction to the closing song, she remembered standing in the pew, singing the song with glad enthusiasm, Ed frowning at her, Nate rolling his eyes and Blythe trying to restrain her with a pleading glance.

Now the familiar words and tune created a desire for that comforting closeness with the God from her past.

She sighed and cut that thought off. God required something she could never afford to give Him, or anyone else— vulnerability and love.

Mark's deep baritone struck out beside her. He held the book loosely in one hand, his other tucked casually in the front pocket of black pants. He sang the words with enthusiasm, and Sheryl felt jealous of his faith and security.

As if he sensed her scrutiny, he glanced sidelong at her, and in between stanzas quirked a half grin at her. An answering flutter of her heart surprised Sheryl, and she turned ahead.

The song wound down to the "Amen," and Sheryl looked ahead, thankful that it was over.

The organist paused a moment then segued into the postlude, and Sheryl steeled herself to face the knowing looks of people who remembered her as a young and willful girl and Jason Kyle's girlfriend.

"Auntie Sheryl," Crystal called out, slipping through the people as they gave way. "Auntie Sheryl, wait for us."

That name again. Auntie. So easily they used it to claim a relationship Sheryl knew wouldn't last longer than the few days she stayed.

But being with them was preferable to facing curious glances and the usual valley nosiness. So Sheryl waited for them as they worked their way through the exiting worshippers.

"Did you see us looking at you," Crystal whispered, as she caught Sheryl's hand in hers.

"I waved, too," Marla put in, trying to wiggle past Crystal to get to Sheryl's other hand.

"Hey, girls," Mark's voice came from behind them, sounding wounded. "Doesn't anyone want to hold my hand?"

"You can carry me," Marla offered just as she got a solid grip on Sheryl's hand.

"Thank you, Your Majesty." Mark swung Marla up in his arms with a laugh.

Marla still clung to Sheryl's hand and because of that, Mark ended up walking close beside Sheryl, his proximity unnerving. Her shoulder bumped his arm, and her hip hit his, but Marla wouldn't release her grip.

They made their way out of church this way, looking for all the world like a little family. Sheryl wondered how the people of the valley would look upon this little scene.

They stepped out into the warm sunshine, people of all ages and sizes milling about below them on the grass surrounding the church.

"Sheryl...Sheryl Kyle?" A woman the same age as Sheryl came up to them, shoulder-length dark hair framing a pleasant face.

Sheryl stared at her blankly, feeling like her mind had shut down.

"Lainie Saunders," the woman prompted. "We used to skip out of Mr. Kuric's class and go swimming in the Horsefly River."

"I remember." Sheryl smiled as happier memories intruded, brushing aside the darker ones from the church service. "I flunked biology because of it."

"So did I." Lainie laughed, glancing curiously at Mark. "My parents were so mad. I ended up taking summer school."

"I spent the entire summer cleaning out calf pens by hand," Sheryl commented dryly, surprised at the quick stab of anger that accompanied the recollection. It had happened almost ten years ago.

"Remember that time we floated all the way down to the lake?" Lainie went on. "And that young Fish-and-Wildlife officer caught us..."

"Anthony Jesperson."

"I think that meeting was meant to be. We've been married four years this spring."

The conversation hit a pause. "And you're expecting?"

Sheryl asked, glancing at Lainie's obviously protruding midriff.

"In two months," Lainie said, with pride tingeing her voice. "I feel like a beached whale, and I'm only seven months along." Lainie smoothed a hand over her stomach self-consciously. "What about you? Did you and Jason…"

"No. No kids." Sheryl withdrew her hand from Marla's and Crystal's, the warmth of their fingers suddenly burning.

"And where is Jason?"

"He passed away about eight months ago." Sheryl felt a tightening around her temples.

"Oh, no. I'm sorry to hear that."

"It's okay." She swallowed, her throat suddenly thickening.

"Do you want to come over for coffee and catch up?" Lainie asked, laying a gentle hand on Sheryl's shoulder, her face expressing concern.

She shook her head, glancing behind her at Mark who still held Marla. "I…I…should get going. I got a ride with Mark, and I think he wants to leave." Sheryl shot Mark a pleading glance, and thankfully he picked up the cue without a pause.

"Sorry, Lainie. My brothers and sisters are coming for the day, and I think we're already late."

"Let's make it another time. I'm sure we've lots to catch up on," Lainie replied, her expression one of concern.

"Sure. I'll give you a call." Sheryl took a step down the stairs, then another and, with a quick wave at her old friend, turned and almost ran to Mark's truck.

"Don't spill, now." Elise handed Marla and Crystal each a cup of juice and added a frown for good measure.

Mark leaned an elbow on the counter of his mother's kitchen, tracing a pattern in the spilled sugar on the gray arborite. "So, Elise, how do you read Sheryl?" he asked.

"Like a closed book." Elise opened one of the many

containers on the counter and began arranging cookies and squares on a tray. "You've spent more time with her than I have."

"She seems like a different person in each different place." Mark pushed the sugar into a neat pile with his pinky, frowning at it. "Lainie talked to her after church today, and I thought I caught a glimpse of what she used to be like. Then it's like someone hit a switch, and she's the girl I met in the bar."

"She lost her husband only eight months ago. A person's emotions are very unstable for almost a year after a death."

"Probably," Mark said, rearranging the sugar again. "But I get the feeling that she's not too sorry her husband's gone."

"Well I know Nate isn't. He's hated Jason for years." Elise set out some cups on the tray, her lips pursed. "From what I've heard he was a pretty hardened character before Sheryl went out with him."

Mark shrugged, pressing a finger on the pile of sugar he had created, still frowning. "What have you heard?"

"He was wild, rough, drank, got into plenty of trouble…" Elise shrugged. "Even if half of the rumors I heard are true, he wasn't husband material."

"So why did Sheryl take off with him and stay with him for eight years?"

"Why don't you ask her?"

Mark curled his lip. "Good idea, 'Lise. She's so talkative."

She flashed him a mischievous grin. "Well, get Mom to ask." Elise closed a sugar container and pushed it aside. "Do you know how long she's going to stay around?"

"I think she's going to make the visit as short as possible."

"What does she have to go back for?"

"Nothing, unless you want to count a run-down apartment." Mark brushed the sugar into his hand and reached over the counter to dump it into the sink. "I guess what she does shouldn't matter."

"Probably not, but I get the sense it does." Elise winked at him. "She's good-looking enough."

"Well as Marla said this morning, 'Grace is defeatful and beauty is a pain'..."

Elise looked puzzled, and as comprehension dawned, she burst out laughing. "That's cute." She pushed the tray of mugs across the counter to Mark. "Anyhow, big brother, here's your chance to show Sheryl what a man of the nineties you are. Don't spill, now," she added with a wicked grin.

"Cute, 'Lise." He picked up the tray and headed from the relative peace of the kitchen to the din of the living room and another Andrews family gathering.

The two couches facing each other were full of bodies, others sat on the floor braced against them, chairs from the kitchen were pulled up, and in one corner of the spacious room a group of teenagers were sprawled on the floor playing an unusually noisy game of Monopoly.

Empty, the room had grace, elegance and style. The fireplace that dominated the center of one wall was built of soft, sand-colored brick and flanked by two floor-to-ceiling windows draped with lace curtains.

Mark almost groaned when he spied Sheryl seated at the opposite end of the living room on a kitchen chair between his parents, Lenore and Nick. As soon as he was done his duties, he would head over and rescue her. Once Lenore got hold of her she wouldn't rest until she got Sheryl's birth weight and grades in school.

"Ah, coffee." Mark's brother, Allen, disentangled himself from his wife and his nephew Benjamin and reached up for the cup that Mark offered him. "You are almost an angel."

"If serving coffee is all that takes then I'm honorary member of the crowd before the throne in heaven," his wife, Diane, said with a laugh. She took a cup and flashed a thankful smile at Mark.

"Saying 'I do' to Allen was enough to bring you there, Diane," Brad, Mark's younger brother, said with a laugh. "Say Mark, we don't have to tip you do we?"

"Just leave donations in the cup when you're done. I'll put them towards the Nate and Mark Eternal Debt Fund." Mark returned.

"Hey, little brother, I'll have a cup of that stuff, too," said Rick, Mark's other brother.

"I don't know how you can still call him 'little,'" sang out Brad. "He's at least five inches taller than you."

"Two," Rick held up two fingers as if to emphasize the point. "Two lousy inches, brat."

"Must be all that hair that makes you think that," said Allen.

Mark shook his head and bent over so Rick could get a cup off the tray. His brother glanced past him toward Sheryl. "Is she the reason you're lowering yourself, brother?"

Mark turned the tray half a turn. "Cream or sugar?" was all he said.

"Right," Rick replied, settling back on the couch with a smirk.

Mark ignored him and worked his way past the younger nieces and nephews leaning against their parents legs, toward the chairs that flanked the fireplace. He felt sorry for Sheryl—she looked a little dazed. And for good reason. Mark had two sisters and three brothers, all married. Only Elaine and Drew had no children. An Andrews gathering was something you eased into, one family at a time, not dived into on a day when all the members were together.

"Noisy enough for you, Mother?" Mark set the tray down on the table, pushing a couple of books out of the way. He spooned some sugar into her cup, poured in some cream and handed it to her.

"It's like music, don't you think, dear?" Lenore asked of her husband as she took her cup from Mark.

"I prefer Bach, myself," Nick grumbled, and raised his eyebrows as a cry went up from the corner of the living room where the teenagers were.

"I've got two hotels on Park Place. You're toast, Jennifer," one of the nephews crowed.

Mark handed his father a cup, offered the tray to Sheryl who shook her head. He took the last cup and eased himself down at his mother's feet.

"How are you feeling, Dad?" he asked, leaning his head back against his mother's chair.

"I got to slow down, doctor said," Nick retorted dryly. "I'm retired. How slow am I supposed to go?"

"He's grumpy because he's not allowed to help you and Nate with the haying," Lenore said, stroking her son's head.

Mark quirked his mother a lazy grin. "I don't know if he's that much help anyhow...."

"Watch what you say, Mark," Lenore admonished, giving his long hair a tug. "You'll goad him into coming out anyway. And when are you going to get your hair cut?"

"I'm trying to save money," returned Mark, winking at Sheryl.

Her only response was to take another sip of coffee.

Elise and the girls set trays of sandwiches and squares on the already-full coffee table, and the noise level immediately decreased.

"How is the ranch doing, Mark?" Brad leaned past his wife to address him. "Nate was saying that you landed a decent hay contract with a guy in Langley?"

"Yeah, Thomason up at the One-Oh-Eight put me on to him. He supplies a lot of hobby farmers and will take all we can give him. If the price is as good as he says, irrigating that hay land will more than pay for itself this year."

Mark popped a cookie in his mouth, and the talk turned toward the weather, loan payments and cattle futures.

Nate wandered into the room and joined in the conversation. Mark glanced at Sheryl who ignored both Nate and him, concentrating on the sandwich she held. Someone asked him a question, but as he answered it, he listened with half an ear to the conversation going on behind him, wondering if the dry wit of his father or the nosiness of his mother could draw Sheryl out.

Her replies were quiet, her manner self-contained, and after half an hour the only new thing Mark discovered was that she'd had chicken pox when she was nine, that she usually didn't have time for lunch and that her visit with her father went fine.

If you could call standing against the wall, arms crossed across her stomach, "fine." Mark knew her answer was an evasion, but with Sheryl, what else did he expect?

The afternoon wore on, and the older men took the kids outside to play volleyball. Diane and Elise were cleaning up in the kitchen, and Brad's wife kept Crystal, Marla and her own youngest son entertained.

Mark felt relaxed, comfortable, the welcoming ambience of his mother's home working its familiar magic. Wherever they had lived, Lenore had made each house a home, each place a focal point for their family to gather, talk and share fellowship.

Sheryl had moved to one of the couches, and as the room emptied, he dropped himself down on the one across from her.

"Oh, honey," his mother said suddenly, spying a red-cheeked Benjamin in the doorway of the living room, blanket tucked under one arm, book under the other. "Couldn't you sleep?"

He shook his head and toddled over toward his grandmother. But when he spied Sheryl, he veered off course and clambered up beside her, slapping his book on her lap.

"Read," he demanded, dragging his blanket up alongside, leaning against her.

Sheryl pulled away, then as she looked down on Benjamin's tousled head Mark could see her soften.

Her hand slowly lifted and touched a wayward lock of
hair, straightening it, and a look of such yearning came over
her it hit Mark deep and low.

The stern lines of her face smoothed, the hardness drifted
away, and she was transformed into the same beautiful girl
that had fussed over Marla's seat belt this morning.

Mark was inexplicably jealous of Benjamin. Jealous of
the way Sheryl's delicate fingers drifted over his head, the
soft smile she bestowed on him when he looked up at her.
Why was it that this young child brought out this soft part
of her, a part she never showed to any adult?

Mark wondered if he would ever know.

Chapter Four

The sun was up; however, the air wafting into the cabin was still cool and laced with the scent of fir and moldering underbrush.

The smell of the mountains. Sheryl stopped sweeping and closed her eyes. Effortlessly she drifted back over the years, remembering walks with her mother as they had discovered this new place. It had been so different from the prairies and the grain farm that Sheryl's first father had worked. These mountains, cradling wide-open valleys, held an elemental fascination for them.

Sheryl smiled as she relived those moments of discovery, happiness and a mother's love.

A quick shake of her head brought her back to the bleak present. Love was a scarce commodity, she reminded herself. God parceled it out in small portions, and it seemed she used up her share as a young child.

She bent over to sweep under the bed, and her broom hit something solid. Puzzled, she got down on her knees. A box.

Sheryl dropped the broom, pulled the box forward and opened the flaps. Loose papers, old scribblers and dog-eared paperback novels filled it. With a rueful grin Sheryl drew out a hard-cover journal that lay on the top. It had been a gift from her mother for her tenth birthday, the first one she'd celebrated here.

Sheryl sat back on her heels, running her fingers over the figure of the old-fashioned lady embossed on the cover. How she'd hated to ruin the clean, white pages when she'd first gotten it. But a need to express herself had overcome her reluctance and soon she'd written in it every day.

Sheryl opened the cover and saw the first words on the page, remembering again what it was like to be ten years old, confused and missing her father:

> I dreamed me and Mom and Dad still lived in Alberta.
> I dreamed Daddy was still alive. But then I woke up.
> I had to cry. I miss him so much.

Sheryl smiled ruefully, touching the childish writing with her finger, remembering the pain of a loss she didn't dare express. Her tears made her mother sad which would bother Ed.

> Mr. Ed Krickson wants me to call him Dad. He's really my stepdad but it sounds funny to call him that.

And that had been the beginning of the conflict, thought Sheryl.

She flipped past long and rambling descriptions of the cows, horses, plants and mountains. She remembered a young girl impressed with her surroundings.

"I like living here now." She had written this a few months later.

> I don't miss Daddy as much. But there's so much to do. I have to feed the orphaned calves, and my hands get so cold. I lost a mitten and Mr. Ed Krickson says

I can't have another one for at least a month. So I stole one from Nate. Just when I feed the calves, though. Then I put it back.

Sheryl closed the book. Now, looking at it from an adult's perspective, the incident seemed even more harsh and cruel than it had as a young child, when she'd been called irresponsible and careless. She put it away, determined to close the box and push it back under the bed, but another book caught her eye. A coiled scribbler. She'd started keeping her diary in leftover scribblers from school, because Ed had found her first diary and had punished her for the sins she had confessed to in it.

Jason smiled at me today. He's so cute, and Lainie thinks so, too. Nate, the daddy's boy, says he's trouble. I hate the way Nate stares at me lately.

As Sheryl read, she remembered how deep their antagonism had run. At first it had been fun having an older brother. But as they got older, Sheryl's battles with Ed escalated, and as a consequence, so did Nate's anger with her.

Sheryl turned over another page.

Jason wants me to go out with him on Friday. I shouldn't go, but I know Jason will talk me into it. Nate still won't talk much to me at the supper table. Just sits there and stares. I was supposed to pray tonight and told Ed I didn't want to. Mom started crying. I like to talk to God, but up in the mountains, away from them, not at the table in front of them where they can criticize what I say.

Sheryl frowned at the last sentences and closed the book. It seemed difficult to believe that she had once had such a simple faith in God.

She looked outside at the sunlight dancing between the branches of the fir trees. That God had made this part of the world was easy to see.

It was harder to see God in a city. It was even harder to talk to God when you were just trying to survive the bleakness.

And now?

Sheryl shrugged as she packed the books back in the box. She had drifted so far from God, it was improbable that she could find her way back to Him.

"Auntie Sheryl." Marla's voice shrilled through the silence. "Auntie Sheryl, you have to help." The voice came closer and as Sheryl got up she saw Marla coming at a dead run up the path.

She made it up the steps and sagged against the door frame.

"What's the matter, honey?" Sheryl ran to the door and fell on her knees before the panting little girl.

"My daddy...fell...down the stairs...in the house."

Sheryl jumped up and took off down the path.

"Wait for me...Auntie Sheryl?" Marla shouted, trying desperately to keep up.

Sheryl grabbed Marla's hand, almost dragging her around the front of the house and through the door.

Nate lay on the floor at the bottom of the stairs. His face was pale, his teeth clenched. Elise was crouched on her knees beside him, and Sheryl recognized her younger sister, Elaine, hovering behind her.

"Just lie still and tell me where it hurts," Elise cried, her hands fluttering over his chest.

"My leg." Nate sucked in a painful breath. "Maybe a broken rib or two."

Marla dropped down in a nearby chair and began to cry.

Elise glanced up at Sheryl, eyes wide, scared. "What do I do?"

Sheryl knelt beside Nate, across from Elise, and carefully felt down his leg. Nate winced when she reached his lower leg, and she stopped.

"Do you have anything long and flat that we can tie his leg to?" Sheryl asked. "We'll have to immobilize it for the trip to the hospital."

Elise covered her mouth with one hand, Marla's sobs increased.

"There's some one-inch boards in the garage," Nate ground out through clenched teeth.

"Elise, get some pieces of cloth we can rip up. Elaine, you help Marla." Sheryl snapped out her orders, turned and ran out to the shed.

When she returned with a suitable length of board, Elise was ripping material into strips, and Elaine was comforting Marla, who stared at her father, eyes wide, mouth still trembling.

With quick but careful movements, Sheryl tied his leg to the board, ordering Elaine to bring the van to the front door so they could load him inside.

"Sheryl," Nate caught her hand.

Sheryl paused, surprised at his acknowledgment of her.

"I'm supposed to drive my tractor to Mark. Can you do that for me?"

Sheryl turned her attention back to the knot she was tying and nodded.

Nate grimaced in pain. "Just go up the road to the old Simpson place. He'll be in the lower fields, along the creek."

"Sure" was all she could say. Nate hadn't spoken more than ten words to her since she had come, and now, even though he was in pain, all he could talk about was the ranch. It shouldn't hurt, but it did.

"I'll need you to help me take the seats out," Elaine called out after she parked the van.

Sheryl left to help, and after they had dragged the bench out, Elise showed up with a sleeping bag to lay down on the floor.

It took the three of them to move him, ignoring his shouts of pain and Marla's increasing tears.

"When are you going on that diet, Nate?" Elise groaned as they finally got him settled.

He smiled wanly at her, his face pale. She leaned over, kissed him lightly and climbed into the driver's seat. Elaine and Sheryl closed the door, and with a rumble of gravel, reminiscent of her brother's driving, Elise tore out of the yard.

The dust from her retreating van still hung in the valley when Sheryl felt reaction set in.

Too vividly she remembered a body at the foot of another set of stairs, a shadowy, menacing figure at the top. After that time Jason had given her a dozen roses. The next time, carnations.

She clutched her stomach as if to hold the memories in and turned to Elaine, pulling in a shaky breath. She was needed and had no time for histrionics.

"Can you stay here with Marla and Benjamin? I should take that tractor to Mark."

"Just give me a minute to check on Benjamin." Elaine ran up the stairs, pausing to pick up the toy truck Nate had slipped on.

Sheryl knelt down in front of Marla, stroking a lock of hair away from her damp cheeks.

"When your daddy comes back he'll have a hard white cast on his leg and a smile on his face." She had an inspiration. "You should make a card for him and when Crystal comes home from school, you could pick some flowers, like you did for me."

"My daddy won't die will he?" Marla sniffed, her eyes shiny with tears.

Sheryl frowned. "Of course not. It's just a broken leg."

"Daddy said Grandpa will probably die in the hospital."

Sheryl caught Marla in a quick hug. "Your daddy is big and strong," she reassured her. "I remember when he fell off the machine shed. He broke his arm, and it got fixed really good."

"Did you and Grandpa pray about it, is that why it got fixed?" Marla wiped her eyes with the heel of her hand, leaving brown smudges on her cheeks.

"I'm sure we did." It was all she could say. She remembered many prayers, but not one for mended arms.

"Well then, Auntie Elaine and I will pray that Daddy's leg gets better, too."

Sheryl smiled at her innocence and stood up. "I better go tell your uncle Mark your daddy won't be coming to help."

"He won't be happy. Uncle Mark said they had to finish this week."

Elaine came back down the stairs. "Benny's still sleeping. Thanks so much for helping," she said to Sheryl. "I don't know what Elise and I would have done without you."

"Managed, I guess." Sheryl shrugged, stroked Marla's cheek once more, then left.

"Conrad, toss me that can of lubricant," Mark strained at a nut under the tractor. The wrench slipped, and his knuckles scraped painfully across a metal bar. He sucked in his breath, and the heavy tool fell out of his hands onto his forehead. Shards of pain shot through his skull.

Conrad hunkered down beside him, holding out the spray can. "It's your p.t.o. clutch, man. That's why the baler don't work."

Mark closed his eyes, rubbing his sore head, stifling the

urge to scream. Could the day get any worse? It had taken him and Nate almost an hour to get the baler they'd rented from Jacksons' to work. Rob had taken his sweet time coming this morning, and now this tractor had broken down after they'd done one whole bale.

He grabbed the tractor tire with one hand, picked up the wrench with the other and dragged himself out from underneath, the hay stubble scratching his back as his shirt pulled up.

"At least we can still drive this piece of junk to the edge of the field. We'll need to pull out the clutch and take it in to get fixed, if Nate doesn't get here pretty quick with the other tractor."

"So what do you figure, Mark?" Conrad hovered beside him, his face expectant. "Do you want me and Rob to head into town?"

"Don't get your hopes up, buster. You guys can start with my tractor. I'll wait for Nate to come."

Conrad sighed and returned to Mark's tractor. He started it and, putting it into gear, roared off toward the other baler.

Mark bent over, snatched his hat off the ground and flipped it on his head. He yanked on his gloves and blew out his breath. A baler that wasn't working properly, one bum tractor and rain in the forecast. And where was Nate? How long did it take to run home and get a tractor, anyhow?

He vaulted up onto the crippled tractor, shoved it into gear and moved it slowly into the shade of the fir trees on the field's edge.

Mark turned around as a tractor roared into the field. That took him long enough, he thought, anxious to get going.

The tractor came closer and Mark leaned forward as if to see better. Since when did Nate have a pink T-shirt and long blond hair?

It was Sheryl.

She rolled noisily past Mark and stopped beside the

baler. Shoving the gearshift into neutral she pushed the throttle down. She waited a moment to make sure the tractor had come to a complete halt and then climbed out.

"I brought the tractor over." Sheryl raised her voice above the roar of the engine, looking up at him as he came closer. She wore the same faded pink T-shirt and blue jeans she'd had on the day they'd driven here. Her hair hung in a braid over one shoulder, but a few wisps had worked loose to blow around her face. Her cheeks had a glow to them, her mouth a soft smile. Mark felt mesmerized, then shook his head, belatedly yanking his hat off his head.

"I'm glad to see you and the tractor, but what happened to Nate?" he asked.

Her smile disappeared. "He broke his leg."

Mark stared her and as her words registered he closed his eyes, wondering what he had done the past few days to deserve this.

"Elise is bringing him into town, and Elaine is staying with Benjamin and Marla," she continued. "I don't know when they'll be back, but I don't suppose he'll be in any condition to drive a tractor for a while."

"That's obvious," Mark said, unable to keep the frustration out of his voice. "Well, thanks for bringing it here in one piece."

Not that it did much good now. Making square bales required two people per tractor, one driving, the other stuking the bales. They didn't have an automatic bale stacker, at least not this year. If they could make enough money on the bales they could look at a more efficient system for next year.

But if they didn't get these fields baled by the end of the week, they might lose the contract entirely. What a time for Nate to break his leg!

Sheryl pointed her chin in the direction of an old, rusted truck parked in the shade beside the broken-down tractor. "Mind if I take that back with me?"

"Go ahead," Mark answered, absently. "Rob can drive the tractor back tonight."

She nodded and turned to leave. Mark watched her go, a sudden inspiration hitting him.

"Hey, Sheryl," he called, running to catch up with her.

She stopped and glanced over at him, lifting one delicately arched eyebrow.

"Nate said you used to help on the farm...." He hesitated in the face of her cool, ever-present self-control.

"Of course. Everyone pitched in when there was hay to be baled." She smiled to take the sting off her words. "Why?"

Mark was hesitant to ask for her help, but the impending rain pushed aside his indecision.

"I don't imagine you would be willing to give me a hand?"

Sheryl tilted her head to one side, as if studying him, then she smiled a soft smile. "I probably could," she said.

Mark pushed his hat back on his head with a surge of relief.

"That's great." he said with a grin. "That's just great. If you just hitch Nate's tractor up to this baler we can get going."

The sun hung directly above them, beating down relentlessly. Sheryl's T-shirt stuck to her back and her head ached in spite of wearing Mark's hat. He'd given it to her when he'd seen her constantly shading her eyes against the glare of the sun. It was too big, but it gave her tired eyes and hot head some measure of relief.

She still didn't know what had come over her when she'd accepted Mark's offer of work. Part of it was his hesitant request. He'd seemed unsure of her response, which seemed a surprisingly unmasculine position.

As well, driving the tractor down the road this morning brought back good memories. These were the kind she cherished and hung on to, to keep the bad ones at bay.

Her eyes swept the golden field ahead. Dust from the baler hung in a soft haze. In the distance Rob drove the tractor and Conrad stuked, making their own circles. She had lost track of how many times she and Mark had gone around.

They followed the cool shade of the trees edging the creek, turned and headed toward the farmyard and corrals. The next turn followed the fence line and Sheryl caught periodic glimpses of the old Simpson house, now Mark's, that she had always admired as a girl. Then they headed back toward the creek, finishing the circle. And hovering over them as they worked, always within view—the mountains.

They were directly ahead of her now. Sheryl followed with her eyes the contours of the land, along the field ahead and up the dark green of the timber that broke here and there, and finally up to the gray unyielding rock swept by white snow, crisp against an achingly blue sky.

She drank it in, a feeling of belonging surging through her as she remembered stolen horseback rides up into their beguiling beauty. As a young girl she often lasted only one day of haying before the mountains called and she stole a quick ride on her horse up them the next morning, promising herself she would be back before Ed and Nate got started the next day.

She never made it.

Sheryl turned away from the view and rubbed her neck. It was sore from turning back and forth, first watching the swath, then the baler and always, in spite of herself, Mark.

The baler spat out another bale, and Mark grabbed it with gloved hands. He flexed his well-muscled shoulders, swing-

ing the bale onto the stuker behind him. His motions were
easy, fluid and as often as Sheryl looked away, her eyes
kept returning to him. His T-shirt clung to his chest and
his back in wet triangles. A red sweat-stained bandana held
his long dark hair down.

Mark glanced up at her then, flashed her a smile, a white
slash against his dark skin, and Sheryl's heart skipped a
beat.

Flustered she looked ahead. He disturbed her even as he
attracted her. It was disconcerting.

"Hey, Sheryl. Stop," Mark yelled. Sheryl jumped and
instinctively stepped on the brakes. She slapped the throttle
down with one hand and the p.t.o. drive with the other,
then turned around. Mark was already at the front of the
baler, yanking the cover off.

"It's jammed. Grab the toolbox, will you?" Mark didn't
even look at her as he pulled hay out of the baler. "Probably busted a shear pin, too," he said with disgust.

The baler must have hit a thick patch in the swath. Angry
at her own inattentiveness, Sheryl grabbed the toolbox and
got off the tractor. She set it beside Mark, annoyed at her
pounding heart and yet unable to quell the coil of fear that
began at the sound of his irate voice.

"Hand me the pliers, would you," Mark said looking up
at her. He straightened, his outstretched hand falling to his
side. "What's the matter?"

He had seen her fear. Sheryl thought all the years of
living with Jason had schooled her into keeping her emotions hidden, concealed. Weakness gave the other person
power. Angry at her lack of self-control, she turned to the
toolbox and found the pliers.

"It's no big deal, Sheryl," Mark said, his voice reassuring as he took the pliers. "Balers jam up all the time."

"I know that," she snapped, stepping back as he turned to the baler.

It was more than the baler, and she knew that, too. It was this place, so rife with memories that created this vulnerability. The mountains, the rivers, the trees. It tricked her into lowering her guard, into hoping that somewhere, somehow she could recapture the brief, happy moments she had once enjoyed.

Mark slammed the lid shut and turned to hand Sheryl the toolbox. "Are you okay, Sheryl?" he asked, his expression puzzled.

"I'm fine." She grabbed the toolbox and set it in the tractor cab, wishing her hands would stop trembling. Adrenaline, that's all it was.

"I wasn't going to hurt you." His voice was soft, his expression observant.

Sheryl took a deep breath. "I know," she said with a careless shrug. "We'd better get back to work." She climbed back onto the sun-warmed seat and glanced back at Mark.

He stood on the stuker, gloved hands on his hips, frowning. But when he caught her glance he quirked a grin at her. Sheryl blinked then started the tractor up, feeling oddly reassured.

Two hot, dusty hours later Mark signaled to her to stop. He jerked a thumb over his shoulder when she frowned, puzzled as to why they stopped.

A truck waited in the shade of the trees alongside the corrals, and Rob and Conrad were already walking toward it.

"Lunchtime, Sheryl," Mark called.

She turned off the tractor and paused a moment, letting her eyes drift over the field and all the triangular stacks of hay bales at regular intervals. It had been a satisfying morning.

She climbed off the tractor, Mark's hat falling over her face, and she pulled it off, lifting her heavy braid from the back of her neck. It had been a while since she had done any work outside, had sweated, had wiped hay dust from her eyes. It sure felt a lot better than aching feet from high heels and a burning throat from cigarette smoke.

Mark waited by the baler for her, and she couldn't help but comment.

"You still trying to prove your point?" she asked dryly as he fell into step with her.

"What point?"

"When we came to the hospital, you said that your mother raised you to be a gentleman and you were going to prove it to me."

"I'd forgotten about that." He flashed her a grin as he wiped off his face with his bandana. "So you think this is part of my campaign?"

"Isn't it?"

Mark paused by an overhanging tree and hung his bandana in it to dry and smiled. "So am I doing it?"

"What?"

"Proving my point to you?"

"Do you always answer questions with a question?" she countered with a sly grin, remembering their first conversation.

Mark laughed.

Funny that the sound of his laughter could kindle this gentle warmth within her, she thought as they walked toward the truck. To make someone laugh was a gift, but she felt as if Mark had just given her something instead.

Elaine had set a picnic cooler on a blanket laid out in the shade of the trees. Marla and Benjamin were jumping all over Rob and Conrad by the time Mark and Sheryl arrived.

"I'm going to throw you in the creek if you don't stop it, Bunny," Rob laughed, throwing Benjamin up in the air.

"He's not Bunny, he's Benjamin," Marla said indignantly, giving Rob's shoulder a push.

"Marla, don't be rude," Mark warned, his voice firm but quiet.

"Yeah, Marla." Conrad stuck his tongue out at her but stopped when he caught Mark's admonishing look.

"You're going to get kids just like you, you know," Mark warned them.

"His poor wife." Elaine laughed, setting out plates and sandwiches.

"Have you heard from Elise?" Mark asked as he took the plate Elaine had filled for him.

"Nate broke some bone in his lower leg, I can't remember which, and bruised some ribs. Elise was waiting for the plaster to dry, and then they were going to head back."

"Poor guy." Mark sighed. "I imagine he'll be out of commission for a few days.

"The cast has to stay on for about six weeks." Elaine smiled up at Sheryl. "I didn't even realize you didn't come back until I picked Benjamin up from his nap. Were you here all morning?"

"I stayed to help when I brought the tractor."

"Good for you. I sure couldn't do this work. Too hot and dusty." Elaine gave her a plate with a sandwich and some vegetables on it. "I think it's bad enough bringing lunch out."

Sheryl just smiled as she took the food and turned around, hesitating.

"Sit by me Auntie Sheryl," Marla dropped down beside Mark and patted the empty spot beside her.

With a shrug, she complied, stepping over Mark's long legs.

As Sheryl lifted her sandwich to take a bite, she saw Mark and Elaine bow their heads. Sheryl paused, not knowing where to look, uncomfortable, feeling like she should do the same but knowing it would be hypocritical.

Mark finished, looked up at her and winked at her as he took a bite out of his sandwich. He turned his attention to Rob and Conrad who had also paused.

"How's the tractor running?" he asked them.

With those prosaic words the spell broke, and Sheryl felt as if something precious had slipped away from her.

"Okay," Conrad mumbled around a mouthful of food. "But I'm going to need some more twine and a couple of extra sheer pins. We busted three so far."

"That's three more than us." Mark said, turning his head to grin at Sheryl.

"What?" Rob sputtered. "How did you pull that off?"

"Skillful driving and close attention to details."

"I would say it had more to do with light swaths," Sheryl said easily.

"And some skill." Mark reached past Marla and gently wiped a trickle of sweat from Sheryl's temple. "How are you feeling now?"

Sheryl's hand halted midway, frozen at his touch. Her heart stopped, did a slow flip and raced on. "I'm sorry, what did you say?"

"You looked flushed before I gave you my hat. I thought you might have a headache."

"No, I'm fine." Sheryl swallowed, still flustered at the casual touch of his callused fingertip on her temple. "Do you want your hat back?"

"No. With your fair skin and hair, you'll burn to a crisp without that hat."

"Is Sheryl going to help you this afternoon, too?" Elaine asked Mark as she fed Benjamin.

Mark turned his head slightly, his gray eyes holding Sheryl's. "That's entirely up to her."

He did it again, she thought. Either he was bound and determined to make his point about chivalry with each thing he did and said or it came naturally to him.

"I'll stay. I like to finish what I start."

She was supposed to have visited Ed this afternoon. That would just have to be put off until tonight. She'd much rather be outside, working, regardless of how dusty, hot and tiring it may be.

Mark smiled, a lazy movement of his well-shaped mouth, and Sheryl's heart skipped again.

"So, Sheryl, how long has it been since you were in the valley?" Elaine asked conversationally.

"I left the Cariboo about eight years ago." Sheryl replied, glad of the diversion.

"And you worked in Edmonton?"

Sheryl turned Mark's hat over in her hands, her elbows resting on her knees. "Yes," she said finally. "I did a number of different jobs but my last one was in a bar."

"Really," Rob lifted his head from his supine position. "Ed must have had asphyxiation when he found out. I just can't feature Ed Krickson's daughter working in a bar."

"Stepdaughter," Sheryl corrected, unable to keep the harsh tone out of her voice.

"How does that work?"

"Sheryl's mother was married before," Mark interjected.

"Oh, right. I remember my mom and dad talking about his stepdaughter. I didn't know that was you, Sheryl." Rob looked as if he wanted to say more.

"We'd better get back to work." Mark stood up, signaling the end of the conversation. Elaine looked disappointed, and Sheryl felt faintly relieved. It didn't seem to matter what the topic was, it always came back to things she didn't want to talk about.

Everyone got up at once. Mark explained to Rob and Conrad what he wanted them to do, and Sheryl helped Elaine clean up.

Benjamin leaned on the cooler, rooting around in the food. Sheryl laid the dirty plates inside and, giving in to an impulse, picked him up. He was so soft and rounded and appealing. She inhaled the sun-warmed smell of him and felt a melting inside of her.

"You're such a cutie, you know," she murmured in his ear. He pulled away, his soft blue eyes fixed intently on her face. One chubby hand reached out and grabbed a fistful of hair and he gurgled his pleasure.

Mark was finished with the boys and he sauntered over, Marla's hand in his. He stopped beside Sheryl and stroked Benjamin's cheek, his finger dark against the baby's fair skin.

"Hey, buddy, how're the teeth coming?" As if in answer, Ben grabbed Mark's finger with his free hand and tried to stick it in his mouth. "I don't think so," Mark warned pulling his hand away. "That's a yucky finger, full of grease and dust."

He wasn't touching her. In fact he stood almost a foot away, yet Sheryl was completely aware of him, the warmth that emanated from him, the faint smell of sweat overlaid with the dusty scent of hay. Unconsciously she took a step away, but Benjamin still held Mark's finger in one hand and her hair in another.

"Here," Mark pulled his finger away from Benjamin and, reaching around, disentangled her hair from the little boy's sticky hand.

Mark's fingers feathered her cheek, sending an unexpected shiver skittering down her back. She tried to keep her head down, but it was as if an unseen force drew her chin up, pulling her eyes toward his.

All the world seemed to drop away as she felt herself melting into soft gray eyes fringed with thick dark lashes. His eyelids drooped, and he came closer, closer.

"C'mon, Uncle Mark, you have to get back to work."

Marla's shrill voice broke the spell his nearness had woven around her, and Sheryl blinked, stepping away.

Benjamin leaned back in her arms, reaching out to Elaine, and Sheryl relinquished her hold on the baby, trying to still the pounding of her heart.

She swung around and walked back to the tractor, her steps brisk, her manner determined. She didn't know what was wrong with her, but somehow Mark was getting under her guard.

Too dangerous, she warned herself as she swung up the steps.

Chapter Five

Sheryl rolled her head to take the tightness out of her neck. A delicious weariness engulfed her. The day had been good, satisfying.

Her plans to visit Ed had, of necessity, been altered. Not that it mattered. It was a relief not to have to face any more of Ed's hesitant declarations of love.

It was only imminent death that had brought them forward, she thought, rubbing her neck. But even as she formulated the doubt, another part of her mind, the one that cried out for family and place, longed to have those words repeated for her to hold to herself.

She shook her head, as if to discard the confusion.

As she pulled her tired shoulders up to ease the persistent ache in them, she glanced across the truck at Mark.

His dusty face was shadowed along his lean jawline, and his hair was still held down by the red bandana he had rolled up and tied around his head that morning.

He looked almost like a pirate in the gathering dusk. Except pirates didn't have such long dark eyelashes, nor did pirates let their mothers stroke their hair, like Lenore had done yesterday. She envied him both his family and the absolute sense of rightness that surrounded his work. He was so obviously a part of this land that it was a stretch to imagine him making his living in the city.

Just then he looked over at her, his dark eyes gleaming in the dusk. His face was expressionless, his eyes piercing, and she looked away, berating herself for entertaining too many thoughts of him.

One more visit with Ed, and she was out of here, she promised herself.

"Looks like Nate is home," Mark said as they pulled into the driveway. He came to a stop and slowly pushed the gearshift into reverse. He turned to Sheryl, "Are you going to come in for something to eat—"

His question was cut off by the piercing honk of a horn as headlights swept behind them and shut off.

Sheryl turned, opening her door. She could see Lenore and Nick getting out of a small car. Nick bent over to take a box out of the back seat, and Lenore walked up to Sheryl her hands outstretched in greeting. "Sheryl, hello," she said with a smile. She caught Sheryl's hands before she had a chance to pull away.

"Goodness gracious, girl, what have you been doing today?" Lenore turned Sheryl's hands over and held them up to the light spilling from the verandah onto the vehicles. "You've got blisters on your palms." She looked over at Mark, who leaned against his truck, chatting with his father. "Mark, how did Sheryl get these blisters on her hands?"

Mark glanced over his shoulder at his mother, one eyebrow quirked at her demanding tone. "She was driving Nate's old Massey. Nate, you will remember, broke his leg and couldn't drive."

"Don't be flippant. Were you baling today?"

"On the fields below my house."

Lenore turned back to Sheryl, her face indignant. "It got up to eighty-five degrees today," Lenore fumed. "Don't tell me you were working in this heat, driving a tractor without a cab on it?''

"I had a hat on," Sheryl replied, bemused at Lenore's anger. What did it matter to Lenore what she did?

Still holding on to Sheryl, Lenore dragged her around the front of the truck, holding out the palms of her hands for Mark's inspection.

"Look at that, Mark. I can't believe you made her help you with such a horrible job. I know you were in a bind, but I'm sure you could have found someone in town."

Sheryl couldn't help but smile at the sight of this five-foot-nothing of a woman glaring up at her son who towered above her.

Mark shrugged helplessly, looking to his father.

"Why don't we do what we came here for, and that's see how Nate is doing and help Elise with supper?" Nick asked, pulling his wife toward him and winking at Mark.

"Are you two coming?" Lenore asked, looking back at them as her husband ushered her up the stairs to the verandah.

Sheryl opened her mouth to protest.

"I know what you're going to say," Mark said, touching her shoulder lightly. "But please don't start with that, Sheryl. Come on in, wash up and have something to eat, or my mother's going to think I'm a total boor."

Sheryl's stomach rumbled, and as she glanced at the brightly lit house a burst of laughter came from within. It was more appealing than her cabin with its meagre propane lantern light.

"As long as Elise doesn't mind dusty blue jeans on her chairs."

"She won't even notice."

The kitchen table was already set. Lenore was unpacking a pot of soup from the box Nick brought in, and Elaine was grilling cheese sandwiches. The smells made Sheryl's stomach clench with hunger.

"Did you want to give the children some of this soup, as well, Elaine?" Lenore asked as she put the pot on the stove.

"Just a bit. They should get to bed."

Lenore looked up as Sheryl and Mark came into the room. "Goodness, you two are even dirtier in the light. Mark you use the sink in the porch, Sheryl you can wash up in the one down the hall...." Lenore waved a spoon in the direction of the bathroom.

"I think Sheryl remembers where it is, Mom," Mark reprimanded his mother his tone light.

Lenore frowned at him, then as comprehension dawned, she laughed. "I forgot. You probably know this house better than I do, Sheryl."

"I used to. It looks so different now." She took a moment to appreciate the changes that Elise had wrought in what was once a dark and run-down room.

The cupboards had been covered with a fresh coat of white paint and trimmed with blue porcelain handles. The dusty-blue countertop was new as were the flowered tiles against the wall. Gaily patterned paper and bunches of dried flower arrangements decorated the wall, and in one corner white chairs with blue cushions were pushed up against a table topped with a blue-and-white-checked cloth.

"I like this kitchen," she said, smiling at Elise, who stood watching her, almost anxiously. "You've made it look fresh and inviting."

"Thank you. It was a bit of a battle to convince Ed and Nate that it needed a woman's touch, but once I started, they came around."

Sheryl smiled wryly, wondering why her mother had never dared to stand up to Ed. Maybe she had too much to lose, she thought as she walked down the hall to the bathroom, another room transformed from dull to bright.

As she washed her hands she caught her reflection in the mirror and grimaced. Rivulets of sweat had dried, leaving dark tracks on her dusty skin. Her eyes were rimmed with brown, her hair dull. Not much to look at now, not much to look at then, she thought, remembering the taunts of childhood.

She soaped down her hands and rinsed off her face.

As the brown water swirled down the drain she remembered a rebellious young girl who had refused to wear the skirts and dresses that Ed had insisted were proper for a young lady. The clothes that had made her classmates laugh at her.

As he had become more determined to bend and shape her and she had become even more determined to stay who she was, the battle had escalated. Push and shove, back and forth, neither yielding.

She looked in the mirror again and picked up a brush, wondering what would have happened if her mom had stood up for her? Or what would have happened if Sheryl had not resented Ed his place in her mother's life.

Sheryl sighed as she ran a brush through her long hair. It was all past, impossible to fix or relive. She rebraided her hair, noting with dismay the flecks of hay that dotted the immaculate floor.

She stepped out of the bathroom to get a broom, almost bumping into Nate.

"Hi," she stammered. "How are you feeling?"

"I ache all over," he mumbled, pulling one crutch closer to let her pass.

He closed his eyes, his face pale. "I didn't say it before, but thanks for what you did."

"You're welcome." She bit her lip, feeling the tension between them. "Do you need any help now?"

"No. I'll manage on my own."

Sheryl hesitated a moment. He still didn't move, so she stepped carefully past him and walked down the hallway to the kitchen.

Marla and Crystal were eating already. One sat on each

side of Mark, as he fed Benjamin some soup. Mark's movements were awkward, the tiny spoon almost lost in his hands, and with each spoonful he gave Benjamin, he unconsciously opened his mouth as well.

Sheryl's steps slowed. He looked far too appealing now, his hair still dented from the bandana he'd worn all day, his lean jaw shadowed with whiskers. He looked darkly handsome, dangerous, the image so at odds with the domestic scene in which he seemed so comfortable.

"Oh, there's Sheryl...and Nate." Lenore rushed past Sheryl to Nate, hovering as Nate clumped down into the kitchen and eased himself into a nearby chair.

"Daddy!" Marla and Crystal cried out in unison. They jumped from their seats, jostling Mark.

"Whoa, girls," he reprimanded, almost spilling the spoonful of soup he was transferring to Benjamin's waiting mouth.

Marla and Crystal eased themselves around him, then scampered over to their dad's side.

Sheryl couldn't help but watch as Nate's children hovered, his wife slipped her arms around his shoulders and his mother-in-law fussed over him. Why did it hurt? Why did it matter that Nate was the one everyone ran to. This was his house, his place.

Swallowing, she slipped into a chair on the opposite end of the table, one over from Mark.

"So your face didn't go permanently brown," he commented with a grin.

"I feel like I left a bale of hay in Elise's bathroom.... Oh, no, I was going to sweep it up." She rose, but was forestalled by Mark's hand on her forearm.

"Don't worry about it. Elaine or Elise can get to it after. The haying crew gets preferential treatment."

"So, can we eat this soup or are we going to live on love?" Nick complained.

In a flurry of people and chairs moving, the family sat

around the table. An expectant pause hovered just before
the meal when Nick looked around, smiling. He held out
his hands to Elise on one side and Lenore on the other.
Marla sat on one side of Sheryl, Crystal on the other, and
they both clasped her hands in theirs, as well.

Nick bowed his head and began to pray.

Sheryl blinked a moment, bowed her head but kept her
eyes fixed on the oil stain on her left leg.

But Nick's gentle voice and soft-spoken prayer drew
Sheryl in. He thanked the Lord for the weather and for the
work that was done. He thanked God that Sheryl could have
helped Nate and that she was able to help Mark, as well.
From thanks he moved on to requests for Ed's return to
health and to spare his life. Nick's words, spoken with a
quiet confidence, were simple and straightforward, more
like a conversation than a listing of confessions.

Sheryl closed her eyes as a faint remembrance of her
own prayers trickled upward. How long had it been since
she'd felt her prayers were getting through to God? She
had winged enough heavenward those first few years.

But here, now, with Nick's soft prayers drawing her up,
she felt the faint touch of eternity. And as Nick said amen,
Sheryl felt bereft. She kept her head down, drawing herself
back into this room, composing herself. When she looked
up it was to smiling faces drawing her into their meal and
their communion.

The first few moments were quiet as Elaine, Elise and
the children finished their interrupted meal. They then excused themselves.

"Kiss your dad good night girls and it's off to bed with
you." Crystal and Marla protested, but Elise held firm.

Nate hugged his daughters, wincing as he did so, gave
Benjamin a soft kiss on his red cheek and watched them
as they left the room. Then he turned back to Mark.

"So how did baling go?"

"We got most of my field done," Mark replied, hunched

over his soup. "We'll be able to move the tractors to the river-bottom land tomorrow."

"What?" Nate looked up from his supper. "How did you manage that with only one tractor and baler?"

"Sheryl brought your tractor over and stayed and helped until we were done."

Nate's spoon hovered in midair, his mouth open. He blinked, looked at Sheryl, frowning. "Why?"

"Why what?" Mark laughed.

"I mean, why did you help, Sheryl?"

Sheryl stirred her soup, lifting one shoulder in a negligent shrug. "I had nothing else to do, and I know how busy haying season can be." She toyed with a noodle, avoiding his eyes.

"And what about tomorrow?" Nate's question hung between them. "I seem to remember that you never seemed to be around the next day."

Sheryl knew he alluded to the times she would steal a quick ride up into the mountains on those glorious mornings that were also perfect haying weather. She chose not to respond.

"You mean to say you helped with the haying when you were young?" Lenore asked.

"I only had to drive the tractor when we were stuking and when we were picking up the bales," Sheryl replied, surprised at the incredulous tone of Lenore's voice.

"How old were you when you started?"

Sheryl pursed her lips, thinking back. "Probably about eleven or twelve."

"What?" Lenore looked first at Sheryl, then at Nate, her eyes wide. "Your feet barely reached the floor at that age. I can't believe Ed actually made her do that, Nate."

"We had a ranch to run. Everyone had to pitch in." Nate's tone was defensive.

"If a ranch depends on twelve-year-old girls driving tractors then I don't think it has a right to keep going," Lenore returned.

"It was only during haying season," Sheryl put in, trying to ease the gathering tension.

Lenore opened her mouth to speak again.

"Can I bother you to get me some more soup, my dear and docile wife?" Nick interrupted.

"Good idea, Dad." Mark held out his bowl, as well, grinning at his mother. "Keep her feet moving and they might not end up in her mouth."

Lenore glared at her husband, then her son, but got up. The rest of the meal passed quickly and soon Sheryl could feel the effect of working outside all day. The room was warm, and the edges of everything in her line of vision grew fuzzy.

She gave her head a shake. She had to get moving or she'd fall asleep. She got up and began stacking the empty bowls, Mark laid a restraining hand on her arm.

"Elaine and Elise can do it. You've had a busy day."

The warmth of his fingers sent a quiver through her stomach. She knew she should pull away, keep moving, but somehow her body wouldn't respond to her mind.

"I...I should go, anyway. I'm tired, and if you need help tomorrow, then I need my sleep."

"You're not going to do that dusty, dirty job tomorrow, too, are you?" Lenore asked.

"I want to, Mrs. Andrews. It's okay." She smiled at Lenore. "Say good night to Elise for me, please. And thanks for the delicious meal."

"You're welcome." Lenore smiled warmly, and Sheryl couldn't help but return it.

Mark got up, as well, leaned over and kissed his mother on the cheek. "I think I'll head back, too. Tomorrow's going to be a long day."

"Are you going to give Sheryl a chance to come in and

see Ed sometime in the next couple of days?'' Lenore asked.

"That's up to her," Mark replied quietly, straightening.

"I can come and get you tomorrow afternoon," Lenore said to Sheryl.

Sheryl threw a questioning look at Mark, who only shrugged.

"How about later on in the day," Mark suggested with a yawn. He rubbed his neck and blinked. "Late afternoon should give us enough time."

"I'll bring a late lunch at two-thirty. Nick could manage a few turns around the field. Couldn't you Nick?"

"As long as I can drive slow," he replied dryly. He grinned at his wife's puzzled look. "Doctor's orders, remember."

Sheryl watched the give-and-take between them, smiling at the total lack of conflict in Mark's family, so different from the atmosphere that had pervaded this kitchen when she and her mother had lived there. She shook her head, dispelling the mood and turned to leave.

The porch door squeaked open behind her. A quick glance over her shoulder showed her that Mark was following her out.

"Wait a sec. I'll walk you home," he said, pausing to pull on his battered cowboy boots.

"It's not that far," Sheryl replied, but she waited anyway, a gentle warmth suffusing her cheeks. She put it down to being outside all day, but as they walked in silence down the darkened pathway to her cabin, a sense of waiting drifted around her.

Leaves rustled as they passed by, and far off a coyote threw its lonesome wail out into the soft night.

Sheryl stopped by the door of her cabin. "This is a first for me, you know," she joked, trying to lighten a mood that felt sombre.

"What's that?" Mark leaned one shoulder against the door frame, his eyes resting on her.

"Having a man walk me to my door."

"Jason never did?"

Sheryl laughed. "Jason would drop me off at the end of the driveway, and I would climb up the verandah and sneak into my room."

"Ed didn't like him, did he?"

"Ed hated him." Sheryl looked away. "Nate didn't like him, either. I guess that's one of the things they were right about."

"What do you mean?" Mark's voice was quiet, prompting, but Sheryl didn't get drawn in.

"It doesn't matter anymore." She took a breath, but to her own surprise it was a little shaky. Fatigue, she thought. "It's all past and things have to move on."

"I don't know if our past is ever past…"

"Please don't start analyzing my life," Sheryl interrupted, trying to soften her words with a light laugh.

"Hobby of mine," was all he said, leaning one shoulder against the door frame. It put him a little too close to her, but she refused to let his size, height and mere presence intimidate her. "I think much of what happened to us in the past shapes the decisions we make for our future."

"So what made you leave Vancouver to come here?" Sheryl verbally sidestepped, changing the direction of the conversation.

Mark rubbed the side of his nose, as if thinking about the answer.

"Well," she prompted.

"When I was a young boy, I used to dream of being a cowboy. Used to sit on a fence, wearing my cowboy hat and boots, just sitting, staring off into the distance. But in my mind I was on the Goodnight-Loving trail, pushing horns, eating dust and fording rivers." He laughed softly.

"I'm sure for a while there my parents thought I was losing it."

"So how did you end up in real estate?"

"It was a place to make money. I spent enough years in college and thought I could make a quick buck on the side."

Sheryl frowned. "You don't seem the avaricious type."

"Thanks for that." Mark pushed his hair out of his eyes and grinned down at her. "I was at that time though. Made a pile of money and thought I had the world by the tail."

"So what made you sell out?"

Mark sighed, staring past her. "I saw what was happening to my friends. Saw the emptiness in their lives and how few of them were really doing what they wanted. As a Christian I couldn't see myself wasting my life like that. So when my parents told me that there was a place for sale beside Nate and Elise's, I chucked it all and came out here." He reached out and touched her hair, his fingers warm on her forehead. In the pale light his eyes seemed to glow, and Sheryl felt a shiver of apprehension. "And here is where I want to stay." He dropped his hand. "And what about you?"

"I have plans."

"College?"

Sheryl nodded.

"And after that?"

"A job as a teacher, I hope."

"No marriage plans?"

"Been there. Done that." She flicked her hands deprecatingly, as if the past eight years were a mere blip in her life.

"Not all men are like Jason, you know."

"I've met more that are than aren't." She replied, uncomfortable with the intensity she saw in his probing gaze. "So we'll just change that subject."

"Okay." Mark smiled lazily at her flippant reply. He

shifted his stance so his back was against the wall of the cabin. "I love this time of the evening," he said, falling in with her request. "I love looking at the stars, even though it makes me feel small and unimportant." He hooked his thumbs in the belt loops of his pants as he stared at the stars strewn across the inky black darkness. "Isn't it amazing how vast the universe is?"

Sheryl bit her lip, sensing where the conversation was going this time, and she didn't know if she liked it anymore. She said nothing.

Mark didn't seem to notice her silence.

"God sure made a beautiful world."

"This part of it, yes," she replied.

He glanced at her as if encouraging her to say more.

"God hasn't been around my part of the world much these past few years," she added, trying to keep her voice matter-of-fact.

"If you seek Him, you will find Him," Mark replied softly.

"I don't want to talk about God, either."

Mark straightened, then turned back to her, lifting her hand, and Sheryl wondered what he was up to. She wasn't used to the casual touches he bestowed so freely. "My mom was right," was all he said. "You do have blisters." He traced them lightly with the tip of his other finger.

"It doesn't matter." She could barely get the words past the constriction of her throat. She tried to pull back, but this time he held firm. Then he bent over and kissed her palm, closing her fingers over the warmth his mouth left behind as if to save it.

Sheryl's heart slammed into her chest, and she snatched her hand away from him, her cheeks burning.

"Thanks for helping," he whispered. "I'll pick you up around eight o'clock tomorrow." And with another wink, he turned and left her.

Unable to keep her eyes off his retreating figure, she

watched him, his soft whistling marking his progress until he disappeared. A few moments later Sheryl heard his truck start and drive away.

She uncurled her hand, looking down at it, expecting to see a mark where his lips had touched her palm. All she saw were lines of grime she couldn't wash out and two red blisters. What was he trying to do to her? she thought as she leaned back against the door, suddenly chilled. She didn't need his solicitous concern, his questions that probed deeper than "Are you free tonight?"

She turned and retreated into her cabin.

But as she lay in bed, all she could think of was hair that almost hung in soft gray eyes, the feel of his mouth on her palm and his quiet faith in God. A faith she knew she could never share.

Chapter Six

Sheryl peeled her orange slowly, her ear attuned for the sound of Mark's truck. The early morning sun finally found its way through the thick foliage, touching the porch with a soft warmth.

Two hours ago she'd given up trying to sleep, and after getting dressed she'd stolen into Elise's kitchen to grab a bite to eat. Thankfully no one had been awake, so she'd helped herself to a couple of bran muffins and an orange and wrote Elise a note.

The moments of wakefulness had given her time to regret her offer to help Mark. She may as well face the fact, she thought, pulling another piece of peel off the orange. Mark scared her. His charm and interest in her life created a potent combination she was unused to dealing with.

Sheryl pulled a face and popped a section into her mouth. She remembered too well each one of Mark's casual touches, his intent looks.

Probably treated all girls the same, she thought, finishing her orange and wiping her hands on her pants. She clung to that notion, because dwelling on any other possibility was too distracting.

She knew she wanted to take this job from start to finish. Nate practically challenged her to last night. She was determined to show him that he was wrong.

Sheryl picked up her orange peels and tossed them deep in the bush. Suddenly restless, she got up and began walking down the driveway. She would finish what she started, she promised herself. As for Mark, well she would treat him with the same lighthearted humor that she did any of the men who had shown interest in her over the years. Guys tended to leave you alone if you treated them like you were a brother, she'd found out.

The muted roar of a truck's engine bounced off the hills, drawing nearer, and suddenly, there he was, dust roiling in his wake as his truck bore down on her.

Mark stopped beside her with a rumble of gravel, and before he could roll down his window, Sheryl ran over to the passenger door and jumped in the cab.

"Aren't you the eager and willing worker?" he said with a grin as he reversed and spun the truck around.

"I like that," she returned, forcing a light tone into her voice. "Demoted from lifesaver to worker. You didn't even try to open my door for me."

"I'd have had to stop twenty feet in front of you in order to beat you to it." He winked at her, stepped on the accelerator and bounced over the cattle guard that divided the yard from the road.

Sheryl sat back, pleased with herself. It was surprisingly easy to sit in his truck, to think of spending the whole day together. Perhaps she had only imagined the undercurrents that seemed to flow around them last night.

At the end of the driveway Mark turned right this time, toward the river.

"Rob and Conrad moved the tractors down to the river-bottom land last night. We'll be working there for a few days," he explained as the truck picked up speed. The scenery flew by, towering fir trees hovering along every curve as they dropped lower into the valley. Ahead of them Sheryl caught a glimpse of the river, flanked by fields ridged with thick swaths of hay.

"How do you get to the fields on the other side?"

"There's a wooden bridge around the next curve of the river. We'll work on this side the next couple of days and if all goes well, we'll cross and spend the rest of the week on the other side."

"Are the cows still in the upper pastures?"

Mark nodded. "I have to check them as soon as haying is done. My family usually organizes a pack trip in conjunction with that and escorts me and whoever is coming along, halfway there."

"Sounds like fun."

"You can come if you want."

"Right."

"Serious." Mark looked at her, his eyes wide. "I bet Elise will ask you, anyway."

"I don't think I'll be around by then." Sheryl couldn't imagine accompanying such a close-knit family on what was obviously a family event. Sunday dinner at Mark's mother and father's place had been difficult enough.

"I see," he said, grinning at her. "You're one of these transient workers who just drifts in and out with the tide, looking for whatever work comes your way."

"That was Jason's line," she replied with a light laugh, trying to get caught up in his banter.

Mark seemed to hesitate a moment, his wrist resting on the steering wheel as he frowned at the road ahead. "What exactly did Jason do for a living?"

Sheryl tilted a wry look his way, puzzled at his interest. "You mean all the helpful gossips in the valley haven't filled you in on Jason Kyle and his famous escapades?"

"I haven't lived here long enough. The only people who I've heard talk about Jason are Ed and Nate."

"I'm sure they had a lot to say about him."

Mark shrugged, his eyes still on the road. "They didn't like him. I gathered that much."

Sheryl said nothing at that. *Hate* was a more apt description than *didn't like,* except good Christian men like Nate and Ed would never admit to feeling that way about another human being.

"So what kind of work did Jason do?"

"You really are persistent...."

"No, I'm an Andrews." Mark tossed her a quick grin. "And I've learned everything I know about asking questions from my mom and sister."

"Well then, I'm out of my league." Sheryl laughed, relaxing around his lighthearted manner. "Jason started out as a helper for a carpenter, and once he figured he knew enough, he started working for himself. And from there things went from worse to worser."

"How did that happen?"

Sheryl sighed, clasping her arms across her stomach, not really wanting to talk about this, but unable to formulate a reason she shouldn't.

"Jason didn't do really well at his business, and he started drinking." She gave a short laugh. "And with the prices of liquor it doesn't take much to drink away a week's wages, especially if your buddies are thirsty, too."

Mark was silent at that. "I'm sorry, Sheryl. I didn't know...."

"That's okay, Mark."

"Maybe." He glanced at her, his expression serious. "I can't explain it, but I have a need to know more about you, to know where you stand with God. It matters to me, but I don't want you to feel that I'm pushing you."

Sheryl held his gaze a moment, touched by his honesty. "You're some kind of guy, Mark Andrews," she said with a rueful shake of her head.

Mark pulled up beside the tractor and baler they used yesterday. The other tractor and baler was parked farther down the field, silent, waiting. Sheryl stepped out of the truck, inhaling the scent of mown hay that still lingered in the morning dew.

The air held a slight chill this far down the valley, and Sheryl hugged herself against it. She took a few steps into the field, dropped her head back and looked around, turning a slow circle. The clouds were hard white against the sharp blue of the sky, the contrast almost painful to see. Purple-tinged mountains, skiffed with a dusting of snow on their peaks surged down to green and brown hills. The shushing sounds of the river at their feet softened and lulled the vastness of the landscape.

She took a deep breath and released it, as if cleansing herself. The years of living in the city had buried these pictures, blurred them. She couldn't stop the smile that curved her lips as the familiar countryside became once more a part of her.

"Ready for some more blisters?" Mark's deep voice beside her made her jump, breaking the moment.

She glanced up at him. His tall figure blocked the sun, casting his features in shadows. Unconsciously Sheryl took a step back.

"Don't be so skittish," he said, holding out a hat. "I just wanted to give you this."

He took a step closer, and Sheryl steeled herself to stand still as he dropped the hat on her head. "Now you have your own." She felt the warmth of his hands through the hat's material as he set it at the correct angle on her head. "It should be straw, but this is all I could find." His gray eyes glinted at her, and as Sheryl held his gaze, something indefinable held them and she couldn't look away.

"Feels good, thanks." Her voice was shaky, and she swallowed, willing her legs to move. If she was smart, she would turn around right now, head down that road and keep going. She was crazy to think that she could keep him at arm's length. Mark was attractive, decent, honest and far too compelling.

"We better get going," she said, trying to keep her voice light and carefree. She scrambled up the steps to the seat of the tractor and concentrated on the job at hand.

Sheryl had picked up the rhythm of the tractor again, slowing down when the swaths were heavier, speeding up along the treeline. The hay didn't grow as thick there because of the nutrients the trees took up from the soil. But everywhere else the swaths were dense and rich, the fragrant dust swirling around the tractor in an ever-present haze.

In the distance Mark saw Rob and Conrad making their own tedious circles, the "chunk, chunk" of their baler and the chug of the tractor's engine, muted by the distance.

He stood easily on the drag, waiting for the baler to spit out another bale. He grabbed it, braced it on one thigh and using the weight of the bale and its momentum, turned and swung it around, dropping it neatly beside the other three so it sat like a square diamond between the pipes, the tops of the bales forming a zigzag pattern. He straightened, paused and grabbed the next one, dropping it neatly into the open triangle formed by two bales side by side, making the next layer. Ten bales to a triangular stuke, hit the release pedal, and the pipes lowered until the bottoms of the bales hit the ground and pulled away from the stuker.

Mark glanced up at Sheryl who sat half-turned on the tractor seat, her long hair tied up in a loose braid, hanging beneath the battered felt hat. She pulled her shoulder up to her chin, wiping a trickle of sweat that reached her chin, leaving a track in the dust on her face. Mentally he compared her to the carefully coiffed and expensively tailored girls he once had squired around Vancouver, trying to imagine any of them perched on a tractor with a brown cowboy hat, two sizes too big shading a dusty face.

The picture made him laugh. As he did so, Sheryl caught his eye, held it for a heartbeat, then blinked and looked away again, and Mark followed the direction of her gaze.

The mountains.

Whenever she had a chance, her gaze would fly to the mountains.

The words of Psalm 100 came to mind. "I lift up mine eyes to the hills, from whence cometh my help." His help came from God. Sheryl claimed she didn't need any help.

He caught another bale, and when he had straightened, she was looking at him again. He smiled back, trying to coax a smile from her, and when she responded, the quickening of his own heart caught him by surprise.

She was completely the wrong person for him, and she made that very clear with each word she spoke in anger against God.

Yet...

When her iron self-control slipped, her vulnerability showed. It was this girl that drew him.

They made a few more rounds when the sound of a horn's insistent honking penetrated the growling of the tractor's engine. He caught sight of his mother, standing in the shade of the trees, her hands on her hips. Even from this distance he could sense her displeasure. Well she could grumble all she wanted. Sheryl seemed determined to finish this job and Mark wasn't going to argue. He needed the help and, curiously, he enjoyed being with her.

The next time Sheryl looked back, Mark pointed to his watch. She waited until the next bale was forced out and stopped the tractor.

Mark dropped the bale into the stuke and pulled his already damp bandana from the release lever of the stuker, wiping his face with it.

Sheryl paused a moment, her eyes wandering over the field, a soft smile teasing the corner of her mouth. Mark watched her, bemused at her obvious love for the land, puzzled that she couldn't see the Creator behind the creation.

He waited until she climbed down off the tractor and fell into step with her.

"Tired?" His voice resonated with concern.

"Yeah." She took off the hat and handed it back to him. "I feel like falling into a tub of water and not coming up for air the rest of the day."

"I get the feeling you're not looking forward to seeing Ed again?"

"It's the reason I made the trip out here." She looked away, her feet dragging in the hay stubble as she rubbed her neck.

"Do you want me to come with you?"

She twisted her head around, her expression puzzled. "Why would you want to do that?"

He didn't know, himself, except that he felt she wasn't ready to face Ed and whatever buried memories might surface, and he felt a curious protectiveness toward her. "I guess I'm not sick of spending time with you yet." His tone was light, but the eyes that held hers were steady.

"I'll be okay." She pushed her hair back from her face, tucking the sweat-dampened tendrils behind her ears, turning away from him, shutting him out. But the trembling of her fingers belied the firm tone of her voice.

"Then why do you look scared?"

She clenched her hands into fists and stared ahead. "I'm not scared," she replied, her voice hard.

Mark only sighed. Why did he keep trying? The precious little she gave away was only what slipped past her control. Nothing was relinquished willingly.

Rob and Conrad were already sitting down eating, by the time Sheryl and Mark came.

"It took you long enough," Lenore scolded. "Come sit here, Sheryl, I've brought a lawn chair for you. Just pull up beside Nick." Lenore handed Sheryl a plate of food, an assortment of cold cuts, a bun and some fruit slices.

"And what about your own son?" Mark complained, an unexpected irritation flickering in his voice.

"My own son is perfectly capable of bringing his own lawn chair in his own truck." Lenore said briskly.

Lunch was quiet, the talk desultory in the energy-sapping heat.

Nick, Mark and Lenore exchanged idle chat, Rob and Conrad dozed and Sheryl said nothing.

Mark tried to catch her eye, but she kept them either on her food or tilted up and away from him, toward the hills that cradled the river. He tried to analyze what it was about her that kept drawing him back to her. She made him feel both frustrated and content, sad and yet peaceful. She seemed to belong here, yet she made it very clear that she would leave once her obligations were fulfilled.

When Lenore got up, Sheryl followed suit, picking up the empty plates, gathering up the remnants of food and repacking the picnic cooler.

"When do you expect to be back?" Mark asked as he tugged on the blanket, waking Rob and Conrad. They stretched and got up, grumbling about slave-driving bosses. He shook the leaves and bits of hay off it and folded it up.

"I thought Sheryl could have supper with us. Then Nick can take her home." Lenore closed the cooler and brushed her hands off on her blue jeans.

"Okay. Just drive carefully."

Lenore shot Mark an oblique glance. "Actually I thought I might go flying through the valley as fast as you usually do."

"Rob and Conrad almost hit a couple of deer close to the bend by the old Newkiwski homestead." Mark lifted up the cooler with a grunt. "That's why I was telling you to be careful." He carried it back to the car, waiting for his father to open it.

"Point taken, son." Lenore smiled at him. "Sheryl, you just sit in the car and take it easy. I'll be there in a minute."

Sheryl hesitated, and Mark saw it again. That brief flash of fear. He took a step toward her, then stopped himself. Why did he always fall for those few scraps of emotion that she allowed to eke out? Why did it take so precious little on her part for him to try so hard to connect with her. He turned back to his parents' car, slamming the trunk closed just a little too hard.

"Easy on my car, son." Lenore frowned at him but he didn't reply. "Are you going to bring your father home? Because if you are, then you can have supper with Sheryl and us."

"Naw." Mark tossed a quick glance at Sheryl, who still hesitated by the door of the car, then turned resolutely away. "Dad can take the old brown truck home. Rob can get it when we need it."

He shouldn't try to spend any more time than he had to with Sheryl. She didn't need anyone. She certainly didn't need him.

"I thought I would give you a chance to visit with Ed for a while, by yourself." Lenore pulled into an empty spot in the parking lot and left the car running.

"Okay." Sheryl put her hand on the door's handle, hesitating.

"Ed has been very eager to see you." Lenore turned to Sheryl, touching her shoulder lightly. "He isn't always the easiest person to be around, but I can assure you he has changed."

Sheryl nodded as the words that whirled around her head all afternoon increased their tempo and finally slipped out. "He told me he loved me," she said, her voice bitter. "The whole time I lived with him and my mom, he never said that to me. Why now?" Sheryl bit her lip, rubbing a trembling finger against her temple, her eyes closed.

Lenore's hand tightened on her shoulder as anger and sorrow contended with each other. She looked sidelong at Lenore. "I wasn't the easiest daughter, I know that, but was I so unlovable?"

"I wish I knew, honey," Lenore said softly. "You should ask Ed."

Sheryl blinked, her finger still pressed against her head as if to draw out the questions that begged answers. "I know I should.... But where do I start?"

"With the question you ask yourself the most." Lenore smiled softly at her. "You won't be going there on your own strength, I'll be praying for you."

"For what that's worth," Sheryl said as she opened the door.

Lenore leaned over, catching the door before Sheryl shut it. "God has the power to change people, Sheryl."

Sheryl held the open door, looking down on Lenore and the assurance she saw there. For a moment she believed her. Just for a moment.

"Thanks, I think." She gave Lenore a wan smile, turned and walked up the sidewalk to the hospital, a soft breeze cooling the heat of her cheeks, teasing her freshly washed hair, enveloping her with the soft fragrance of the shampoo she had used at Lenore's.

As she approached the glass doors, she stopped. What was she doing here? she thought, her hand resting on the sun-warmed handle. It wouldn't change anything, either in the past or present. She could just turn around and go back.

Just then brisk steps sounded behind her, and a work-roughened hand reached around her to open the door.

Sheryl spun around, the bright sun blinding her. All she saw was a tall figure wearing a cowboy hat.

Mark.

Her heart skipped, she began to smile in greeting, surprised to see him here.

"Do you need some help?" The figure spoke, and Sheryl felt the keen edge of disappointment.

She stepped back as the man opened the door and waited for her to go in. The singular smell of the hospital assailed her nostrils, and she hesitated.

"Well, if you won't go in, I will," the man growled, stepping past her. Sheryl caught the door on the backswing, berating herself for her foolish notions. Mark was in the field, baling, and she was on her own. Taking a fortifying breath of fresh air, she stepped into the darkened hallway.

Ed sat by the window when the nurse ushered her into his room. The loose hospital gown was covered with a brown bathrobe that hung loosely on his large frame, and he wore leather slippers.

He looked like an old tired man, and as he turned, Sheryl swallowed. For a fleeting moment she thought she saw pain in his eyes.

"How...are you?" he asked, his words slurred by his misshapen mouth.

"Fine." Sheryl sat down in the hard vinyl chair across from him, the daylight from the window further illuminating the ravages the stroke had wrought in this once-proud man. The droop of his eye was more noticeable in the unforgiving light of the sun, the gray in his hair more pronounced. His entire body listed to one side, propped up by pillows.

Sheryl leaned back, crossing her arms as she faced the man she had so many questions to ask. It was easy for Lenore to encourage her to start with the one she asked herself most. It was also the one that caused the most anguish.

"How are you feeling?" she asked, opting for safe ground even though the question sounded trite in the face of his obvious decline. Lenore also said that God had the power to change people. Well if that's what had happened to Ed Krickson, then she didn't know if she wanted to get too close to God.

"I…wanted so bad…to see…you." Ed shifted his weight, trying to lean forward, his one good eye piercing, probing. "How are you? Are you…right…with…God?"

"What does it matter to you, Dad?" She hadn't meant to call him that, but the situation hearkened so strongly back to her past the name slipped out. "God and I understand each other. He leaves me alone, and I leave him alone."

"No…no…Sheryl." He reached out to her looking distressed, his hand barely lifting off the arm of the chair. "You…can't leave…God alone. He'll find…you."

Sheryl closed her eyes, wishing she could as easily shut out the all-too-familiar words. "I've been in deep and dark places since I left, Dad, and God hasn't found me in them."

"What…places?"

Sheryl shook her head. *Tell him*, her thoughts urged. *Let him know what it's been like for you.*

"Sheryl…I wish…I could…help you. I was…so wrong."

She sat up at that, leaning forward now, his confession bringing questions to the fore.

"Why did you turn me away, Dad? Why did you let me down when I needed you?"

Ed shifted, trying to move, as Sheryl got up, her arms wrapped tightly around her middle, wrinkling her T-shirt. Slow down, she warned herself. You're all alone, no one will help you through this. She took a deep breath to still the voices and her beating heart.

"I'm sorry…"

Sheryl rubbed her upper arm again and again as if to erase the memory of the pain. "Sorry." The word came out in a burst of disbelieving anger. "You think you can get rid of it all with that feeble word." She bit her lip. This wasn't going at all as she had thought it should. She was supposed to be in control, calmly asking him about the letter he returned, asking for some kind of restitution. But what could she ask from this frail man who could barely talk? What could he give her now that would change anything?

"Mark said...Jason's dead." Ed's words came out in a tortured sound, and when Sheryl turned to him a lone tear sparkled on his wrinkled cheek.

She only nodded, unable to tear her gaze away from the path of the tear as it slowly drifted down to his chin, puzzled that the news of Jason's death should cause it.

"How?"

"Car accident." She clutched herself harder, concentrating on the color of his hair, the droop of his shoulders. She had to be strong, his tears were too late and didn't help her now.

"Do you...miss...him?"

Sheryl looked away, biting her lip. Her stepfather, the man who had hated Jason before they'd left, now looked as if he was grieving Jason's death, whereas she, his wife, had not shed a tear. She pressed her fingers to her eyes as if to force something from them. "I don't miss him, Dad."

"Did you...love him?" Ed tried to lean forward.

Sheryl felt the beginnings of a headache building behind her eyes. This was even harder than she had envisioned. Ed challenging her, blustering at her—these she had ready answers for.

Not this unexpected concern, his probing questions—these she wasn't prepared for. They came around behind her and pushed away all the defenses she had built against him. Now he could be proved right, and while her prideful nature didn't want to admit it, she knew that if she was to have any kind of peace in her life, if she was to regain any kind of power over her future, she had to admit her part in what had happened in the past.

"Did...he love...you?" Ed asked this time.

Sheryl felt a catch in her throat. Had anyone cared in the past few years whether she had received love? "I think he wanted to," she replied carefully. Slowly she lowered herself into the chair across from Ed. "Jason wasn't a good husband, Dad. But I stayed with him because that's what wives do. That's what you taught me."

Ed said nothing, his eyes holding hers as another tear formed. "I'm sorry."

Sheryl only nodded, his tears touching her emotions in a place she didn't think Ed would ever have access to again. "I'm glad you're sorry, Dad. I'm sorry, too. Sorry that I ever married him. Hard as it is for me to say it, you were right about him." She smoothed the wrinkles out of the worn skirt, the confession draining her.

She had come for vindication, for this chance to find out whys and why nots and suddenly it became wearying, draining. But she pressed on. The threat of his death demanded that the events of her past find some kind of finish, closure. "I just wish I could know why you and Nate couldn't let me be part of your family."

"I never...had a girl."

But you had a son, Sheryl thought. You loved him.

"I don't think...I even...knew how to love Nate."

Sheryl's heart skipped at his response. It was as if he'd read her mind. "Why did you marry my mom?" Sheryl avoided his eyes, pleating her skirt, her voice soft as she moved on to other questions.

"She was pretty...and so sad." Ed sighed. "I wanted...to help her...help you."

Sheryl rubbed her finger over the crease she had made in her skirt, his confessions settling into her memories.

"I needed...her," Ed said softly.

"And what about me?" She looked up at him, questioning. "Did you need me, too?"

"Yes. I loved her...I love you. Please believe...I love...you."

Sheryl sighed, rubbing her forehead. She stood, looking down at this broken man. She couldn't dredge up enough anger to hate him. Tucking her hair behind her ear she tilted her head to one side. "Well you had a strange way of showing it," she said quietly.

Ed blinked slowly, concentrating on her, shaking his head with long tired movements. "I'm sorry...so sorry..."

Sheryl felt a strange thickening in her throat. She swallowed it down, willing the emotions back where she had consigned so many more.

And as she forced her emotions back to equilibrium, as she battled with old dull pain, Ed closed his eyes.

Sheryl felt her heart stop, and she rushed over to his side, almost praying that it wasn't so. Frantically she grabbed his hand, searching for his pulse.

He twitched and his head fell forward as Sheryl felt the faint, but regular heartbeat. She sat back on her heels, her own heart bursting in her chest. He had fallen asleep and there was nothing left for her to say, so she quietly left.

Chapter Seven

Mark reached back and pulled his shirt off in one easy motion, ignoring the buttons. Balling it up he tossed it in a corner of the kitchen, joining the rest of his laundry.

Scratching his chest, he wandered to the fridge, pulled it open and grimaced at the contents. He took an apple out of a broken cellophane bag and took a quick swig of milk right out of the carton.

Another nourishing meal, he thought as he kicked the door of the fridge closed behind him.

He walked into the living room. Should clean this up, too, he thought, munching on his apple.

A wood stove sat smugly on a brick pad, awaiting chilly fall nights and cold winter days when it would radiate welcome heat. For now it held an assortment of dust-laden pictures: wedding portraits, family pictures and school pictures from nieces and nephews.

A wave of melancholy washed over Mark as he walked through the empty room on his way upstairs to his bedroom. When he'd first seen the house, the Simpson family had lived here, and kids and furniture had filled it. It looked better then.

He finished his apple as he trudged up the stairs. It was still early in the evening. The dew came down too soon to hay longer into the night. Tomorrow, after two dry days, they would be able to go until dark.

The rest of the evening stretched before him, empty, quiet…boring. His dad had repeated his mother's invitation to supper, but he'd declined. In spite of his better judgment he found himself inexplicably drawn to Sheryl, and he couldn't understand her. She made it fairly clear any time he tried to get past her guard that she didn't want his concern.

But he couldn't stop thinking about her. Better that he stay at home instead of subjecting himself to more of the same. Humiliation wasn't an emotion that sat well with him, so why seek it out. It had taken a while to get over Tanya's rejection, he shouldn't be in such a hurry to let another woman give him more of the same.

Mark walked over to the window, opened it and threw his apple core out, pausing to appreciate the view. Five years he had lived here, yet he never tired of the view.

The corrals lay below him, laid out in squares of graduating sizes. It had taken almost an entire summer to build up his corral system to make it easier for him to sort his cows. The work reaped its own rewards, he thought, remembering the past fall and how much quicker he and Nate had separated the heifers from the steers and the calves from the cows.

Beyond the corrals lay the hay fields, neat triangles of stuked hay dotting the clipped field. In two days they would have the lower fields done and then they could haul the bales to Nate's place where they would await the trucks from Langley. It had taken a few years and a lot of hard work. This hay contract and the increase in cattle prices should help the ranch turn a healthy profit, for a change. If things held, the partnership would be well able to support two families.

Mark laughed ruefully. Make that one family and one bachelor.

He glanced over his shoulder at the spacious bedroom behind him. A mattress pushed against one wall served as his bed, the rumpled sheets mocking his mother's constant nagging as he grew up. It looked lost in the room.

The condo he'd owned in Vancouver had come furnished, and a cleaning lady used to come in once a week. It had never felt like a home, but at least it had been neater than this place, he thought, running a finger through the dust that layered the windowsill.

This house needs a family.

In spite of his earlier resolve, his thoughts wandered to Sheryl. In his mind he saw her again on a tractor seat, working in heat and dust, never complaining, a faint smile curving her lips, softening the hard lines of her face. She looked more appealing all dusty and dirty, manhandling Nate's old Massey around the corners, than Tanya or any of the women before her ever could after spending an afternoon in their salons. In Sheryl he sensed a love for the land that so closely echoed his own, and it called to a deeper part of him.

Tanya had never wanted to share this life, had wanted no part of it. Whenever he'd brought her out here, she'd complained about the distance, politely declined offers to go riding and smiled deprecatingly at his family. Tanya fit in Vancouver, but not out here.

With a short laugh, he spun away from the window and off to a much-needed shower. Sheryl had her own plans, as well, and they didn't include a bachelor rancher.

But as the hot water poured down over him he couldn't help but remember those brief moments of vulnerability that seemed to call out to him.

Lenore's house exuded a quiet peace that enveloped Sheryl as soon as she stepped inside. It was as if the house, which had held so many people on Sunday, had shrunk down, pulled into itself. The living room was symmetrical again, the couches neatly facing each other across a delicate Queen Anne coffee table, whose legs seemed to barely touch the deep pile of the carpet, wing chairs flanking the fireplace presiding over the room.

In the kitchen the counters were visible again, an oak table had also shrunk down, four chairs neatly surrounding it, the crystal vase of flowers reflected in the gleaming surface of the table.

"Just sit down, Sheryl. I'll make some tea while we wait for Nick to come back." Lenore dropped her bags of groceries on the countertop with a muted clunk. "I'll phone Elise to tell her you're here for supper, so she and Nate don't worry."

Sheryl almost laughed at that. "That's not necessary. I'm sure it doesn't matter whether I show up or not."

Lenore paused, her hand still holding on to a cupboard door. She let it slip shut and leaned back against the cupboard, her arms crossed over each other.

"Now I know you're not a whiner, so I don't think that's one of those 'feel sorry for me' kinds of statements. They do worry about you."

Sheryl didn't want to get into a discussion over Nate's lack of fraternal devotion—he obviously had Lenore fooled—so she merely shrugged in answer.

"Nate and Elise often wondered how you were doing when you lived in Edmonton," Lenore continued, concern furrowing her forehead. "He tried to get hold of you..."

"Please, Lenore," Sheryl interrupted, suddenly tired of seeing Nate as the blue-eyed boy. "Nate knew Jason's last name, he knew where we lived. He never once tried to contact me." She caught Lenore's eyes and held them, the emotions of the day catching up on her. She felt a sob begin way down in her chest.

Then the all-too-familiar invisible hand closed off her

throat, pushed closed the crack in her defenses, and the heartache subsided. For a fleeting moment Sheryl wished the tears would come, wished the pain could be lanced, but knew that her solitary life could not allow her to get swept up in the ensuing emotional storm.

"Are you okay?" Lenore came around the counter to kneel beside her, gentle hands covering Sheryl's tightly clenched fingers. "Is it Ed?"

Sheryl shook her head. "I don't know what's wrong with me these days." She drew in a shaky breath, forcing herself to relax. "Ed told me..." But she stopped. What could she possibly gain from opening up to Lenore? She didn't need to hear confessions from someone who was such a small part of her life. "Sorry," Sheryl said, drawing her hands away. "It's been a tiring day."

The back door opened just then, deep voices laughing, bursting into the house, bringing vitality and breaking the quiet.

"That sounds like Mark." Frowning, Lenore got up, leaving Sheryl to compose herself and at the same time try to stop the foolish trill of her heart at the sound of Mark's voice, the mention of his name.

"How fast did you have to drive to get here the same time as your father, Mark?" Lenore asked as both men walked into the kitchen at the same time.

"Dad drives like an old lady," Mark said, quirking a tired smile at his mother.

"I thought I'd give you enough time to get supper on the table, but I see I should have driven even slower," Nick joked. He turned to Sheryl. "So how's Ed?"

Sheryl got up, suddenly self-conscious of her faded denim skirt and too-large white T-shirt. Strange that a pair of gray eyes focused on her should bring that out. She never cared what she looked like before. "He was sitting up today. They took him off the monitors."

It bothered her that it mattered, and as she looked past

Nick's smiling face to Mark's serious one, things other than her clothes took precedence: like the clean sweep of his freshly shaven jaw; how his brown hair, still damp from his shower, swept just above his dark eyebrows; how his eyes seemed to delve into hers, seeking, drawing her out. She faintly heard Lenore's laughter, Nick's dry answer. On the periphery of her vision she saw them move past her, but she couldn't take her eyes away from Mark's, couldn't break the connection that seemed to grow with each step he took closer to her until he stood in front of her.

"Hi," he said, his deep voice soft, the single word winging home to a heart that hungered for more.

"I thought you were going home?" she replied, her voice unsteady.

"I did and then changed my mind."

Her heart lifted and thrummed as time slowed and all else seemed to fade. She caught herself, blinked, swallowed and forced her leaden feet to step away.

Mark was a complication she could ill afford. Solid, secure in his faith and surrounded by family and community.

She turned away, breaking the contact by force of her will. "Do you need any help with supper, Mrs. Andrews?" Sheryl offered, her voice rough edged. She cleared her throat and caught Lenore's scrutinizing glance.

"You can start browning the hamburger," she said, handing Sheryl a fork.

Sheryl had a hard time working, knowing that Mark's eyes followed her every move. It was disconcerting, puzzling and exciting, and she didn't know which emotion took precedence.

By the time they sat down to supper she felt wound up tighter than a spring.

Lenore was well organized and in less than twenty minutes managed to pull together a Stroganoff-based sauce over buttered noodles with a crisp salad on the side. They seated themselves around the table, Sheryl between Lenore and Mark, and as Nick paused, she knew what was coming. Too late she tried to drop her hands to her lap. Lenore had already captured one and Mark held out his hand for the other one. She hesitated, and he laid his hand, callused palm up, on the table, inviting yet not pushing. It would have looked ungracious to refuse, so, reluctantly she laid her hand in his large one, quenching the light trill that quivered up her arm at his touch.

Then his fingers wrapped around hers, firm, hard, secure, and as they bowed their heads Sheryl felt peace flow through her that was a combination of Mark holding her hand and the communion of four people united in prayer.

When Nick quietly said amen, Sheryl carefully slid her hand out of Mark's, thankful that he loosened his hold on her and, picking up her fork, tried to eat.

"How much more baling do you have to do?" Nick asked Mark.

"Three more days, tops. I'm thankful it's been going so well."

"I can't come tomorrow and help you, I'm afraid," Nick began.

"I'll help again." Sheryl interrupted, her voice quiet.

Mark almost dropped his fork. He had been hoping, praying, that she would offer. He didn't dare ask.

"You don't have to," Lenore said. "I'm sure Nick can…"

Sheryl smiled at Lenore. "I'm sure he can, too, but this time I want to finish what I start."

"Now what do you mean by that?" Lenore asked.

Sheryl looked down at her plate. "When I was younger I used to drive the tractor, but could only last a few days. Then I would take off…" She let the sentence hang, and Mark tried to decipher her expression, but a heavy swag of golden hair hid her face from him.

"I still think it's a bit much to expect a young girl like you to help with that dusty, dirty job." Lenore placed her knife and fork together on her plate and pushed it slightly away from her.

"Well I'm glad she doesn't mind," Mark replied. "It sure helps me out a lot."

"I don't imagine you worked on a farm in Edmonton?" Lenore asked, ignoring Mark's warning glance.

Sheryl pushed the noodles around her plate as if contemplating the easiest way to answer the question. "I worked in a bar."

"How did you like that?"

Mark stifled a groan. His mother, soft-spoken though she pretended to be, could never manage to get away from her tendency to be nosy.

Surprisingly, Sheryl smiled. "I disliked it thoroughly. I can't imagine a more futile occupation than serving drinks."

"How long did you do that?" Lenore asked, resting her elbows on the table, her chin propped on her hands.

"Too long." Sheryl looked up and smiled a wry smile. "When we first moved to Edmonton, I took some secretarial courses, then got a job working at a lawyer's office." For a moment she seemed far away, then with a shrug she looked down at her supper. "But things slowed down, and I got laid off."

"Mark tells me that you are studying again."

Mark almost groaned. Sheryl must think that she was discussed at every possible moment. As if to confirm that, she glanced sidelong at him.

Mark paused as their eyes held. It was like a reaching out and touching, he was so aware of her. He swallowed and, trying to relieve the tension that sprang between them, winked. She blinked, smiled back.

Something inside of him turned slowly over then. So many things that should matter didn't. Against his better judgment, he was falling for her. The signs were clear to him. The urge to touch, the constant seeking out of her company, the feeling of completeness when they were together.

He looked away, breaking the connection, suddenly sorry he had.

She was wrong for him in so many different ways. She gave nothing of herself. She claimed no relationship with God, she had no intention of pursuing one. Her stay here was only temporary; that point she made very clear.

Mark listed all the reasons, trying to be rational about his feelings for her.

He looked at her again, watching her hands, the cuticles of her nails still lined with dirt that he knew would only come out after the season was over.

In his mind he saw again her hands clutching the steering wheel of the tractor as she manhandled it around the corner, leaning into the turn, a smile tugging the corners of her mouth.

In as many ways as she was wrong for him, she was right. She loved the land as he did; the work didn't bother her. She was independent and self-contained enough to be able to endure being isolated....

"Are you done, Mark?" His mother was asking.

With a jolt he pulled himself back to the present. "Sorry," he mumbled, handing his mother his plate.

"And where were you?" she asked as she gathered up the remains of the supper.

Mark said nothing, realizing that the question needn't be answered.

Bible reading followed dessert, Mark studiously avoiding eye contact with Sheryl. When prayers were over, he got up, feeling suddenly self-conscious.

"What's your rush?" Nick asked as he leaned back in his chair, a cup of steaming coffee resting in front of him.

"With the warm weather we've been having, the dew will be off the swaths early tomorrow," Mark said, pushing his chair carefully under the table. "I want to get an early start."

"Well, then, maybe you should drive Sheryl home. I had planned on taking her myself, but it would be easier if you did," Nick said.

"She might not want to come right now...." The excuse sounded lame in his ears. The prospect of having her in the truck with him for another hour, coming so close on the heels of his own discovery, would be awkward.

A silence greeted his remark, and Mark realized the difficult position he'd put Sheryl in. To agree would inconvenience his parents, to disagree would sound ungracious. "I guess it does make more sense, if I take her home," he amended. Great, Mark, he thought, now she'll feel like it's too much trouble.

"Will Elise be bringing you lunch tomorrow?" Lenore asked as he bent over to kiss her goodbye.

"I hope so." He waved to his father and waited for Sheryl to get up and say her goodbyes, wondering why this reticent girl could make him feel like an inept teenager.

"You're welcome to come anytime, Sheryl," his mother said, taking her hand. "Just ask Mark to bring you, he'll use any excuse to get some of his mom's cooking."

"Thank you." She smiled, said her farewells to Mark's father and walked past Mark out to the truck.

The ride was made in silence, broken only by the ping of gravel on the truck's undercarriage.

Sheryl looked out the window, fully aware of Mark lounging behind the wheel beside her as he drove in his usual full-speed-ahead fashion. It still frightened her to see the scenery fly by in a green and blue blur, so she kept her eyes fastened on the mountains above them, which moved past at a more sedate pace.

"How did your visit with your father go?"

Sheryl jumped at the sound of Mark's voice breaking her concentration.

"It went," she replied, as a fresh pain clutched her heart at the thought of Ed and his declaration of love. Why now? Had God truly changed his heart? "I didn't stay long...he fell asleep."

Mark slowed and turned into the Kricksons' driveway, pulling up to the house and switching off the lights.

"Thanks again for helping me." He half turned, tapping his fingers on the steering wheel. "You seem to enjoy the work."

She shrugged, wanting to leave, yet loath to exchange the cozy intimacy of the cab and his company for her lonely cabin.

Mark studied her, his head tilted to one side as if trying to figure her out. "You know, I've heard Ed and Nate talk about you, and I have to confess that for a time I didn't think particularly well of you." He shrugged. "I'm sorry about that. Since I've met you I know there's another side to this story of rebellion and mistrust."

Sheryl sighed, her usual reticence wearing away under the concern and caring shown her by Mark's family and, yes, Mark himself. "I don't know if it's worth delving into. It's over...."

"Maybe. But whatever happened is affecting your relationships now." Mark leaned back and smiled encouragingly at her. "Tell me about your first father. Wasn't his name Bill?"

And in that moment, Sheryl felt she could unburden herself. No one had ever asked about Bill Reilly before.

"Bill Reilly," she replied, pleased that he knew her father's name. "He was a good father, a caring man." Sheryl sat back, not realizing until then how tense she was. "We had a ranch in Southern Alberta, the most beautiful part of the country."

"Prettier than this part?" he asked with a soft laugh.

Sheryl turned to Mark, smiling. "It's pretty in a different way. You should go there once, to see the sweep of the land as it moves toward the mountains. It's majestic, open and different…and the same.''

"I might do that," Mark said, his voice quiet, his whole posture relaxed.

"My dad and I went everywhere together. We covered a lot of country." Sheryl sighed, drifting back to a happy, almost magical time. "He used to take me with him on the tractor, in front of him on the horse. I was an only child, and probably spoiled, though I never felt that way until I moved here. I just know, for that time in my life I was safe, secure and loved." She clasped her hands in her lap, circling her thumbs slowly. "When he died I felt as if I would never laugh again, never be happy again."

"That must have been a difficult time for you and your mother." Mark's soft voice was sympathetic.

Sheryl only nodded, remembering an old sorrow made less painful by the passage of time.

"So how did you end up in Williams Lake?"

"My mom's cousin had a rental house there, and she found my mom a job. So we moved."

"Why didn't you stay on the ranch?"

"My dad, though loving to a fault, was not much of a manager. The ranch had to be sold to pay the debts. My mother was ill prepared for making a living, and things got very tight. My mom's cousin introduced her to Ed, and that ended her brief but short career in the Laundromat." Sheryl pressed her thumbs together, watching her nails turn white under the pressure. "They got married, and Ed started his campaign to change what he saw as a willful and spoiled child."

"Didn't he love you?"

Ed's words from this afternoon reverberated through her head. She glanced over at Mark. He lay back against his door, one arm resting along the back of the seat his other hand supporting his head.

"I suppose he wanted to," she continued, reassured by

his casual pose. "Though I don't think he quite knew what to do with me. He loved my mother, in his own way, though I saw early on that she was intimidated by him." Sheryl sighed, recalling frowns and puzzlement on his part, resentment on hers. "I never wanted him to take the place of my father, and I have to confess that my part in the whole relationship was to defy him just for the sake of staying loyal to my father's memory and showing Ed that he would never replace Bill Reilly in my life."

"How long after your father died did you mother remarry?"

Sheryl frowned, thinking. "About six months."

Mark lifted his eyebrows. "So soon?"

"Like I said, money was tight, and my mother didn't seem able to cope without a man to support her."

"And you moved right onto the ranch from Williams Lake?"

"I loved it at first. And at first I suppose Ed did try. He taught me how to saddle and care for a horse, something my father always did for me. I was allowed to ride whenever I wanted, as long as my chores were done for the day."

"And that included baling hay…"

"Among other things. I fed orphaned calves, mucked out the calving pens, helped with the fencing, rode out with Nate to check on upper pastures…"

"And you were ten years old?" Mark lifted his head, frowning at her.

"Yes."

"And as you grew older…"

"Things went from difficult to worse. I didn't mind the work at first, but it seemed that the rides became fewer and farther between." Sheryl pulled her hands over her face as angry confrontations between her, Nate and Ed came to mind. "I would sneak off whenever I could, leaving them to do the work. This of course created more anger and punishment, which meant more chores, which made me more determined to fight them, and away we went. Soon we were fighting over what I wore, how I acted. God was drawn into every discussion on my hell-bent nature. I didn't like God very much. He seemed an angry dictator at best, a despot at worst.''

"How did your mother deal with it all?''

"I think she was afraid to oppose Ed and stand up for me. She was a good mother, but not a strong woman.''

"And where did Jason come into the equation?''

"Early on.'' Sheryl scratched her head with one finger, sighing. "Jason was exactly the opposite of what Ed saw as fine and upstanding in a young man.''

"I've heard about Jason....''

"Everything you have heard is true.'' Mark hadn't moved but his stillness created an air of waiting, listening. He hadn't made any judgments on her behavior, hadn't offered any comments. He just asked those quiet questions that encouraged.

"At first I saw him as a misunderstood young man. But he wasn't. Those who knew him understood him completely. He was angry, rebellious and sadistic.''

"What do you mean?''

"He used to hit me.'' She kept her voice even, glossing over the humiliation.

Mark said nothing, but Sheryl could see his hands tightening on the steering wheel.

"But that was only for the first few years.''

"What do you mean?'' Mark's voice was harsh, controlled.

Sheryl lifted her mouth in a cynical parody of a smile, turning to face Mark as if challenging him. "I started fighting back.''

Mark's gaze was level, his eyes slightly narrowed. "Why didn't you leave him?''

"And go where?" Sheryl laughed shortly. "I had no place and no money."

"Why didn't you tell Ed? No matter what you may think of him, he would have helped you, let you come back...."

"I tried to tell him..." Sheryl turned away. She had said enough, had said too much. She was venturing too close to the true pain, buried deep where she didn't dare venture. "Look, I've got to go." She fumbled for the door, unable to find the latch in the darkened cab.

Mark reached across her and opened the door for her and she slipped out.

"Hey wait a minute." His voice was suddenly quiet.

Sheryl stopped, biting her lip, not wanting to break the moment they had shared, but knowing she had to.

"Aren't you even going to say thanks for the ride?"

She turned back, studying him. His hair framed his face, and in the glow of the dash, his features were all angles and shadows. He was handsome and appealing in a very frightening way. His questions had given her a first chance to tell someone her part of the story, and her ensuing confidences had made her feel vulnerable to him.

"You look scared again," Mark continued, his gray eyes holding her. "It makes me sad for you."

She said nothing, thinking of Jason, Ed, Nate—men who, as far as she could remember, had never felt sad for her—a painful breathlessness pulling on her chest as she faced one who did. Sighing, she leaned her head against the door, clutching the frame as she felt herself drift into his smoldering eyes.

"My mom was right, you know," he said, his voice hushed.

Sheryl frowned, not comprehending the direction of his words.

"I don't think twelve-year-old girls should be driving tractors, either." His level gaze and serious expression gave

Sheryl approbation while creating a newer anger for the pain she now lived with.

"Don't do this," she whispered, almost pleading.

"Don't do what?" Mark leaned forward. "Don't try to understand what you lived with? Don't try to figure out what made you who you are now?"

"I can't do this. I can't give you what you want...." She pushed down the pain and memories. "I'm not going to delve any deeper and open myself to anyone again." But she could only look as far as the open vee of his gleaming white shirt as she spoke.

"I still haven't heard the whole story, Sheryl. I know you aren't the selfish person Nate led me to believe you were." He ran a finger along the steering wheel, then looked up at her. "I'm sorry I prejudged you. It wasn't Christlike, and it wasn't right. I guess I've come to respect you and know there's more that you're not telling me."

"Please..."

"I won't dig anymore. I'll leave you alone." He quirked her a wry smile. "For now."

Sheryl felt again the unwelcome prick of tears behind her eyelids. Why did he do this to her? What did her life matter to him? How did he manage to make her feel vulnerable, when she promised herself it would never happen again?

She slammed the door shut, the sound ricocheting off the buildings in the yard. Without a second glance, she strode away, her hands shoved in the pockets of her skirt, head down. She would finish what she started and thereby prove to Nate and herself that she was dependable and worthy. Then she would return to Edmonton, back to her studies, back to...

Sheryl bit her lip, her step faltering. Clenching her teeth, she reminded herself of her plans, her first small steps to an independent life.

Chapter Eight

As the tractor slowed, Mark watched the last bale clunk its way out of the baler, a grin lifting his mouth. He caught the bale, winked at Sheryl, who watched him over her shoulder, and dropped it on the top of the last stuke.

Relief, fulfillment and just plain happiness surged through him, and with a whoop he jumped off the stuker and ran toward the tractor. He caught Sheryl around the waist just as she was getting down and set her on the ground.

"We're done," he shouted. He caught her hands in his, pressing them against his stubbled face. He looked heavenward and called out "Thank you, Lord." As he looked back down, he grinned at Sheryl's incredulous face. She blinked and grinned back, her sea green eyes limned with dust, her hair sticking out, dust smears on her cheek.

She looked gorgeous.

"You are a wonder, my girl," he exulted, catching her by her slender waist and swinging her up and around, his own happiness overcoming his resolve to be careful with her. Her hat flew off in one direction and her feet in another.

By the time she touched ground again, she was laughing, her white teeth a sharp contrast to her tanned and dirty face. "I don't suppose you do this to Nate, when the first cut is baled," she called out.

"Nate isn't nearly as good-looking as you are." He winked at her. Giving in to an impulse, he dropped a kiss on her forehead. He thought she would jerk away, but to his surprise she only blinked and then smiled back. "I don't know if I've said it enough, but thanks," he added, suddenly serious.

"I enjoyed it."

"I know." He couldn't seem to stop himself—the need to connect with her was too strong—and he reached up and palmed her hair away from her face, cupping it gently, his gloved hand looking incongruous against her delicate features. "I've never met anyone like you before."

"I believe that." She stepped away then, breaking the contact. "Here come Rob and Conrad."

Mark glanced over his shoulder at the approaching tractor, frustrated at the intrusion.

Rob drove, and Conrad hung from the cab, singing. They pulled up beside Mark with a hoot.

"All done, slave driver." Rob called down from his perch. "We'll bring this rig to your place and then me and Conrad are heading to town."

Mark pulled his gloves off and shoved them in his back pocket. "I'll have a cheque for both of you in the mail in the next couple of days."

He sighed as they jumped back on the tractor, wondering again at the exuberance and stupidity of youth. They were probably headed off to the bar where they would promptly drink away half of what they made in the past week.

"I guess baling's thirsty work," said Sheryl with a wry note in her voice. "I wish they could see what they are wasting."

Mark glanced over at her, and she caught his look. With

a deprecating shrug she turned back to the still-running tractor. "We should get this unit back to the farm. I imagine you'll want to service the tractor, return the baler…"

Mark caught her arm, and she turned to face him, her eyebrows lifted in question.

"Thanks a lot for helping."

"You already said it."

"But I don't know if you realize what this means to me and to Nate.…"

"I didn't do it for him, I did it to help you out. I like the work…I love being outside." She laughed shortly and turned her gaze back to him. "I guess I just spent too many years here, hating it when I had to help, hating where I lived, that I never really appreciated it like I should."

"You probably didn't have a chance to appreciate it."

Sheryl shrugged. "You don't need to defend my actions. In a way Nate was right. I wasn't always dependable." She smiled at Mark. "Now I've made up for that."

Back at the farm Sheryl helped him clean up the baler, grease the tractor and gas it up. She hadn't forgotten what needed to be done and was quick, efficient and capable. Nate and Ed had taught her well, Mark conceded.

She returned from parking the tractor, brushing loose bits of hay off her pants. "I guess I'm done."

Mark nodded, watching the play of sun and wind in her hair, wishing he had the nerve to reach over and take the braid out, to see it loose again.

"Do you need to return the baler right away?" she asked, quirking him a questioning look.

He pulled his thoughts together. "No," he answered shortly. "I'll return it when we come back."

"Come back…?"

"From the pack trip."

Sheryl nodded as comprehension dawned on her face. "I forgot about that."

"Aren't you coming?"

"No, I can't."

Mark felt disappointment cut through him. He had so hoped she was coming, had hoped that once she was on a horse in the mountains she so clearly loved, she would lower her defenses, would open up...

To what? he thought deprecatingly. Your suaveness and irresistible charm?

"So what were you going to do?"

She shoved her hands in her pockets, pursing her lips. "I was going to head back to Edmonton."

"For what?"

"My apartment...my studies."

Mark nodded, dropping the rag into the empty pail beside him. "Of course. I forgot."

He sighed, cleaned up the tools, Sheryl helping him of course, and when they were done he drove her back to Nate's place. The drive was quiet.

He pulled up to Nate's house and stopped.

"So," he said, turning to Sheryl, the truck still running. "Thanks again."

She looked down at the old felt hat she still held and nodded. "You're welcome again." Then she caught his eyes and smiled. "I really enjoyed it, truly."

"So when are you heading back?"

She shrugged, "A bus leaves from Williams Lake at midnight for Prince George. I can visit Ed once more before I leave."

"Tomorrow night?"

She frowned at him. "No. Tonight."

"What?" He couldn't stop the exclamation of surprise. "Why didn't you tell me?"

"I knew we'd be finished early today..."

"I don't care about the baling. I just thought you might let me know..." His voice trailed off.

She glanced at him, her expression surprised, and as their eyes met Mark felt it again, that clutch in the pit of his stomach that hurt and made him angry at the same time. Couldn't she see what effect she had on him? Didn't it matter to her?

"Mark, what's the matter?"

He shook his head, wondering whether she was just blind or indifferent. "I can't believe you didn't tell me when you were going." He shoved his hair out of his eyes with a quick movement, unable to keep the words down. "I mean, we spent the entire week working together, and I didn't have a clue."

"You knew I was only going to be here awhile…"

"Of course I knew that, I just thought you might want to stay and spend some time here without having to work like a dog."

"I told you already I enjoyed it." She handed him his hat and reached for the door handle. "Anyhow I have to leave sometime."

Mark couldn't stop himself and caught her arm. "I don't want you to go. Come on the pack trip, spend some time in the mountains.

She said nothing, only stared ahead, her face suddenly harsh.

"Nate won't be coming, if that's what you're afraid of."

She shook her head and then turned to him, her face drawn and tight. Mark felt a chill shiver through him as he faced again the same withdrawn Sheryl he had met in the bar over a week ago.

"It doesn't matter, Mark. I can't go."

And before he could challenge her comment, she stepped out of the truck without a backward glance.

But as Mark watched her, he felt as if she'd taken part of him with her.

Sheryl waited until she heard Mark's truck reverse and tear down the driveway. Only then did she dare turn around, watching him hungrily as he left, just as she did each night he brought her home, knowing this would be her last glimpse of him. The red bandana still held down his long hair, and from his posture, Sheryl knew he was angry.

She was fully aware of the undercurrents that flowed between them, she knew he was attracted to her, even though it seemed that to recognize it was a type of pride.

But it was there, and to ignore it would be to encourage him. He was not for her. The very things that made him so incredibly appealing also pushed her away. He had a place, security, but more importantly, a sincere faith. His spontaneous prayer that morning had shown her more clearly than anything he could say that he had a real and solid relationship with God.

She turned, her feet dragging, knowing if she had given him any encouragement at all, things might have been different. But then what? She knew that the most basic ingredient of any relationship was the ability to open up to each other.

And she knew she couldn't give any man any kind of power over her.

She pushed open the door of her cabin, surprised to see Marla and Crystal sitting on her bed, crying.

"Auntie Sheryl," they called out when she entered the cabin, launching themselves at her.

She took the full brunt of two small but compact bodies catching her around the waist, almost causing her to stagger.

"What's wrong?" She disentangled herself from their arms, suddenly worried. "What happened, tell me quick."

"Daddy says you're going away tonight," Marla wailed, clutching Sheryl's hand, her tear-streaked face turned up to hers. "And that you're not coming on the pack trip with us."

"Why do you have to go?" Crystal complained, stamping her foot. "It doesn't make sense."

"Come and sit on the bed with me, before you push your foot through the floor like Rumplestiltskin," said Sheryl, trying to make this very angry bundle of girl laugh.

Crystal managed a faint smile, then frowned again and dropped onto Sheryl's bed so hard the springs sang.

Sheryl sat beside her and pulled Marla onto her lap.

"We asked Daddy to ask you to stay longer, but he said you had to leave," Marla sniffed.

"Mommy said you were leaving tonight," Crystal said, suddenly turning on Sheryl. "You can't go. We didn't even see much of you. Uncle Mark had you to himself all the time."

"I had to help with the baling. Your daddy had a broken leg, and Uncle Mark couldn't afford to hire anyone else."

"But now you have to go right away."

"Please," added Marla. "We didn't see you at all..."

Any further entreaty was broken off by the opening of the door.

"Here you are, you two urchins." Elise scolded, her hands on her hips. "Sorry about this, Sheryl. I couldn't find them and finally clued in to where they went." She turned to the girls and stepped aside, pointing out the door. "Now off to the house and the bathtub, on the double."

Crystal glanced at Marla who sniffed again. Sheryl gave her a quick hug and then let her slide off her lap. They walked to the door, making each step seem like a monumental effort. At the door Crystal hesitated and turned back to Sheryl.

"If you stay one more day, we can get to know each other better." Crystal added. "Maybe you can even come on the pack trip with us. Daddy says we can't go this year because he has a broken leg and Mommy has to cook."

"Don't bother Auntie Sheryl with all of your troubles, Crystal. She has had a busy day and a long night ahead of her." Elise admonished.

"Don't you like us at all, Auntie Sheryl?"

A stab of pain pierced her heart at the innocent question. The only time she saw them was a brief glimpse of their heads each evening against the light of their bedroom window when Mark drove away.

"I suppose I could leave tomorrow instead." She hesitated. "That is if it's not too much trouble."

"Of course not," Elise said warmly. "I'd love to have you around."

Crystal and Marla looked at each other, mouths open, then whirled around and ran back to Sheryl. Again she was engulfed by arms and surrounded by cries, this time of happiness. She caught her balance and, reaching out, stroked their heads, missing Elise's smirk.

"I think you'd better go, girls. Your mom is waiting," she said, squatting down to look them in the eye.

Marla smiled at her and hugged her again.

"We can go riding tomorrow if you want," Crystal said. "Or we can go for a walk."

"Whatever you want," Sheryl replied with a smile.

Crystal nodded and turned.

"Let's go, Marla," she said with a grin.

"I'm sorry about that, Sheryl," Elise said as the girls ran down the walk, their whoops of delight drifting behind them on the night air. "They have been wanting to spend time with you all week, and when they found out you were going away tonight they were desolate."

"I just didn't want to impose on you."

Elise walked over to Sheryl's side and gave her a quick hug. "You're not imposing at all. Like the girls were complaining, we've hardly seen you at all. Mark had you to himself, and all he did was make you work. I'd like you to have at least some time to go riding. It's the least we can do after you helped us out."

"Well I suppose one more day wouldn't matter much."

"No, probably not." Elise smiled, then turning, left.

* * *

"The next bus doesn't leave until five Tuesday afternoon?" Sheryl frowned, winding the telephone cord around her finger. "Is there any other connection I can make before that?" She sighed, grimacing at Elise who lifted her eyebrows in sympathy. "Okay. Thanks a lot."

Sheryl hung up the phone and turned to Elise, wondering if she knew all of this when she'd convinced her to stay another day. "Well, unless I hitchhike, it looks like you're stuck with me until Tuesday." She bit her lip, planning. Her rent was paid until the end of next month. All she needed was a job, badly.

Elise shook her head. "Don't even think about hitchhiking. Mark would have a fit if he found out you were even considering it, and he'd end up driving you himself."

"So what must I do the next few days?"

"You can come on the pack trip with me and Crystal," Marla said, looking up from her coloring. "Daddy says we can't go if he isn't coming, because Mommy has too much work to do."

Sheryl looked at Marla's innocent blue eyes, then at Elise's gray ones, so like Mark's, and wondered if this hadn't been the plan all along.

"Catch Roany and F5 and get them ready to be rigged up." Mark handed two halters to Conrad. "Tie them to the south hitching rail. I don't want F5 to get too close to Tia. She's ornery today."

Conrad took the halters and headed off. Mark watched to make sure he shut the gate properly behind him and then shouldered himself between Two Bits and Tia. He began buckling up the rigging on Tia who pranced around. A warning thwack on her haunches made her settle down.

"Where should I put these?" Elaine stood beside him holding a pannier. Mark glanced up from the latigo he was tightening and almost ground his teeth in frustration.

"Just set them against the tack shed for now," he answered shortly, "and make sure you put them where they won't get kicked over."

He turned back to Tia, giving her a shove, wondering for the thousandth time how he'd managed to let Allen and Elise talk him into moving the trip up a couple of days.

"Hey, Mark," Brad called from the other side of Two Bits. "The buckles on this rigging are wrecked."

"I thought you were farther along than that." Mark called over his shoulder, snugging up the latigo. Tia jerked back, and her rope flew loose. Mark grabbed for it, but she trod on the end, grinding it into the mud from the rain last night.

"Move over you ornery critter." Mark shouldered the horse aside, but she wouldn't budge. Two Bits sidestepped and almost crushed him between the two horses. Mark elbowed Two Bits in the ribs and, with one final heave, managed to move Tia and tied her snug to the rail.

"Just stay put you miserable creature," he warned, hoping he had used up his catastrophe quota.

He ducked under Two Bits' head, trying without success to quell his rising frustration.

"The breeching is too tight," he said shortly, running a practiced eye over the rigging. "You shouldn't snug it up till you're ready to pack the horse."

"Now you're going to be ticked," sighed Brad, resting a hand on Two Bits' haunches. "Which one is the breeching?"

"Breast collar goes across the chest of the horse, breeching across the rear end...like britches?" Mark loosened the buckles, wishing, almost praying for one person who knew what they were doing, instead of these weekend cowboys who made up his family.

"Well I'm glad enough I got it on the right way," Brad huffed, picking up on Mark's mood. "Anyhow, the buckles on the *breast collar*—" he put emphasis on the word "—are the ones that are broken."

Mark ignored him, praying as he felt the all-too-familiar tightening of his chest as he struggled with a mixture of impatience and frustration. He wished again he'd had four days instead of two to get everything ready.

"You have to ream out the hole on the strap," he told his brother. As he ducked under Two Bits' head, he knew that his underlying problem wasn't horses and inept wranglers, it was Sheryl.

She had dropped the news of her leaving on him without any preparation. They'd spent four days working together, talking in the evening each time he'd dropped her off, but never a hint of her departure until four hours before she left.

Mark tugged on a strap on Tia's rigging a bit too hard, netting him an antsy horse, and he took a deep breath, stifling the rising clutch of panic. He didn't know if he would ever see her again. She doubted she would expend a lot of energy on familial visits in the future. He paused a moment, looking past the horses, past his house to the hills beyond that so captured her fancy. He wished he could take her riding through them. He wished he could bring her to the very place where he instinctively knew she might drop her guard and show him the girl he had only caught tantalizing glimpses of. He knew there was a hungering within her for love, for God, for security, but she covered that need with a hard shell of independence because much as she yearned for these things, she feared them more.

"Yo, Mark." Rob's loud yell pulled him back to reality and the work at hand. Biting back a sigh, he vaulted over the hitching rail to handle yet another crisis.

"Oh, no," Brad yelled out. "Someone catch that horse!"

Mark looked up just as Tia thundered past, ropes trailing, loose rigging flopping around, kicking up great clods of mud. Three horses were right on her heels as Conrad let out a mighty yowl.

"I told you to watch that gate, Conrad," Mark cried out, running to the gate that Conrad was desperately trying to push shut.

Conrad eyed him warily, and Mark stifled his anger. He'd been owly the past couple of days. He knew it, and try as he might, he couldn't seem to keep from sniping at everyone. He dug in his pockets and tossed Conrad a set of keys.

"Take my truck and head them off before they hit Sweet Creek."

Conrad was over the fence and hit the ground running.

"And don't pump the gas," Mark called out after his retreating figure.

Everyone had stopped what they were doing, watching the latest drama unfold. Conrad got in, leaned over to turn the key, his head bobbing. It wouldn't start.

Mark groaned and dragged his hands over his face. Flooded. "What are you trying to teach me, Lord?" he sighed, drawing in a steadying breath and counting to ten.

"Hey, Mark," Brad called out.

Mark looked up in time to see a set of car keys arcing toward him. He caught them against his chest.

"Just remember it's a car, not a farm truck," Brad yelled as Mark ran toward the gleaming white vehicle.

Mark got in, pushed the key into the ignition and was about to turn it when he looked up and saw the three runaway horses galloping back down the drive toward the corrals.

"What in the world..." he muttered, jumping out of the car. What miracle had occurred to make the horses turn around? He jumped out of the car and snapped out orders. "Someone get in the corral and keep the other horses away from the gate. Brad, Allen, funnel the loose horses down. Don't let them get on the wrong side of the hitching posts. Elaine you open the gate."

Conrad came at a dead run, vaulted over the corral fence

and herded the horses into a corner. As the gate swung open the three free horses paused a moment, as if pondering their next move. Then a whinny sounded from behind them, and there was Tia being urged on by Sheryl riding Nate's gelding.

Mark stopped, shock and surprise coursing through him as Sheryl easily herded the horses through the gate. Tia stopped.

"Shut the gate," Sheryl called out as she swooped down and caught Tia's halter rope, preventing her from escaping one more time. Elaine pushed the gate closed, and all was under control.

Except Mark's heart. It lifted and ran at the sight of Sheryl's long blond hair, flushed cheeks and soft green eyes, unable to believe that she was actually here. Questions stumbled through his mind, all eager to be voiced.

Why hadn't she left on Thursday like she said she would? Why had she changed her mind?

Then she looked down at him. He sensed hesitation and indecision. Whatever her reasons were for coming he wouldn't find out directly.

It didn't matter. Her presence was an unexpected answer to a prayer he hadn't even dared to utter. It was nothing short of a miracle.

He held out his hand for Tia's rope. Wordlessly she gave it to him, and their gazes locked, neither able to look away. Mark rubbed Nate's horse, Spanky, with one hand, smiling up at her.

"Miss your bus?" he asked, his voice quiet.

Sheryl nodded. "Crystal and Marla managed to make me feel guilty for not spending any time with them, and since the next bus isn't leaving until Tuesday afternoon, they conned me into taking them on the pack trip."

"Good girls." Tia pranced away from him and Mark tugged on her halter rope. "And you returned my horses."

"I thought I'd ride Spanky here to get a feel of him, and

when I saw the horses coming down the road, I figured they weren't supposed to be there.''

Mark took refuge in humor. "Wow. Smart *and* good-looking.''

A smile teased the corner of her mouth, but she seemed to ignore his comment. "Elise is bringing the girls and their horses right away. I hope it's okay they come. Nate thought they'd get in the way, but I promised to look out for them.''

"I'm glad they're coming,'' he replied, leading her horse to the hitching rail. The entire congregation of Sweet Creek church could come along, if they had anything to do with her being here. "But I'm even happier that you're here.''

Sheryl bit her lip and then dismounted, fiddling with Spanky's cinch. "So what can I do?''

Mark tied up Tia next to Spanky and leaned back against the rail, watching her. "Why don't you tell me?''

She looked him squarely in the eye as if challenging him. "Throw the diamond hitch.''

"Now I'm really impressed,'' he said, a heaviness inexplicably falling off his shoulders. Ed was the only one who could throw a faultless diamond hitch that caught all the parts of the pack and held them with an even snugness on the pack horse. He hadn't managed to teach Nate, so packing up the horses invariably fell totally on Mark's shoulders.

"Well that's easy to do to some people,'' she joked, loosening the latigo on Spanky's saddle.

Mark pushed himself away from the rail and stopped directly in front of Sheryl, taking a chance and tipping her chin up.

"I'm really glad you came, Sheryl.''

She only shrugged in answer, keeping her eyes down.

Mark let his glance idle over her hair as the sun danced off it. It was tied up again in her now-familiar braid. She was beautiful and she was here. For now that was enough. The rest was in God's hands.

Chapter Nine

"Here, I'll help you with that."

Rick, Mark's older brother, stopped and helped Sheryl heave the tarp over the packed horse.

"I can't believe you know how to do this stuff," he said as he straightened it.

"I'm a little rusty, but it's coming back." Sheryl smiled at him. Mark's family accepted her sudden appearance with an equanimity that still surprised her.

"Are you hassling the help, Rick?" Mark poked his head over the horse's rump, handing Sheryl a rope.

"Don't be getting greedy, Mark. You've got at least thirty-five years of escapades to share."

Mark slanted him a warning glance, and with a laugh Rick sauntered off, whistling.

"Don't I just love my family," he sighed, handing Sheryl the lash cinch to which the forty-foot rope was tied. "Do you want me to help you?"

"It'll go faster." Sheryl answered.

They fell into the same easy rhythm they shared baling hay. Sheryl felt an accord that she didn't want to analyze.

She murmured softly to the horse as he danced around, and he settled down.

"Are you this good with cows?" Mark asked as she tied the final half hitches under the pack and they moved on to the next horse.

"Cows used to petrify me." Sheryl laughed. "Nate always got mad at me when a cow charged and I'd run the other way. Then he'd be stuck with a bawling calf and a protective mother." Sheryl laughed, setting the pack pad high up on the horse's withers and sliding it down.

"Nate tends to overreact," Mark responded. He bent over and handed her an extra pad. "Use this on F5. He's a bit high withered as well as high-strung."

They finished packing up the horses and together helped the others finish saddling, checking stirrups, adjusting cinches. Sheryl was amazed at Mark's patience, how easily he worked with the horses, not against them.

By early afternoon the horses were packed and everyone mounted up and ready to go. Mark walked down the line checking ropes, adjusting bridles.

Sheryl handed Brad the lead rope for one of the pack horses, Roany. "Don't tie this to the saddle horn," she warned as he took the rope. "If you meet up with a bear you'll have a rodeo you don't want to be in the middle of. Better to let Roany fend for himself rather than get tangled up in ropes and hooves."

"That makes sense." Brad mounted his horse. "Mark just hands me the rope, lowers his eyebrows and growls 'tie that rope to your saddle and you're wolf bait' so I don't ask why."

"I'm sorry," Sheryl apologized. "I didn't mean to preach."

"No problem. I'd sooner listen to you than Mark's yowling anyhow," Brad said loudly, as Mark drew nearer.

"Unlike yours, my yowling makes sense," Mark answered dryly, running a quick eye over Brad's saddle horse. "Check your cinch ten minutes after you've been riding."

Mark turned to Sheryl, the soft breeze lifting his long hair away from his face, a smile curving his well-shaped mouth.

"Ready to go, partner? I've got you leading F5. He seems quieter around you."

Mark's voice took on a teasing tone, then his rough finger brushed a few wisps of hair out of her face, further confusing her.

Sheryl glanced at him, trying to gauge his mood. He smiled crookedly, his head tilted to one side. He let his fingers trail down her cheek, and his expression became serious.

A sixth sense warned her of his intention, and she silently pleaded with him not to. Then his head blotted out the sun and he brushed his lips lightly over hers. He straightened, winking at her, as if challenging her.

"Lets get the show on the road," he said quietly. He turned and ambled down the line of horses to Toby, his own mount, leaving Sheryl, her emotions in a turmoil.

Somehow Sheryl found her way back to Spanky, Nate's horse, ignoring Elise's approving smile. She untied F5's lead rope and mounted up, her cheeks burning.

She managed a quick wave at Lenore who had elected to stay behind with Benjamin.

"Have fun," Lenore called out as the line moved past her, out of the yard. "See you in a few days."

Sheryl drew in a steadying breath, wondering what she had gotten herself into, wondering what the next few days would bring.

The horses had been climbing for about twenty minutes, the trail winding through the dusky coolness of the towering fir trees. In the light-strewn openings in the foliage,

Sheryl caught glimpses of the hay fields that lay below them, dotted with small stukes of hay.

Now and again she saw Mark at the head of the column. He rode easily, moving with his horse, the hand holding the pack horse's rope resting on his thigh. She let herself watch him, let herself wonder about him. She couldn't imagine that he hadn't been swamped by other girls. He was the kind of man her fellow waitresses would fantasize about during coffee breaks. If Tory could see her now, she would think her crazy for not taking advantage of the situation.

As if you had a chance, she chided herself.

He did kiss you, the other insidious voice reminded her.

"Hi, there." Elise fell back and drew abreast of Sheryl. "Isn't the weather great?"

Sheryl welcomed the intrusion into her thoughts and turned to Elise. "Have you done this trip in the rain?"

"Oh, yes. That's when we really depend on Mark's even temperament." Elise paused, as if waiting. "He's such a great guy," she added hopefully.

Sheryl recognized her underlying purpose and decided to humor Elise a little.

"So how long has Mark lived out here?"

Elise brightened at Sheryl's question, and Sheryl stifled a chuckle. They were good people, but they couldn't get away from their straightforward heritage, so different from her stepfather and brother's.

"Mark moved out here about seven years ago, the same year Nate and I got married, and bought out the Simpson place a year later." Elise sighed, looked ahead, as if making sure no one else was listening and drew her horse a little closer to Sheryl's. "He bought the place for Tanya but she wouldn't move from Vancouver. Guess she could get engaged to a manager of a successful real estate office, but couldn't marry a rancher."

Sheryl straightened as she absorbed this hitherto-unknown piece of information.

"Did she ever come out here?" Sheryl couldn't stop herself from asking. She had a sudden inexplicable need to fill in the spaces in Mark's own past.

"She tried to talk him out of it, but he wouldn't listen. He bought the ranch, and she came out once in a while, but we could see it was coming apart a little more each time she visited. When he had to make a choice, he chose the ranch."

"How did the girl take it?"

Elise sighed, biting her lip. "Badly. Mark was considered quite a catch. She finally offered to live here for half a year at a time, but Mark didn't want that. He is pretty even tempered but when it comes to the ranch, he is pretty definite."

Sheryl looked past the other riders to the trail that wound upward through the silent trees, remembering semitrailers, airplanes and the constant smell of exhaust. How could anyone choose that over this?

"So he's been unattached since then," Elise added hopefully. She settled back with a smile, moving easily with the rhythm of her horse. "There have been a number of girls who imagined themselves in love with Mark, but none of them have the temperament to live out here on their own, and Mark knows that."

Sheryl only nodded, which was all the encouragement Elise seemed to need.

"He seems to enjoy being with you, though."

"And what am I supposed to say about that, Elise?" Sheryl laughed, unable to feel uncomfortable around Elise's straightforward manners.

"You could get coy and accuse me of kidding you, meanwhile hoping that I'll reassure you, or you could freeze me out with a 'you're exaggerating' and since you did neither, I'm going to say it again." Elise tossed Sheryl a sideways glance, suddenly serious. "I haven't seen him this interested in anyone in a long time."

Sheryl decided to change the line of questioning. "Did you send the girls into my cabin or was it their own idea?"

Elise pursed her lips, tilting her head to one side, eyes glinting with amusement. "It was a group project."

Sheryl stifled a groan. The way the Andrews family operated everyone was in on the plan except her and Mark, of that she was sure. His surprise this morning was genuine.

"But that wasn't the only thing we had on our mind when we cooked up this scheme." Elise continued. "I guess we wanted you to spend some time with us as a family, to spend some time up in the mountains. Mark says you love them so much, and Nate has told me enough about how you used to spend hours riding up here."

Sheryl returned Elise's now-serious look with a smile. "You are really an interesting family," she said.

"I'm glad you feel that way," said Elise as if Sheryl had just bestowed the ultimate compliment.

They rode on in companionable silence, Sheryl enjoying the ease she shared with Elise and literally soaking in the smells and sounds of riding up the mountain trails. It had been years since she'd been on the back of a horse. The creak of the saddle, the jingle of reins, the soft sounds of hooves falling on packed ground as they worked their way up the hills brought back good memories.

The trail, guarded by fir and pine trees, angled upward now, and would continue until they crested the first range. From what Sheryl remembered they would be at the upper pastures and the first camp by late afternoon.

She shifted in the saddle, turning back occasionally to check her pack horse, who plodded along expending the minimum amount of energy required.

A sigh lifted her shoulders as she looked around, the sun warm on her neck and back, the occasional shade welcome.

Elise stayed close, and now and then Sheryl made a comment on the landscape, pointing out birds and some of the different plants.

"You love this country, don't you?" Elise asked finally.

Sheryl nodded. "I spent a lot of time up in these hills. My poor mom didn't get much help from me in the house. Nate always said he pitied the man who married me."

Elise was quiet, then turned to her. "You never really got along with Nate, did you?"

Sheryl felt as if it was her chance to spill out the injustice of what had happened. For eight years all her anger and frustration and guilt had been directed at Nate and Ed. It waited, stewing, and now she was given a chance to tell her side.

But Elise was married to Nate, and Sheryl didn't know if it was fair to push on the foundations of what Nate had built here, just to satisfy her own anger.

Sheryl shook her head. "Please don't ask me about that."

But Elise wouldn't quit. "Sheryl, he's my husband and I love him, but I also know he's not perfect." Elise bit her lip, nodding. "I guess it would help me understand him a little more if you could tell me your side of the story."

Sheryl tightened her hands on the reins, trying to balance her own memories with the changes that she had seen in Ed and even in Nate.

Sheryl looked ahead of them, at the long, drawn-out line of riders and pack horses as they meandered down the hill to a dried-out creek bed. It was almost symbolic of this family. A dependence, a caring, and Nate had a part in all of this.

"Please," Elise encouraged. "I think it's sad and wrong that you've been away from them so long without a word."

Sheryl cleared her throat and began. "It was difficult when we first moved to the farm." Her voice trailed off as she tried to catch the right memory. "But once I got over losing my dad, I realized that it could be a lot of fun. Nate and I had to work with each other a lot, and I didn't mind the first few years. But there was always work to do on the land, and my mom didn't help out much. She was busy enough running the house, but I think Nate resented that.''

"Nate always said that Ed was a perfectionist...." Elise let the sentence hang as if encouraging Sheryl.

Sheryl felt tempted to leave it there, but somehow Elise's raised eyebrows and tilted head seemed to draw her out. She sighed, then said, "I don't think there were many things either Nate or I did that met with his approval. But Nate kept trying. I didn't. And that was when the trouble began.''

"I guess Nate kept at it because he always knew he would get the ranch someday.''

"And that's why I resented all the work after a while,'' Sheryl added quietly. "As a stepdaughter, I figured there was nothing in it for me.''

Elise nodded in understanding, and Sheryl experienced the same feeling of relief she'd felt with Mark. And again she felt as if part of the burden she had been carrying had shifted a little, felt a little lighter.

"How did Jason come into the picture?''

"Through my own stubbornness.''

"How did that happen?''

Sheryl shrugged. "I was talking to him once, and Ed found out,'' she continued. "He warned me away from this evil boy and I, of course, ran in the opposite direction.'' She fell silent, remembering how dangerously exciting it was at first to be with Jason, the thrill of defying Ed, but she also remembered her mother's anguished look each morning after she slipped in late.

"How old were you when you started going with him?''

"About sixteen. We went out for about two years, until I graduated from high school, then Jason and I eloped.''

"When did your mother die?''

The unexpected question was spoken in gentle tones, but

the words cut and hurt. Sheryl thinned her lips, looked ahead and shut off her memories.

"I'm sorry, Elise, I don't want to talk anymore."

"No," Elise said quietly, "*I'm* sorry. I shouldn't pry and dig." She reached over, and squeezed Sheryl's hand. "I'm glad you came and I'm glad you're here and I won't ask any more questions—" she lifted her eyebrows as if she didn't quite believe the statement herself "—if I can keep my mouth shut that long."

In spite of the momentary tension, Sheryl smiled. Elise was uncomplicated and easy to be with. But the pain she felt at Elise's question showed her that she was better off to keep her thoughts to herself.

Mark dismounted, looking over his shoulder gauging the hours until sunset. Glancing around the site, he noted with approval the firm hitching rails and clear camping area. He hadn't had the time to supervise Rob, and he'd sent him up here right after the haying was done. He'd done a good job.

Mark tied up his mount and pack horse, easing the cinch on his saddle for now.

"I'll get you something to eat in a bit, Toby." He stroked his horse's nose, stepping back as the animal tried to rub the side of his head against him. "Just settle down, now," he warned with a smile. He walked around to his pack horse, loosening the rope, keeping a lookout for Sheryl.

One by one riders pulled in, laughing, chattering. Horses shook and blew, riders dismounted, stretching, groaning.

"Watch that horse, Jennifer," Mark called out to his niece as she dismounted. "He's a little too interested in the ground for my liking."

Her father, Allen, looked up and jogged over. "Whoa, you mongrel." He caught him by the bridle. "Don't you go rolling over on my best riding saddle." He held the horse a moment while his daughter dismounted, then tied him up.

"The tents are on Brad's pack horse," Mark said to Allen, pulling the tarp off his own. "Get Diane and Lois to set them up while we unpack these horses. Those teenagers can help."

He carefully untied the boxes, making sure he took the same weight off each side to keep the pack frame from slipping. By the time Elise pulled up, all the boxes and containers were off the horse, lying in a neat pile.

"Working already, brother?" she asked, dismay tingeing her voice as she looked down.

"Don't wimp out on me now, sister. We're hungry, and since you're the chief cook, we have to wait for you."

Elise slipped off her horse with a groan. "Well, the least you can do is take care of this poor critter for me. I'll see what's on the menu for tonight."

Mark caught the reins, looking up just as Sheryl rode in, a curious half smile on her face.

He had spent most of the afternoon glancing past his family to the end of the train, catching only glimpses of her blond hair as it caught rays of the sun through the gentle dapple of the pine trees. Now that she was in front of him, he felt suddenly tongue-tied, an unfamiliar feeling for an Andrews.

"This really is God's country," she sighed as she slipped off her horse, running her pack horse's rope through her hands.

Mark felt a thrill at her words. That she could acknowledge God as Creator was a beginning. He smiled at her as she brought her horses around to the hitching rail.

"So how does it feel to be back up in the mountains?" he asked, watching her slim hands working at the latigo of her saddle, pulling it loose, her head bent. He half turned, still watching her, resisting the temptation to kiss her exposed neck.

She paused a moment, looking up again. "I've forgotten how much I missed this." Her voice caught on the last words, and she looked down again, busying herself with the saddle, the bridle and moving on to her pack horse.

Mark let her go, sensing her need for space, encouraged by the emotion in her voice. He returned to Elise's horse, thoughtful. If spending only one afternoon riding in the hills could open up even one tiny crack, he wondered what he might learn about her after two days.

Open her heart to You, Lord, he prayed, his mind imploring as his hands worked. *Let Your creation show her Your power and let us show her Your love. Help us to show her Your forgiveness and teach her to forgive.*

Mark paused, glancing over his shoulder once again. Brad and his wife, Lois, were helping Sheryl unpack, their voices carrying a murmur punctuated by an occasional laugh from Lois. Drew and Elaine were gathering the tack, and Allen and Diane helped Elise set up the kitchen. Their teenagers had found a frying pan lid and were already playing frisbee with the younger kids.

He felt the tension ease in his shoulders. He had been dreading this trip, and when Nate broke his leg, it put that much more on him. He had come so close to canceling, but now, as he saw his family so thoroughly enjoying themselves, he realized that all the trouble was worthwhile.

And when he heard Sheryl laugh softly, he knew that the patience he had unexpectedly received to finish the preparations for the trip was God-given, possibly for another reason.

Soon the clearing was full of tents, and Elise was ringing the gong for supper. Mark stretched, pushing a kink out of his back. The horses were hobbled, the more aggressive mares picketed to prevent them heading back home. Folded tarps hung over rails alongside saddles, blankets and bridles. He quickly scanned the sky. No clouds, but in the mountains you never knew. He would cover everything with the tarps before he went to sleep.

With a satisfied nod, he turned back to the camp, where his family had now gathered, waiting. They stood in a circle, a steady buzz of chatter flowing comfortably around them. He approached them and took his place beside Sheryl who stood off to one side, her hands clasped behind her back.

"Allen, can you say grace?" Elise asked as she held out her hands.

Mark saw Sheryl hesitate as a circle formed. Marla pulled Sheryl's one hand to herself and, with a wry grin, Mark reached over and caught her other.

She pulled away as Mark had known she would, but he only looked at her, his hand holding her smaller one firmly. When she looked up at him, a slight frown marred her forehead.

"Shall we pray?" Allen said, looking around the circle with a smile. Mark bent his head, still holding Sheryl's hand. She relaxed.

Allen's words were hushed, almost muffled by the largeness of the space they were in. His voice flowed, counterpointed by the whispering wind teasing the leaves of the trees above.

As Allen prayed, Mark added his own silent supplication, holding Sheryl's hand tighter, praying that she might be able to see God in nature around them, be able to see His love and His forgiveness.

When Allen said amen he felt Sheryl's fingers cling to his almost desperately. When he turned to her, her head was bent, eyes squeezed shut, lips clamped between her teeth. Mark resisted the urge to pull her close to him, to ease the tension that held her so stiff.

But then she pulled her hand away and looked up, not at him or anyone else, but at the leaves above them as if in supplication.

"We'll eat the usual way." Elise's voice broke the moment. "Parents help the little kids, and then the adults can eat once they're settled."

Sheryl turned to Marla and away from Mark, as if shutting him off.

He waited, watching her as she ushered her stepniece to the line, helping her select a plate and cutlery and then get served by Elise. Sheryl found them a spot on a fallen log and sat down.

Mark waited until everyone was served, intending on sitting at the table. He had envisioned sitting with Sheryl, but sensed that she wanted to be left alone. Crystal suddenly appeared beside him.

"Come and sit with us, Uncle Mark?" she asked, an overly bright smile wreathing her face.

"Why?" he asked, looking past her to where Sheryl sat with Marla, her head bent over the little girl's.

Crystal leaned closer, her voice lowered to a theatrical whisper. "Sheryl has tears in her eyes," she whispered.

Mark straightened, his fingers tightening on the plate he held. Ignoring his family's knowing looks, he affected a casual air, got up and sauntered across the clearing to where Sheryl sat.

He lowered himself slowly to the ground beside her, leaning against the log she sat on. "Hope you don't mind that I sit here?" he asked, glancing up at her.

"No, go ahead." Her voice was quiet, almost strained. Beside him he could see her legs stretched out, the toes of her scuffed running shoes tapping against each other in agitation.

Crystal joined them with a plate of food for Sheryl, and between the two little girls, they managed to fill up the silence that loomed between the two adults.

When Mark finished eating, he gave Crystal his plate, sent Marla on an errand and pushed himself up on the log beside Sheryl. She sat, head bent over her plate, her fork pushing around the remnants of stew that he knew was now cold.

"You don't have to eat it if you don't want to," he told her, his hands dangling between his knees.

"But if I don't, the bears will," she said with an attempt at humor.

Mark took the plate from her and with two spoonfuls finished it off. Then he handed it back to her. "Now just wipe it with your bread and you're done."

She did as she was told. "Thanks," she said quietly.

Giving in to an impulse, Mark slipped an arm around her shoulders and squeezed her.

Her answering smile surprised and pleased him. She didn't resist. It was as if she was content to have him hold her beside him. She took a slow breath, and Mark saw the shimmer of tears on the corner of one eye. With a gentle forefinger he touched it and one slipped out.

Mark pulled her closer, wondering, praying, knowing that somehow she had been touched, but knowing, as well, that he would have to trust and wait.

Chapter Ten

The crackle and snap of the fire broke the stillness of the night. Sparks spiraled upward into the darkness then chased by others.

Sheryl watched the flames, her hands cupped around a coffee mug, her restlessness easing.

She had helped Elise put her girls to bed, told them a story about when she was young and then kissed them good-night. She had dawdled, hesitant to step out of the safety of the little girls' company and join the adults sitting outside, their words an indistinct murmur punctuated by the snapping fire. The single tear that had slipped out at suppertime was a mistake, she didn't know what to do about it.

Mark had wiped it away, and she knew he wouldn't leave her alone. So when she stepped out of the tent, safely out of the circle of the firelight, she scanned the bodies around it, checking for his distinctive hair, but she couldn't see him.

So why had she felt a twinge of disappointment as she stepped closer to the fire?

The circle had opened for her, and she had found a spot

just within reach of the warmth of the flames, but slightly back from the group.

Sheryl took another sip of her tea, followed by a deep, cleansing sigh. She enjoyed watching Mark's family, enjoyed listening to their light banter. Unfinished jokes circulated, memories interrupted by laughter and other remembrances, the conversation a stream of consciousness that meandered over past and present.

"Where are you?" A gravelly voice murmured in her ear. Joy sluiced through her at the familiar sound. A large hand rested on her shoulder, long fingers curling around it. Sighing lightly she gave in to an impulse and laid her head back, enjoying the feeling of belonging that surged through her at his touch. He liked her, and she had to admit she was attracted to him. Why not just enjoy it?

"My mind's just wandering," she replied.

"Well, put this on and come and wander with me instead." Mark drew back and dropped her heavy jacket over her shoulders and turned her around to face him.

His eyes glowed with reflected firelight, his finely chiseled features accented by the shadows. "I have to check the horses and thought you might want to come with me," he said, pulling the collar of the coat up around her neck.

Sheryl hesitated.

"Please," he urged, his rough finger caressing her neck.

She felt her skin warm under his touch and, pushing aside the last of her own objections, slipped her arms into the overlarge sleeves, pulling the coat close to her and nodded. "Sure. If my expert opinion is any good." Keep it light and superficial and just savor, she reminded herself.

Mark smiled, dropped an arm over her shoulders and drew her away from the campfire and his family. "You can tell me if I have the hobbles on upside down."

"Well if you're worried about that, you probably tied the horses to the picket with the wrong end of the rope," Sheryl retorted, a teasing note entering her voice. It was time she proved that she could hold her own, play the game and not get involved.

The fire was behind them now, the noises of his family receding as they walked.

"Listen, I had a hard enough time finding a picket that had the point on the right end," Mark said, slipping his hands in his coat pockets, his eyes on her as they walked.

Sheryl laughed, the sound softened by the darkness. The sighing of the wind in the trees above them and the occasional nicker or snort from the horses beyond them were the only sounds accompanying their muted footfalls.

He reached out and took her hand in his, intertwining their fingers, and Sheryl let him, content to relish in his attention. When he stopped and leaned back against a tree and drew her close to him, she didn't stop him, either.

She laid her head against his chest, feeling more than hearing the steady thump of his heartbeat, the slow rise and fall of his breathing. He touched her hair and pulled her braid out from the jacket.

"Do you always tie it up?" he asked, toying with it.

"Usually. It gets in the way otherwise." She was pleasantly surprised at how easy it was to just enjoy his company.

"Can I undo it?"

"Sure."

"I've wanted to do this for days," he sighed, combing her hair with his fingers. "It's so beautiful."

Sheryl leaned back, her hands pressed against his chest, watching him as his eyes followed his own hands as they wrapped themselves in her hair. It felt good to be treated so gently, but she had to be careful to keep the situation under her control. "What do you want, Mark?"

Mark looked bemused, his eyes still on his hands. "I want a lot of things. A square-bale stacker, some more land..." He paused, looking down into her eyes, his own glinting in the weak light of the moon. "Lots of money," he whispered dramatically.

"Who doesn't?" she replied softly, her tone bantering, her mouth curved up in a smile.

Mark tilted his head. As his smile faded away, his expression became serious, and against her will Sheryl felt her heart still. Don't let him do it, she thought grimly, remembering his unexpected kiss that morning.

But his gentle fingers rested lightly on her forehead, his other hand held her even closer.

"I want a lot of things," he whispered, his eyes intent. "But what I need is you."

He waited a moment as the words sank in, dropping so quickly past her guard, she couldn't stop them. They shot straight as an arrow to that deep, empty place in Sheryl's life that yearned for love and affection. No one had ever needed her before. Wanted, used, but needed?

She looked up into his soft gray eyes trying to discern what he really meant.

Stop this now, commanded the angry part of her.

But Sheryl was suddenly tired of anger, tired of fighting. This moment, this time up in the mountain was like a dream. Mark's family, the fellowship, the beauty of the surroundings, Mark's arms around her—all of this was so unreal it was easy to think that no matter what happened it wouldn't affect her, once she returned to the valley and reality.

He needed her.

His arm tightened about her, his hand slid over her cheek and suddenly his mouth was on hers creating an ache within her heart that almost hurt. His lips were warm, soft, and she drifted against him, clinging to him.

"Sheryl," he murmured against her mouth, his own moving to her cheeks, her eyes, his fingers following, touching, tasting.

She slipped her hands around his neck, tangling her fingers in his hair, her mouth seeking his hungrily.

Reluctantly he pulled away, tucking her head close to his chest, his mouth brushing her temple.

"Oh, Sheryl, I wish I could tell you how much I care about you," he whispered against her hair, his lips warm on her skin. "I think I'm falling in love with you."

That word, more than any, was sufficient to wake her, and she pulled back. "Don't talk like that," she warned.

Mark tilted his head to one side, brushing her hair out of her face. "But I have to," he said. "I feel like I found someone who belongs with me...you're the part of me that has been missing all this time."

"Please stop."

"I can't," he murmured, tracing the line of her eyebrows. "I want to tell you what you mean to me, how much I like just watching you. I like seeing you work with the horses, driving a tractor. You look beautiful with dust streaking your face and straw in your hair. And when you smile—" he kissed the corner of her mouth, as if to encourage it "—that's what I want to do."

Sheryl felt confusion warring within her. Physical actions she could deal with, but not words. She had no defense against what he said. He wasn't supposed to be making her bones melt and her blood thin with words. This was just supposed to be an interlude, a brief moment, a light flirtation.

Her mind fought with the pleasure of what he said and the humility of feeling undeserving. Jason and, even earlier, Ed both had tried to pound the feeling into her without success, and now Mark, with only a few words, had succeeded where Jason and Ed had failed. She didn't want to feel unworthy, yet around Mark she knew she was.

Caught between her wavering emotions she looked up into Mark's glowing eyes and slowly shook her head. "We don't fit at all, Mark," she whispered, desperately fighting his attraction, trying to keep her emotions under control. What he said was too beautiful, too wonderful, to be meant for her. It gently pried open cracks in her protective covering that let out the remembering. "You're too different," *Too good for me,* she added silently to herself, *too wonderful, too much God's child.*

"Not so different, Sheryl," he admonished, running a callused finger down her cheek. "We both love the same things…"

"No," she said, her voice suddenly thick with emotions that came so easily to the surface when she was with him, mocking her earlier intentions. "I can't love…. I don't have it in me."

Mark tilted his head to one side, his hand cupping her chin, slipping down her neck. "Yes you do. I've seen you with Crystal and Marla, with Benjamin…"

"Stop it," she said, her voice tightening. "You don't know what you're talking about…"

"You don't mind it when I kiss you," he continued undaunted, gently caressing her neck.

Sheryl stiffened as his hands drifted over her shoulder, reminding her. She stepped away, and Mark's hands dropped to his side. His chest lifted in a protracted sigh.

"You do that so well, Sheryl."

She ignored him, pulling her jacket around her.

"What does it take to crack that shell you have so firmly around yourself?" Mark's voice was soft, but his tone suggested he wasn't going to let her pull back this time. "I care about you, Sheryl, and I want to help."

"What can you do," she cried out. "You're just a man, just another lousy man, and what has any man ever done for me?"

Mark paused, reached out and touched her cheek, tracing the track of the lone tear that slid unheeded down her cheek.

"One man gave up his life for you, Sheryl."

She blinked, swiping the moisture from her eyes with the palm of her hand, watching him, suddenly still as she listened.

"Jesus took all that pain you're carrying around, all those burdens, all the mistakes, the punishment that we deserve…" He dropped his hand, his eyes watching her. "He took it all with him and then he died—just for you."

It was there again. That hovering feeling, that sense of great love waiting. But she knew too well what God wanted. Subjugation.

"Well I can't give him what he wants, Mark," she said suddenly, closing her eyes against his image, concentrating on who she was. "God wants too much from me. And so do you. I can't give you what you want, what you need. You need someone who can share that faith you have, someone you can pray with, not someone who is hauling around all this other garbage.…"

"Then dump it," he replied softly.

She looked at him then, "What?"

"Dump it. I've told you what Christ has done for you, what he's waiting to do for you…"

"It's not that easy," she faltered.

"It's a whole lot easier than packing it around yourself." Mark pushed himself away from the tree, but he didn't touch her.

Sheryl bit her lip, her arms clasped tightly across her stomach. She couldn't look at him, but she could hear him breathing, saw his hands hanging loosely at his sides, his feet slightly spraddled. It was as if he expected her to turn and run.

She couldn't.

There was no place left to go. God seemed determined to find her and He would use anyone who came in her path.

Sheryl looked up at Mark. The slight breeze that came with evening in the mountains lifted his hair and dropped it gently. As she watched him, he laid his hand on her shoulder again.

"I can only guess at what happened to you. I know it's more than what you've said," Mark sighed, tilting his head to one side, his eyes gleaming in the soft night. "I just know that I care for you in a way I've never cared for anyone." He tightened his hold on her, lifting his other hand to her waist as if to pull her closer.

She resisted; she had to. If she let him hold her again she wouldn't be able to keep herself aloof, and her last barrier would be pulled down.

"Sheryl, please tell me about Jason."

She stiffened, then forced herself to relax, to adopt a light tone. "I told you already. He wasn't a good husband." She ran her finger down the front of his T-shirt, feeling the warmth of him through it. "It doesn't matter anymore...."

"Yes, it does. It's a part of you that you keep hidden. I don't like that. I want to know—"

"All the details?" she asked, her voice tight. She didn't pull away, but wouldn't meet his gaze. "Is it important for you to know exactly how many times he humiliated me?" She suddenly grabbed the front of Mark's jacket, the metal ridges of the button cutting into her hand. "Why is it so important to hear how many times he hit me, how stupid I was, how helpless? Do you want to see the scars?"

Mark closed his eyes and drew in a deep breath. Sheryl felt his chest rise and stifled a clench of instinctive panic.

"No." He ground the single word out, his rough voice harsh. "I want to share the burden you're carrying, to help you. I want you to see what God wants to do for you. But you have to tell me. You have to open up."

Sheryl swallowed, feeling as if she hovered on the brink of a dark abyss, unsure of what emotions waited below— pain, sorrow, regret, fear...

"I can only guess at what happened to you. I just want

to help you," Mark's rough voice softened as his words tugged on her barriers. "Please let me help."

Sheryl closed her eyes at his words. They were so tempting. Did she dare let go? Who could she trust to catch her?

I'll be there. The still, small voice slid into her mind out of another part of her life. A soft and gentle part that was always there, a part she never dared acknowledge in her battles to be strong. *I'll bear you up on eagle's wings,* the voice continued.

Sheryl felt a wave of pure love, pure devotion, pure tenderness wash over her as if erasing and removing all the stains and wearing down all the bars that she had held so tightly over her soul.

A sob shuddered through her. Then another. She tried to stop it, tried to pull it back, but it was as if she tried to hold back the sea.

A wave of sorrow washed over her.

"Just let go," Mark's voice whispered, somewhere above her, piercing the darkness of her soul. "God will carry you through."

Suddenly she went slack. Strong arms caught her, supported her. Then the tightness that always constricted her throat, loosened its grip.

Sheryl clutched her chest, trying to stop the knot of pain unraveling in her chest. "Where were you?"

"It's okay," Mark whispered, pulling her close, wrapping his arms around her. "I'm here."

Strength. Warmth. She felt a melting.

Then the sound came. First a narrow keen, weak and meager. As Mark's arms held her the sound built in her throat, harder, heavier.

Then, with the swiftness of a summer storm, the sorrow poured out. A grief larger than she could articulate threw her around, sucking her in the maelstrom.

"Mama," was all she could say. "I want my mama."

Huge, heaving sobs racked her body, sorrow held down too long engulfed her, trying to come out all at once.

She clutched her head as tears coursed down her heated cheeks. Mark pulled her tighter against him, drawing her head against his chest. She clung to him as her anguish grew, the sorrow threatening to rip her in two.

"Why, Lord?" she cried out clutching Mark's jacket, the metal ridges of his buttons digging in her hands. "Why did you take her away from me?"

She could say no more, her face pressed against his shirt as she wept away months of repressed grief and sorrow.

She cried for the loss of her mother, for the brokenness of her relationships, for the loss of her own innocence in the reality of living with Jason. Time drifted on, meaningless, as she unburdened herself, her mind empty of all but grief.

The sobs lessened, but still the tears flowed. She wanted to stop but knew she couldn't until the pain was lanced out…for now.

After what seemed like hours, the tears subsided and she felt strength surrounding her through her sorrow. Strong arms held her, hands pressed her close. Mark had become an anchor in the storm that had just washed over her. But even with her heated cheek pressed against his now-damp T-shirt, she knew that a greater strength had comforted and held her firm.

She had tried to run away, but God had found her.

Mark closed his eyes, his own emotions in a turmoil. He rocked Sheryl slowly, soothing her, praying for the right words, knowing he would never forget the sounds of her anguish or the feel of her now-pliant body resting against him, trusting him.

"Dear Lord, please grant her healing," he whispered, his hand holding her head close to him, "Let her tears cleanse her."

He felt a tremor drift through her as she drew in a shaky breath, her cries a soft mewling sound. He wanted to absorb her pain into himself, take it away from her. Their relationship had taken another turn, and now the bond between them could not so easily be ignored or brushed aside.

"Oh, Sheryl," he whispered against her hair, kissing her damp temple, tucking her head under his chin. "I do love you."

His leg was cramping. He tried to loosen Sheryl's grip on his waist but she clung harder.

"I just want to sit down, Sheryl," he whispered, stroking her hair away from her face.

Reassured she released her hold on him, and when he sat down he drew her onto his lap, wrapping his arms all the way around her as if she were a child, holding her as close to him as he could.

"Do you want to talk about it?" he asked, his voice quiet as he stared off into the dark, surprised that his family had not heard the sound of her crying and come to investigate.

Sheryl took in a breath, shuddering. "I'm afraid to."

"Why?" he prompted softly, laying his head against the rough bark of the tree he sat against.

"It's so hard," Sheryl said simply, her hands resting against his chest. "I tried to push everything out of my mind, tried not to think."

He hesitated, feeling as if he took advantage of her, but deeper than that was a need to know everything about her, everything that she tried to conceal. "You said something about your mother and Jason..." he said gently, stroking her head with his chin.

Sheryl drew a slow, deep breath. "I missed her so much," she said softly. "I wasn't the daughter I should have been. I made things so hard. Then Jason..." she shuddered. "The times he beat me...I felt I deserved it for what I did to my mom."

Mark closed his eyes, feeling her pain, sharing her sorrow, swallowing down his own. She had lost so much, had endured so much, how could he comfort her?

"I wanted to be a good wife and I wanted a baby so badly," she continued, her voice quavering. "He didn't. And now I have nobody."

Mark held her, his own emotions a disarray of feelings, thoughts, questions. She had borne this sadness and grief on her own. Now her restraint and self-control took on another meaning, became pitiable instead of a source of frustration. Who did she have to help share her burden? She had pulled away from God, she had no family support, and he wondered what kind of friends she could have made living with Jason.

"Can I pray with you, Sheryl?" he whispered, stroking her head, his fingers tangling in her hair.

"I don't know," she murmured. "It's been so long since I prayed." She drew back, looking up at Mark, the darkness unable to conceal her puffy eyes, the tracks of her tears on her cheeks. "I'd feel like an uninvited guest barging in...."

Mark palmed away the moisture from her cheeks, smiling down on her. "He's waiting for you, Sheryl. He wants to be with you. His love is never ending, don't you remember?"

Sheryl shook her head slowly. "I remember believing it when I was little, but somehow I haven't seen a whole lot of it lately."

Mark almost cried, himself, at her honest declaration, and he struggled for the right words. He took a breath and pressed a quick kiss on her heated forehead. "God has never promised us an easy life, without problems," he said slowly, "but He does promise that whatever things come our way He will use for our own good."

Sheryl blinked up at him and lifted her hand to his face. Her cool fingers ran down his cheek and cupped his chin as she watched him, a sad smile trembling on her lips. "You make it sound so neat and tidy," she whispered.

"But right about now the only good thing that has come out of this is meeting you."

Mark's heart skipped a beat. He was unable to tear his gaze away from her shimmering eyes. She blinked, and another tear coursed down her face. Bending over her, he kissed it away, and suddenly she clung to him, desperation in her movements.

"Please stop being so good to me, Mark," she whispered, her voice urgent. "I have nothing to give back to you."

He laid his chin on her hair, staring into the darkened forest, afraid to think that life had indeed sucked her empty. Was what he offered enough to fill it? All he could do now was pray her heart would open to what God could give her.

Without warning she suddenly straightened, drawing away from Mark.

"I must look a fright," she said with a curt laugh, pulling her hair away from her face. With one easy motion she stood up, finger combing her hair, looking anywhere but at Mark.

He stayed where he was, drawing one leg up, resting his wrist on his knee as he watched her hurried movements. How quickly she pulled back, drew her defenses around her. It would be admirable if it wasn't so heart-wrenchingly sad.

"Do you have my hair elastic band?" she asked suddenly, her fingers weaving her hair back into a braid.

He stretched his leg out as he dug in his pants pocket for it. He handed it to her, and wordlessly she took it, still looking everywhere but at him.

"So what happens now, Sheryl?" he asked, unable to keep silent.

She paused, her head bent, then resolutely twisted the elastic around the bottom of her braid, her movements erratic. Tucking it into her coat, she shoved her hands in the pockets pulling her coat closer around her. "I don't know," she answered finally, sniffing lightly, wiping her nose with the back of her hand.

Mark pushed himself off the ground and came near to her, standing close enough, but not touching her.

"I can't say I do, either," he replied softly. "We shared something tonight, God touched you tonight, and I don't think you will ever be the same."

"Probably not." She looked up at him, her face confused. "But old habits die hard. Maybe I just need some time."

Mark kissed her lightly on the top of her head and drew her alongside him, walking back to the campfire. "Then we'll wait," he said, comforted by her hesitant acknowledgment, praying, wondering, but also realizing that she was right.

They walked back in silence, the wind whispering above them, the cool darkness enveloping them. In the distance Mark could hear the snap of the fire, the murmur of his family's voices punctuated by occasional laughter. Unconsciously his arm tightened around Sheryl's shoulders as if to give her strength. She lifted her head to look at him.

"You look scared," he said, smiling down at her.

Her step faltered, and she looked away from him, her hands still buried in her pockets. "I am."

Mark stopped turning her to face him. "Why?"

Sheryl shrugged, chewing on her bottom lip. "What am I supposed to say, how do I act?"

Mark frowned, trying to find the meaning under the oblique words. "Normal, I guess."

"But that's the trouble, Mark," she looked back up at him, her face tight with suppressed emotion, "I don't know what's normal. I don't know who I am anymore."

As Mark watched her he remembered the cold, hardened girl he had met in the bar only a couple of weeks ago. Now she stood before him, her clothes and manner totally at odds with that same girl. He had gotten past her hard veneer to the soft and hurting core of her. But by doing this he had also taken away her own natural defenses, and she was lost.

"You're Sheryl—" he started.

"But which one?" she broke in. "Reilly, Krickson or Kyle?" She broke away from him. "Who do I belong to?"

"First and foremost you belong to God," he replied without hesitating.

Sheryl said nothing, but when she turned back to him, she was smiling lightly. "I guess that's where I'll have to start then." She looked over her shoulder at the soft glow of the fire through the trees. "We better go. Your family is going to wonder what happened to us."

As soon as they stepped into the clearing, Elise stood up and looked past Sheryl to Mark with a knowing smirk on her face.

Mark shook his head imperceptibly as he pushed a stump into the circle with his boot.

Elise frowned, but when she sat down Mark knew she got his silent message. He just hoped the rest of his family would leave Sheryl and give her the space and time that she needed.

He prayed that he would be able to, as well.

Chapter Eleven

The early-morning sun warmed the tent, and Sheryl rolled over, pain slashing through her head and right behind it, her memories.

Sheryl slung her arm over her eyes as if to keep both at bay. But images danced through her mind, painful, mournful. Her mother's sad face as Sheryl and Ed once again faced off over Jason. Jason's angry face when she hit him back for the first time. The screech of metal, the glass flying.

Sheryl rolled onto her side, pulling her arms close to her chest, wishing she could drift back to the painless void that was her life the past year. It had taken years of living with Ed and Nate to build a defense against emotions. When her mother died, she hadn't been able to cry. While being married to Jason, she hadn't allowed herself to.

Now Mark had peeled away the protective layers, had made a mockery of her strength.

She rubbed her temples, now damp with tears as she pulled herself into the present. Her pain still hung in her mind, and she knew that no matter what happened, by tomorrow she would be alone again.

The thought propelled her out of her lethargy. With a quick motion, she pushed back the sleeping bag and got up.

Elise stood by the table, yawning as she mixed up pancake batter, smoke wafting from the stoked-up fire. Sheryl pulled up her mouth in a semblance of a smile and walked resolutely over, her offer to help received with enthusiasm. As she kept busy, Sheryl felt the blessed return of equilibrium and control.

Until Mark appeared in the clearing. He said nothing, but as he walked past her he trailed his hand casually over her shoulder sending shivers down her spine and confusion through her mind, mocking what she thought she had just attained.

Breakfast was over quickly and devotions followed. Allen read from the Old Testament this time. "'For the Lord searches every heart and understands every motive behind the thoughts. If you seek him, he will be found by you.'" The words were unfamiliar but, much like Mark's words of last night, they found and filled an empty spot in Sheryl's life. And much like Mark's words they made her feel unworthy.

After devotions came the work. Sheryl quickly haltered Marla's and Crystal's horses, then tied them up.

As she snugged up cinches, adjusted stirrups and packed the horses she felt surrounded by Mark's family as they moved, asked her for advice and exchanged laughing comments with each other.

"How's it going?" The soft voice behind her startled her. Sheryl glanced over her shoulder at Elise who stood beside her horse, her hand resting on its rump, concern showing in her face.

"Fine," Sheryl replied, her tone noncommittal, determined not to answer the questions that she saw in Elise's eyes. "I just have to snug this up and F5 is all packed."

She turned her attention back to the ropes, making sure the loops were taut, the pressure on them even.

"You look tired," Elise persisted, tilting her head so she could better see Sheryl's face.

Sheryl shook her head, pulling the last rope through and making it taut. "I'm okay, really."

Elise took a step closer and placed her hand on Sheryl's shoulder. "You don't sound okay."

Sheryl bit her lip, still holding the end of the rope. She swallowed and swallowed, willing the myriad of emotions that were roiling beneath her fragile self-control to settle down. "Please don't ask, Elise," Sheryl whispered finally, still unable to face her friend.

"There you are, sis." Mark's voice broke into the silence. "Rick told me you were pestering my chief wrangler." He ducked under the hitching rail, and Sheryl didn't know if having him around was any better. "Is your horse all ready to go, sis?"

"Yes," returned Elise, sounding peeved. "And so is Crystal, Marla and all the others."

"Good, then we can head out." Mark untied F5, speaking to Sheryl as he did. "I didn't think you minded if I got Allen to lead this critter."

"Fine by me," she said, risking a glance up at him. Their eyes met, Mark's hands stilled, and she felt herself drifting toward him. She had to almost clench her fists to keep from laying them against his chest.

He blinked then cleared his throat. "Good," he replied, his own voice unsteady. "Elise, can you take up the rear. Sheryl is going to ride up front with me."

"Sure..." It wasn't hard to hear the smirk in Elise's voice, and Sheryl knew that the inquisition Elise tried to begin a moment ago was only forestalled. She took a breath and turned away from both of them, reminding herself that tomorrow she would be leaving.

* * *

"Do you remember that place?" Mark drew his horse alongside Sheryl, pointing out a steep slide visible between the trees.

"Frying pan ridge," Sheryl replied. "Nate and I were out riding when we found that old frying pan up there."

The early-morning mountain air had had a gentle bite, which the sun had since warmed off. The hills spread away from the riders, their undulating stretches ridged with pine trees. Above them, the grassy slopes gave way to harsh, unyielding rock and benignly deceptive rock slides.

She glanced sidelong at Mark, disconcerted to see him studying her with a bemused look on his face. Up till now his comments had been superficial and she had been grateful for his casual attitude.

"What?"

"You look beautiful this morning," he said softly, reaching out. But Sheryl's horse shied and his hand missed its target.

"My eyes are red, my hair is a mess…" Sheryl shook her head taking refuge in humor.

"You look softer, warmer, more approachable," he returned, refuting her deprecating remarks. "And you look great sitting on the back of a horse," he finished with a smile.

"Well, I guess the horse can take some credit for that."

"I said *you* look great, not the horse."

She only nodded.

"How are you feeling this morning?" he said his expression suddenly serious.

"I woke up with a headache."

Mark drew his horse closer, taking her hand in his, squeezing. "I was praying for you last night."

"What for?" Sheryl replied, trying to cover the jolt his words gave her. Not now, she thought, please don't talk about that now.

Mark winked at her, threading his callused fingers through hers. "That you would sleep well."

Sheryl knew she should take her hand out of his, but she couldn't break the connection. She enjoyed the feel of his large work-roughened fingers, as an undefinable peace flowed over her. She knew it couldn't last and was determined not to let the future intrude on this time out of time.

Mark looked ahead, his hand swinging Sheryl's, his hat pushed back on his head, eyes narrowed against the bright morning sun. Small wrinkles fanned out from the corners of his eyes, light lines in his tanned face, and a smile lifted one corner of his mouth. He moved easily with his horse, unconsciously attuned to its movements.

His jacket hung open, the ever-present mountain breeze ruffling his hair. Above him was the hard blue sky, behind him the rugged mountains.

The rightness of the scene gave Sheryl a stab of pleasure, almost painful in its intensity. As if he sensed her regard, he turned, his dark eyebrows frowning a moment, questioning.

"What's wrong?"

Sheryl shook her head, smiling as she squeezed his hand. "Nothing at all," she returned, losing herself in eyes as gray as a soft summer rain.

They reached Mark's camp by lunchtime. Everyone dismounted, and pulled out the sandwiches and ate them standing, sitting or lounging against the wall of the cabin. Sheryl sat with Crystal and Marla, content to watch and listen. The girls found a ready ear for their excited jabber about their horses and near encounters with death on the trip up.

All too soon it was time to return to the main camp. A few moans and groans accompanied the mounting up. Brad, Allen and their wives said their goodbyes to Mark. It would be a while until they saw him again. Elise gave him a quick peck on the cheek, and he gave the girls a hug.

Sheryl helped Crystal and Marla into the saddles. Elise was already on her horse, and at a signal from her, they rode off, leaving Mark and Sheryl alone.

Sheryl toyed with the reins of her horse, unsure of what to say. How do you say goodbye to the first man you met that you felt at one with? How do you tell him that you can never be together?

Then his hand lifted up her chin, and she looked once again into soft gray eyes.

"I'm glad you came along, Sheryl," he said, his voice rough with unexpected emotion. He smiled carefully at her, his fingers caressing her cheek. "If it wasn't so terribly improper, I'd ask you to stay with me out here and ride with me, help me gather the cows."

Sheryl managed a shaky grin at his words, trying to grasp some kind of equilibrium in her own emotions, now so tender and vulnerable.

"Thanks for letting me come. It was good to be out here again." She bit her lip as she felt a sob rise in her chest, remembering last night, not wanting to think what lay ahead. She blinked carefully, but a tear coursed down her cheek.

"Oh, Sheryl," Mark sighed, drawing her suddenly against him in a fierce hug. "I'd say don't cry but you have so much sadness that has to come out."

She leaned against him, drawing from his strength, saying nothing.

"Whatever happens, Sheryl," he said, "please remember that Jesus's love is greater than mine."

Fresh tears flowed at his words, and Sheryl fought to regain control. She couldn't start crying now. She had to get on her horse and ride down to their camp and then down into the valley and then...

She straightened, palming her cheeks and wiping the moisture off on her pant legs. "I'm sorry," she murmured,

"I don't know what's happening to me. I never used to be weepy."

"You never had the chance," Mark said softly, reaching into his pocket and pulling out a red polka-dotted hanky. Carefully, he lifted her chin with his fingers and dried the rest of her tears. He took his time, his gentleness almost setting her off again. When he was done, he folded the hanky in her hands.

"So, what happens now, Sheryl?" he asked.

Sheryl looked away, wrapping his handkerchief around her hands, clenching them tightly. "I still have an apartment in Edmonton. I'm enrolled in classes this fall, and I'll need to go job hunting."

"I still owe you for the one you lost." He shifted his weight, tugging on his ear. "And what about Nate and Ed?"

"I'll visit Ed just before I go and as for Nate..." She lifted her shoulders in a shrug. "Nothing much has changed. I don't imagine it will between now and when I leave."

"And forgiveness...?" His words were soft, but they cut.

"I don't know if I can do that, Mark."

"Not on your own, of course."

Sheryl bit her lip. "I don't think I have to forgive them. They have to live with what they've done, just as I have to live with the consequences of my own decisions."

"But you can't build a relationship until forgiveness has been granted," he urged, touching her cheek with one finger.

Sheryl looked up at him, shaking her head regretfully. "I don't know if I want a relationship...."

"You have all that you need," he finished for her.

Sheryl avoided the steady deepness of his gaze and said nothing.

"And now you have to leave?"

"Yes."

Mark sighed, shoving his hat back on his head. "Can you wait until I'm done up here?" he asked, then hurried on before she could reply. "I know I'm asking a lot of you, but can you stay at Nate and Elise's until I get back? I'll be finished here in a couple of days. It will only be four more days, tops. Could you wait that much longer?"

Sheryl's heart flipped over, stopped and then began to race. She couldn't think about what he asked, didn't dare let her thoughts venture further.

Mark caught her by the arms, as if sensing her withdrawal. "I'm not asking you to stay forever, at least not yet. But something's happening here and I don't know exactly where it's going." His voice became pleading. "Sheryl, you can't just go back without having settled what you know is building between us. Stay and let's give it a chance."

Sheryl closed her eyes, fighting the temptation to drift against him, to let him kiss her like she knew he wanted to.

"Please, Sheryl. Stop fighting, stop trying to be so independent."

"I don't know, Mark. I get confused by you." She looked up at him, pleading. "You want things from me, things I'm not ready to give."

"Give-and-take is all part of normal interaction."

"But that doesn't come easily for me." She almost cried the words out. "Do you think this trip has been easy? Do you think it's easy for me to jump from a life with Jason, Nate and Ed, into a trip like this with a family like yours?"

"What's wrong with my family?"

"Don't get all defensive." She pulled away, reaching out to settle her horse, jumpy from the rising sound of their voices. "Your family is perfect. Too perfect," she added softly.

"No, we're not. We fight and bicker and get angry with

each other. I have just as hard a time getting along with Nate as I'm sure you used to."

Sheryl frowned up at him, surprised to hear that.

"But we keep on going because he's family and he's been placed in my life for a reason," he continued.

"And what about the things that happened to me? I still haven't found the reason I lost my father, my mother." Sheryl halted. "Everyone who I ever loved…"

So many of her barriers had already been broken down by this darkly handsome man. So much she'd held so tightly had been pried open, leaving her vulnerable and scared. He talked easily of forgiving things that happened in the past, but it wasn't that easy. "You talk about God having a reason for what happens. Was Jason placed in my life for a reason? And is there a reason you and I met?"

Mark laughed shortly. "Yes, I know there is."

"Well, God has a sense of humor, I guess." She turned away from him, wanting to get this parting out of the way, afraid to prolong it. But just before she could get her foot into the stirrup, Mark pulled her back, held her by the shoulders and looked down into her eyes, his brows meeting in a frown.

"There's a plan for us, Sheryl. I know it. You belong here as much as I do. Think about that when you're trying to find a job in Edmonton." And without any warning he pulled her against him and caught her mouth in a brief, hard kiss.

Sheryl turned away, stifling a sob, jumped on her horse and rode and rode and rode.

Sheryl slipped her jacket on and shook out the wrinkles of her skirt. She flipped her backpack over her shoulder, hefted her suitcase off the bed and took a last, lingering look around the cabin. Was it only ten days ago she had come here?

It seemed like weeks.

Nate waited in the driveway, she could hear the low thrum of the engine of their minivan. She wished Elise could have taken her to Sweet Creek. So many unresolved feelings hung between her and Nate. Their relationship was still wary, watching and unforgiving. It was easy for Mark to talk of forgiveness, but surely something had to come from Nate?

With a sigh Sheryl left, closing the door softly behind her. Moisture drizzled down through the trees, and Sheryl picked her way carefully through the puddles, heedless of the water that misted her hair.

She came around the corner of the cabin, and Marla and Crystal jumped off their perch on the verandah rail and came to her at a dead run, calling her name.

Dropping her suitcase, Sheryl bent over to catch them against her.

"Why do you have to go, Auntie Sheryl, why don't you stay with us?" Crystal cried, clinging to her waist.

Marla said nothing, only hung on to Sheryl her face pressed against her side.

Sheryl stroked their heads as a bleakness settled inside her. How much she wanted to stay, how much she needed to leave.

"I'm sorry sweethearts, but I have to go back to my own home. That's in Edmonton." And maybe there, she thought, away from the memories, she'd have the space to seek God.

"But you can have a new home here?" Crystal cried out, giving Sheryl a shake. "Uncle Mark wants you to stay, I know he does."

Funny that those innocent words could create anew the aching hunger that had gnawed at her yesterday with each fall of the horse's hooves, taking her farther and farther away from Mark.

"It's okay, Crystal. I might come back again," she promised quickly.

"When?" Marla's head shot up, her eyes expectant.

Sheryl bit her lip and shrugged lightly. "I don't know. I have to get a job and save up some more money." The explanation sounded lame in Sheryl's ears, but Marla seemed to accept it.

"You could work here," Marla offered.

Sheryl only smiled and stroked Marla's head, a rush of love flowing through her.

The door slapped against the frame, and Elise stepped onto the verandah, holding Benjamin. Sheryl released the girls and walked across the verandah toward them.

"So, you're going, then?" Elise said quietly, her eyes sorrowful.

Sheryl didn't trust her voice and only nodded. She held out her hands for Benjamin who leaned toward her, the drool on his chin rolling down the soft fuzz of his blue sleeper, his bright eyes wide. She wrapped her arms around his soft warmth, holding him close, inhaling the sweet baby smell of him. She swallowed down a lump of pain, not wanting to cry again, not with a long trip beside Nate ahead of her.

Benjamin placed his chubby hands against her shoulders, pushing back, his blue eyes focused on her as if memorizing her. He gurgled and grabbed the braid that hung over one shoulder.

"You are such a sweetheart," she murmured, pressing a kiss on his warm cheek. Giving him another quick hug, she returned him to Elise's arms.

"Run upstairs, Crystal, and get that package on the bed," Elise said over her shoulder. She looked back at Sheryl with a sad smile, then hooked an arm around Sheryl's neck, drawing her close. "I sure hope we can see you again," Elise murmured against her hair.

Sheryl returned Elise's hug, Benjamin hanging awkwardly between them, her backpack slipping down her arm.

When she straightened she was surprised to see tears in Elise's eyes.

"Please don't start," she said, her voice breaking.

"Oh, Sheryl. I had so hoped you could stay."

Sheryl shook her head. "I don't belong here, Elise. There's too much history…" And pain, she added silently.

"I guess we've just asked too much of you, me and Mark," Elise replied softly, blinking back her tears. "But you have to keep in touch. Promise me you will?"

"Maybe," Sheryl said vaguely, avoiding the steady deepness of her eyes, too much like Mark's for comfort.

The screen door flew open, Crystal and Marla tumbling through the opening. "Here, this is for you, Auntie Sheryl." Crystal ran up to Sheryl, breathless, handing her a small, wrapped parcel.

"It's just a little something for the trip." Elise shrugged, pulling Benjamin close. "I hope you enjoy it."

"You have to open it on the bus," Marla piped up.

Sheryl looked down at the brightly wrapped package, trimmed with ribbons and a bow, swallowing down a knot of emotion. She couldn't remember the last time someone had bought her a gift, and she was afraid she was going to cry again.

"Thank you, very much," she replied softly, touching the springy curls of ribbon.

The blare of a horn broke the moment. She reached out and gave Elise another quick hug and, pressing a kiss on each of the girls' heads, she rearranged her backpack on her shoulder and picked up her suitcase. With a quick wave to the assembled group she ran down the steps of the verandah, through the drizzle to the waiting van.

She threw her knapsack and suitcase in the back seat, got in, and before the door closed behind her, Nate took off. She turned to look back. Elise's and the children's figures were indistinct blurs through the water than ran down the windows, but she waved anyhow.

The van topped the rise, turned the corner onto the road, and the ranch was hidden from view.

Chapter Twelve

Sheryl turned around, buckling up her seat belt, fussing with it, straightening her coat, trying to avoid Nate's gaze. The atmosphere in the van was heavy, weighted with memories and recriminations that neither had dared voice over the past week.

Finally she settled into the seat and stared resolutely at the windshield wipers slapping back and forth across the window, watching familiar landmarks slip by, now blurred with the haze of rain.

The silence bothered her. She and Nate had spent many years together, and now they couldn't even share more than a few mumbled questions and answers. It wasn't right. Especially after spending three days with the Andrews family and their constant chatter, the silence in the van felt unnatural.

"I'd like to thank you for letting me stay in the cabin, Nate," she said finally.

Nate only nodded in reply.

She bit her lip and tried again. "Did you visit Ed while we were gone?"

At that Nate turned to her, his mouth curled up in derision. "Spare me the false concern, Sheryl."

His comment, all too familiar, wouldn't have hurt a week ago. She had grown soft in the past few days. "It wasn't false concern," she said as her fingers tightened around the buckle.

"You were here ten days," he replied looking ahead again, his jaw clenched. "You managed to see him three times."

"You want it both ways, don't you, Nate." She drew in a deep breath. "You've accused me of not finishing a job, and because I did, I couldn't see Ed as often as I might have."

Nate bit his lip and changed tack. "Why did you go on the pack trip?"

"I was invited."

"The girls seemed to enjoy the trip. Although they said you didn't spend much time with them." He glanced at her, his eyes slightly narrowed. "They said you had someone else you wanted to be with."

"As in?" As if she didn't know.

"Mark."

"Well I guess now we're getting down to what you really wanted to talk about."

He turned on her, his face angry. "He's my friend, brother-in-law and partner and that makes his concerns mine."

"I think Mark can take care of himself."

"Mark is a different man from the kind of man you're used to...."

"How do you know what I'm used to? I've only ever had one boyfriend." She smiled derisively, "And *one* husband."

"The worst man in the county."

Sheryl said nothing to that.

"Mark is a good man, Sheryl," Nate continued, his tone condescending. "He's a sincere Christian."

"Something I've never been, right?"

"And I've found out that marriage is difficult enough," he interrupted. "And if one partner is a Christian and the other isn't, well that just makes it even more difficult."

"He hasn't proposed to me, Nate."

"Mark's a romantic," Nate continued, a white line edging his lips. "I know he's fascinated with you." He spared her a brief glance. "You're an attractive girl. I know where he's headed with you, even if you don't seem to care."

Mark's words drifted over the anger that slipped so easily into her mind at Nate's words. "Anger drains you, Sheryl, it eats away at you until nothing is left." She didn't want to hear them. Didn't want to let go of her anger, because then what would she have left? Only sadness and an emptiness that yawned ahead of her, bleak and unwelcoming.

But Nate wasn't finished. "When Mark bought the ranch he made plans to live on it with someone else…"

"Tanya," Sheryl said with quiet determination.

"So you know the story."

Sheryl nodded, her hands clenched tightly together.

"Then you know what he is going through right now. You know how hard it must be for him to have met someone who seems to have the same interests as he does."

Sheryl turned on him at that. "What do you mean when you say *seems?*"

Nate plunged a hand through his hair with a quick sigh. "You helped him with the haying, you went on the pack trip. Mark thinks you enjoy that kind of work."

Sheryl shook her head in dismay. "Your idea that I was a lazy girl who never lifted a finger is old, tired and untrue."

"I didn't say that."

"No, of course you didn't. You never come right out and say what you think, you skirt around it with vague words." Sheryl slowly unclenched her fists, almost afraid of her anger. "Why don't you just come right out and admit to yourself that your feelings for me aren't the kind a Christian should have."

Nate bit his lip; his eyes narrowed as he seemed to fight some internal battle. "I've never known exactly what I've felt for you, Sheryl."

More ambiguous words, more pieces to try to fit together.

Sheryl looked away, fixing her eyes on the hills that undulated away from them. This whole trip had been a waste of time. She would have been better off to have stayed in Edmonton.

And what about Mark?

Sheryl pressed her fingers against her lips. She couldn't think about Mark. Because much as Nate's words cut and hurt, she knew he was right.

"He asked me to wait for him, Nate," she said softly, wanting to prick his self-righteous hauteur. "Just before we rode away, he said that something was happening between us and that he wanted time to figure out what it really was."

Nate turned suddenly at that, eyes wide. "And what was your answer?"

"I'm in your van, heading out to Williams Lake," she replied, her voice tight. "I don't know why you see it necessary to point out how unsuitable I am for him. But somehow, by showing me that he cares for me and by giving me what you and Ed never would, Mark has shown me, more clearly than you and Ed ever could, that I don't deserve him." She looked down, rubbing her hands over her skirt, forcing herself to relax. She wished she could appeal to their past, to the part of him that might remember rides up to a slide, finding a frying pan.

"I left because I know even better than you do that I can't give him what he needs." And as she spoke the words Nate had only hinted at, her anger seemed to dissipate, leaving only sorrow that even when they agreed on something, she ended up feeling vanquished.

Nate blinked, stupefied. He opened his mouth to speak, seemed to think better of it and looked ahead again.

As they drove, the silent swish of the wipers vied with the splashing of the tires through the puddles in the rocky road. The mountains, misted and gloomy, hung over Sheryl's shoulder, and as the river plateau broadened, she couldn't help turn for one last glimpse of them.

An hour later they pulled into the parking lot of the hospital. Sheryl swallowed, a heaviness weighing her down. Her first impulse was to tell Nate she wanted to wait in the van instead of seeing Ed. But deep within her she hungered for what he had offered on their first visit and much as she doubted his sincerity, she still yearned for it. Mark's love she couldn't give in to, but the love her stepfather belatedly offered her was her due.

She drew a deep breath, opened the door and stepped out into the rain.

"I've got to see the doctor," Nate said as he hobbled down the wet sidewalk to the front doors of the hospital. "I'll meet you at Dad's room." His tone was brusque and he didn't look at her.

She followed Nate until without a second glance he headed to the outpatient section of the hospital. Sheryl watched him go, wondering again what single event, if any, had created such antagonism.

With a sigh, she shook the moisture off her coat, shoved her hands in the pockets of her jeans and walked away, her measured tread squeaking lightly on the waxed floor. Each step brought her nearer to Ed, each footfall seemed to be a harbinger of an epiphany.

Sheryl knew her experiences in the mountain had buffeted her protective cover, had exposed her own weaknesses. And now what would her reaction be to her stepfather, given what happened?

He sat in the same place he had during her previous visit, the dull light softening the harsh angles of his now-thin face. Today he looked more alert, his eyes brighter, and when he saw her, his smile was a little broader.

"Sheryl…" He lifted his good hand and held it out to her.

She paused in the doorway, trying to let this actual image of Ed drift past her own memories.

All that was left was this old broken man, this old lonely man. She took a steadying breath and stepped into the room. He looked up at her entrance, and a tentative smile lifted one corner of his mouth.

"I've…been waiting." He spoke his words carefully, each sound an effort. "Please…sit…here."

Sheryl pulled her purse close to her and once again sat across from her stepfather, studying him with other eyes, other emotions. The sorrow that had engulfed her up in the mountains seemed to have smudged the clarity of her memories and feelings.

"Glad…you…came." Ed smiled his crooked smile at her, one side of his face staying resolutely in place. He tried to reach out to her, but Sheryl kept her hands stiffly folded in her lap.

But as she looked at his face, she saw sorrow and regret etched clearly in the lines. She remembered the tears he had shed the last visit she'd made, when she'd told him of Jason's death.

She remembered the words of love spoken each time and felt her own tense shoulders sag. It was so much work to keep up her anger against him. Each time she saw him he became more pathetic and less powerful.

He pushed himself up in his chair, his pillow falling off the chair. Sheryl got off her chair and picked it up, crouching down to tuck it between the metal arm of the chair and his frail body. As she did, she felt his good hand on her hair.

"I wanted…to love you," he said softly.

Sheryl looked up at him. "What do you mean by that?" she asked. "Why do you talk of love now?"

"Wrong…Sheryl…I've been so wrong."

Sheryl edged backward, lifting herself up onto her chair, her eyes never leaving his face. "How have you been wrong, Dad?" she whispered, wishing he could speak clearer, faster.

"When you were little…you were so strong…" Ed leaned back and sighed. "You loved your dad so much…I was jealous."

Sheryl lifted her eyebrows. Sad that she had never considered that aspect, she thought. Looking back, it made sense.

"Is that why I was never allowed to talk about him?"

Ed frowned. "I loved your mom…she was…everything…Nate's mom wasn't. Soft…warm…kind. I was…everything Bill Reilly…wasn't. I…know I never… treated her…like I should…." He paused, his brow furrowed in concentration.

Sheryl clasped her hands around her knees, mentally urging the words out of him.

"I was…jealous of your dad…I gave you…a home…a place…and you had…to move because of him. I don't…know if your…mom ever loved me…the same way."

"She wasn't in love with you?"

Ed shook his head sorrowfully. "She didn't love me…like I loved her." He looked up at Sheryl, his mouth curved up in a smile of memory. "She seemed to love you more. I was jealous of you. I thought you were spoiled…willful." His voice grew quiet. "I was so wrong. I'm so…sorry."

"I tried, Dad, I really did." She felt a need to tell him that, to make it clear that it wasn't all her fault.

"I know now." He reached out for her. "I've learned a lot...from Mark...from Elise...about love."

Sheryl closed her eyes. Mark again. Perfect, loving Mark. How much farther was he to be put beyond her reach?

"They showed me...loving is giving...it's letting yourself become weak." Ed sighed, a soft exhalation. "I didn't give...to your mother...to you...like I should have...like God did to me. I have been so...wrong."

Sheryl bent her head, still afraid to look at Ed and take what he so belatedly offered. It wasn't enough to fill the emptiness of her life, but it would take away the hollowness of it.

His hand touched hers and with her head still down, she wrapped her fingers around his. They squeezed hers with surprising strength. She looked at his hands, the raised veins, the heavy knuckles of a man who had worked hard. It had been difficult for him, as well. She knew he'd had a desire to get ahead. These ambitions were universal. It was just that Ed's were stronger than some, his motivation more powerful. How he had gone about it was questionable, but after working for a living, she understood so much better its daily struggle.

"Sheryl, I always loved you...just not the right way. I shouldn't...have driven you away. Can you please forgive me?"

Again Mark's words came back to her. "You can't build a relationship until forgiveness has been granted."

She looked up at him and saw such pain and regret in his face that it pulled at the bleak emptiness in her, opening it. She had no father, mother or husband. No one. And now a small part of her past was being given back to her.

She thought back to eight years ago, to the last days she'd spent with Ed and Nate before she'd left with Jason. She had always known that the decision to marry Jason was hers and hers alone. Suddenly she realized it was no longer right to put all the fault for the mess of her life on his shoulders.

"Jesus told us we had to forgive seventy times seven," she whispered suddenly. "I haven't filled my quota yet."

Ed smiled tremulously. He could say nothing, but the hand that clutched hers and the tears that drifted down his sunken cheeks said more than his halting words ever could.

"You always had...a big heart." He shook his head as his tears flowed more freely now.

Sheryl felt as if that same heart was being squeezed down to a small knot, and suddenly she leaned over and kissed Ed on the cheek. He reached up and held her neck, and it seemed only natural to put her arms around him.

Sheryl hugged him carefully, feeling the changes her eyes had noted. It suddenly struck her that he, too, had lost much.

"I didn't want...you to marry...Jason."

"I know, Daddy, I know," she said, her voice thick. She pulled away, reaching into her pocket for a handkerchief and came up with the same red polka-dotted one Mark had given her just the day before. She quickly blew her nose, wiped the spilled tears, a pain knifing through her as she caught the scent of Mark on the scrap of material. "I made a mistake leaving with Jason," she said, her voice hoarse with emotion. Sheryl stopped at that, afraid that if she spoke more she would be putting unnecessary burdens on his frail shoulders. "I guess you need to know that what happened was as much my fault. When my mother died..."

She shouldn't have ventured that far, she thought, swallowing down the tears. Ed could not help her; she needed to be strong on her own.

"It wasn't your...fault...Sheryl. She always loved you...always."

Sheryl wiped her face once more, sitting up. As she sucked in a deep breath, controlling her sorrow, she let Ed's words flow over her. She had received love, in different ways, she had just been too full of anger to see what had been happening. It wasn't all her fault, she knew that, but she also knew she wasn't innocent.

"Thank you for telling me that, Dad."

Ed smiled at her, reaching out for her hand. She took his again, tracing the blue veins. He still wore his wedding ring, and Sheryl rubbed it lightly.

"I have to also confess that you were always right about Jason. I should never have married him, and I admit that I did it all on my own." Sheryl paused, hoping he would understand her confession. "What happened was my own fault. I tried to explain that to you in the letter I sent."

Ed frowned, straightening. "Which...letter?"

Sheryl shook her head, not wanting to destroy the moment of harmony between them by bringing up something he had obviously forgotten.

"Did you send me a letter?" he continued.

"Hi, Dad."

Sheryl jumped as Nate's overly loud voice broke the moment. He hobbled into the room, the clump of his crutches the only sound.

Ed frowned as if wanting to ask more questions, but Sheryl turned to her stepbrother.

"So what did the doctor have to say?" Not that she cared, but she needed to change the subject. Nate's entrance couldn't have been better planned.

Nate glanced quickly at her, his expression wary as if he didn't quite trust her. "I have to be on this walking cast for another two weeks, and then it can come off."

"Good thing...haying is over," Ed put in.

Nate looked away and nodded.

Ed turned to Sheryl. "How long...are you staying yet?"

"I'm leaving tonight."

Ed frowned and looked back at Nate who merely shrugged. "So soon?" Ed asked of Sheryl.

"I have to, Dad. I'm taking some courses, and if I don't

get them done, I can't be admitted to university this fall.''
Sheryl spoke hurriedly, hoping her explanation would satisfy him. His words sounded suddenly empty and mundane
to her, sitting across from her dying stepfather.

"I thought you...were moving back home?"

Home. The word sounded so comfortable. She had no
home in Edmonton, but she knew she could not live here.

"Sheryl only came up to see you, because she knew that
it was only a matter of time for you." Nate said.

"And I haven't...conveniently died yet." Ed smiled, but
Sheryl couldn't share the macabre joke.

"I'll try to come back again, Dad," she reassured him.
If I can get a job, she added silently, wondering how she
was going to work up the nerve to ask Nate to pay for her
bus ticket to get her home. She didn't have enough cash to
pay for it herself. "I'll keep in touch."

Ed nodded and turned back to Nate. "Did Mark...go to
the upper...pastures?"

"A few days ago. He should be back by tomorrow or
the day after if all goes well."

"How much...hay did you...get?"

"We did really well. Our banker will be pleased, anyhow. Looks like things are finally pulling ahead a little for
us."

Sheryl smiled to herself. Bankers and crops and weather.
The eternal tug-of-war that went on with ranching. Nate's
and Ed's conversation hearkened back to many made over
supper tables at the end of the day. When she'd lived at
home, she'd been a part of it—how many bales today, how
much do we need to put up, will we have to borrow money
to buy more, will we have enough to sell, will the rain stay
away, will cattle prices hold?

Ed lay back, his face pale. Sweat beaded his brow, his
weariness obvious to Sheryl.

She let him and Nate talk for a while, and after a few
minutes reminded Nate that the bus would be leaving soon.

"Okay," he replied, getting up, still avoiding any eye contact with her. "I'll wait for you in the van."

He left and Sheryl turned to Ed, surprised again at the change that had occurred from her first visit to now. A certain lightness and peace had entered a small part of her life, and she treasured it. One more time she leaned over to hug Ed, this time her motions easier, more spontaneous.

"I love...you, Sheryl." He drew back, cradling her cheek in his one good hand. "But you have to know...God loves you more. Let Him love you...take His love...take it and live...."

Sheryl only nodded, afraid to speak, afraid to think too hard of the supreme irony of finding peace with him just before he was to die. "I'll keep in touch with you, Dad," she whispered. She kissed him again. "I love you."

He smiled at that, nodding his thanks.

Sheryl straightened, turned and resolutely left the room. She walked down the hall, through the doors and stepped into the van that Nate had driven up to the door, her movements mechanical, her thoughts fully occupied.

Maybe the fact that she might never see him again gave his words so much weight. Maybe it was his closeness to death that made her mull over what he had said about God. But as they drove down the rain-soaked street, Ed's words resonated through her head.

They reached the bus depot, and much to Sheryl's surprise Nate paid for her bus ticket. She thanked him and, flinging her backpack over her shoulder, picked up her small suitcase and walked over to the empty chairs in the waiting area.

Her bus wouldn't leave for another hour.

Nate clumped behind her, and after hesitating a moment he sat down in the empty chair across from her, holding his crutches across his leg.

"Here," he said, handing her a few bills. "Some cash

for the trip. You'll need to eat I guess. Wages for the haying season," he told her gruffly.

Sheryl pocketed it, thankful for the small buffer the money would give her when she got home. "I appreciate that," she said.

Nate nodded in acknowledgment, his fingers clenching and unclenching the crutches.

Nate sighed, fidgeted then blurted out, "What did Dad say about the letter?"

Sheryl frowned. "What letter?"

"You sent a letter to him asking to come back. I heard you asking about it. What did he say?"

"How did you know what my letter said? Dad didn't seem to."

Nate turned red. "I couldn't let him see it."

Sheryl's mouth fell open. "You read my letter? You kept it from Ed?" She blinked, feeling the full extent of his repressed fury. "Why?"

"After all you did to him, to me, you took what we were offering and threw it all back in our faces when you took up with Jason. You didn't want to be a part of our family, you never wanted to help."

"I was ten years old when I came…"

"And at your age I was already pitching bales, stuking, riding fence." Nate stared at her, his blue eyes so much like his father's. But where Ed's had been softened by sorrow, Nate's were hardened with anger. "I was fourteen when you came and in all the years I worked side by side with my father, he never cut me the slack he cut you. And how do you thank him? You take off with the one guy guaranteed to make him so angry that I had to suffer for it. And then you have the nerve to ask if you could come back."

Nate spat the words at her so quickly Sheryl barely had a chance to absorb the shock of them before he threw more at her.

"I thought you knew how I felt, how I cared about you, but all you could think of was ways to hurt us. I loved you, but I don't think you even knew."

Sheryl's breath left her, she stared at him, the busyness of the bus terminal receding in a rush of black, with Nate's face at its center.

What was he talking about?

"Nate, I don't understand." She grasped for coherency, trying desperately to make sense of what he had just spilled on her. "You said you loved me?"

"To my shame, yes." Nate's fingers on his crutches were almost white. "I loved you from the moment you were old enough. But you made it clear that you preferred Jason's company."

"I never knew, Nate." Sheryl stared at him in disbelief. "I really didn't know."

"Well neither does Elise or anyone else." He tapped his fingers against the wood of his crutches as he looked past her, not seeing. "I love Elise, and I'll do anything for her. I don't want her to know this. It's not something I'm proud of."

Sheryl pulled her hands over her face, as if trying to absorb what he had just said. Casting back over the past events, looks, comments thrown her way, it now made sense. Why didn't she see it before?

His words seemed to hover, buffeted by the emotions that swirled around both of them. But Sheryl wasn't finished.

"And what about my letter?"

Nate looked away, chewing his lip. Behind him a neon sign flashed red, then white, then red, each change synchronized with the pounding of Sheryl's heart.

"You knew what was in it…" she urged.

He turned to her then. "Yes I read it. I had to protect my dad from more hurt. I needed to know what you wanted after three years of silence."

"And you found out." Sheryl was surprised at how quiet her voice came out. "You found out what I had to live with. You read my pleas, my fear. You coldheartedly sent it back. I had to live with the consequences." She simply stared at him, her arms clasped tightly across her stomach, her fingers clenching the thin fabric of her coat. "Do you know what I had to live with after that?"

Nate tried to shrug. Sorrow coiled like a snake through Sheryl, anger twisting her face. She drew back, and with quick, jerky motions pulled off her jacket and rolled up the sleeve of her shirt, exposing the two-inch scar on the inside of her upper arm. It was only a fine line now, a row of dots marching up either side of it from the sutures.

"Beer bottle, busted across the bedpost," she said, her voice flat as she struggled for control, remembering the pain, the humiliation. "He discovered I had hidden my tips from him. It was my grocery money for that month. He blew it in an hour." She ignored his look of surprise as she drew up her skirt, exposing her thigh. "This one is a souvenir of the one time he picked up the mail and found the letter that you decided to send back." She bent her head as she dropped her skirt. "I'm sorry, but the broken arm doesn't show, or the bruises from the accident when—" Her voice broke and she pressed her fingers against her mouth, wishing, praying, her silent pleas desperate.

Nate sat still as a statue while Sheryl battled her emotions. Around them life swirled on—people talking and laughing, saying hello and farewell. A baby cried and a father hushed it. Someone dropped a glass bottle, the brittle sound of smashing glass breaking in on Sheryl's pain.

"Last call for the five o'clock bus to Quesnel and Prince George."

Sheryl glanced over at Nate, anger and bitterness vying with her sorrow and regret. "That's what I had to live with. That was the consequence of your sending my letter back." As she watched him, she saw his face tighten, and he bit his lips, his gaze still downcast, his hands clutching his crutches.

Sheryl got up as the tinny voice over the intercom propelled her into movement. She bent over and picked up her knapsack.

"Sheryl." Nate's voice made her straighten. She looked over at him, wondering what he would have to say. Their eyes met. Was that pain she saw in his eyes? Regret? Sorrow? Or only her deep desire that he show some kind of emotion? But he said nothing more, his face devoid of expression.

For a moment she stared at Nate as he sat, still holding on to his crutches as if they were his only defense.

Sheryl drew in a trembling breath, flipped her knapsack over her shoulder and walked away without a backward glance.

Chapter Thirteen

The steady thump of the wheels as they hit the frost heaves on the Yellowhead would have lulled Sheryl to sleep at any other time. But each time she closed her eyes thoughts, memories and events flipped and whirled around her mind like a kaleidoscope.

Almost two weeks had passed since she and Mark had driven down this road, and she felt as if she had lived a lifetime.

With a resigned sigh she turned her head and looked out the tinted windows watching the fields flow past. The grain had already turned a pale gold, and here and there swaths of hay lay, awaiting the baler.

In a month the harvest would begin, and back at Sweet Creek, Mark would have one more cut of hay. A month after that the cattle would be ready to be brought home, calves weaned and shipped. When she'd lived in Sweet Creek she had helped with each part of the operation.

In her mind she already saw Mark on his horse, herding the cattle down the trails from the far pastures, she could hear the din of the cows and calves bawling as they got separated for weaning, taste the dust of their milling feet as they were squeezed down to smaller and smaller pens until they were finally run through the chute one at a time for their shots and treatments.

And what would she be doing at that time?

Sheryl closed her eyes, trying to alleviate the momentary flash of panic. She was headed home to no job and an apartment she knew she had to move out of before it got condemned. All she had to show for eight years of living away from Sweet Creek was a pile of schoolbooks and mismatched furniture. She hoped she could find a job. Government and businesses all were downsizing, and the last time she had gone job hunting, there were thirty applicants for each of the jobs she had applied for.

I won't be scared, she thought, biting her lip. She looked down at her knapsack and pulled out the gift Elise and the girls had given her. She hadn't unwrapped it yet, preferring to savor the mystery of it and to just enjoy the notion that someone had thought enough about her to set something aside and wrap it up.

Now would be as good a time as any to unwrap it, she thought, carefully peeling off the ribbons and putting them in her knapsack. The tape was next, each piece meticulously pulled off, and then with a smile she folded back the paper.

A couple of bars of soap wrapped in a pretty handkerchief and a worn book. She sniffed the soap and turned over the book.

It was a Bible. Her old one.

Inside it was a short note from Elise. Sheryl unfolded it and read it. Elise and the girls had found the Bible when they'd cleaned up the cabin for her arrival. They thought she might like to have it back. On the bottom of the letter Crystal and Marla had scrawled their names, and Elise had signed the letter simply "Elise" and put their phone number and address on the bottom.

Sheryl folded up the letter and set it aside. She opened

the Bible to the flyleaf, tracing the inscription there with
trembling fingers. Ed's delicate handwriting, so at odds
with his character, showed that the Bible had been pre-
sented to her on the day of her mother's marriage to him,
sixteen years ago, and given to her with the hope that they
might become a family that feared God.

They had feared God, at least Sheryl had learned to, she
thought, flipping the delicate parchment pages of the Bible.
And as for the family part...

Sheryl sighed lightly. It was no longer as easily decided
who and what to blame. She had other experiences and
other views to meld in with her own. She smoothed out a
wrinkled page, her eyes falling on a childish scrawl in the
margin. It simply said, "I love God and he loves me."

She remembered again the peace that had flowed over
her whenever she'd prayed with the Andrews family and
knew it wasn't just their presence that had created that.

How she longed for that peace now, she thought, turning
the pages randomly, glancing at passages, remembering the
cadences and the rhythms of words buried deep in her past.

She came to the New Testament. Partway through she
found a paper wedged between the pages of 2 Corinthians.
Curious to see what she had put there, she opened it up. It
was an old church bulletin dated the same week she and
Jason had left. She glanced over the familiar names, the
announcements. Suddenly she noticed under the heading
"Church Family," "Welcome to the Andrews family who
will be moving from Vanderhoef and will be making their
home here with their children, Brad, Elaine and Elise." Her
heart thudded heavily in her chest as she read and reread
it. She hadn't realized that their coming had been that close.
Missed each other by days!

Her throat felt dry as she folded it up again, her fingers
shaking.

God has a plan, Mark had said, a reason for things happening the way they did. What would have happened had

she waited? Would she have met Mark? What would he have thought of her?

She knew the answer to that. Cocky, rebellious and angry. He would have had nothing to do with her then. So what had changed? She had spent eight years with Jason, she had been refused sanctuary from her father…correction her stepbrother…

Sheryl slipped the paper back into the Bible, trying to sort out her confused feelings. She should hate her stepbrother for what he did.

But somehow she couldn't. She had spent too much time hating, fighting down fears and trying to be strong. It only took from her and left her feeling empty.

Sheryl looked down at the Bible again, her eyes glancing over the familiar passage, and suddenly her eye caught it. A verse with a star inked beside it. God's words: "My grace is sufficient for you, for my power is made perfect in weakness." And then a little further on Paul speaking: "When I am weak then I am strong."

It didn't seem to make sense and yet it did. When she had broken down in Mark's arms, when she'd allowed someone to give to her, allowed herself to become weak, that was when she had felt renewal come into her.

When she'd allowed herself to forgive her stepfather, when she had confessed her part in what had happened, shown her weakness, then she'd felt peace and love overcome her.

Releasing her breath in a cleansing sigh, Sheryl laid her head back, her hand resting on the words she had just read. She didn't know what lay ahead, but she felt she would just have to trust that somehow maybe Mark and Ed were right. Maybe God did have a reason for things happening the way they did.

"Tory, this is Sheryl." She rubbed her forehead with her index finger, clutching the handset of the pay phone as she stared at the building across the street. If this was any indication of some great plan of God, she wondered if maybe the blueprint wasn't upside down.

The blackened hulk of her apartment block stared back at her, the acrid smell of smoke still lingering in the air. It had burned down last night, she was told. Had she come home when she'd originally planned she might have been able to salvage her books, the expensive correspondence courses that she had scrimped to buy.

"Hi, Sheryl." Tory's excited voice reassured her that she had done the right thing in calling. "How are you?"

Sheryl shook her head, grimacing. "Don't ask."

"Well, where are you?"

"Standing across from what's left of my apartment block…"

"Oh, no!" Tory's gasp came clearly across the line. "I wondered if that was your place when I heard it on the news this morning."

"Well, wonder no more. I've officially joined the ranks of the homeless…." Sheryl stopped herself, vowing she wasn't going to cry over a pile of rubble that had never been a home to her, only a dwelling.

"You stay right there. Don't move. I'll come and get you right away."

"No, Tory, that's okay. I just…" *Just needed to connect with someone, needed to talk to you,* she added to herself, *and I didn't dare ask.*

"Sheryl," Tory said her voice angry. "Don't you dare even protest or I'll get even angrier. Now promise me you won't move?"

Sheryl nodded. She couldn't speak.

"Sheryl?"

"I won't," she whispered. "Thanks." She hung up the phone, biting her lip. *I won't cry,* she thought, pressing her fist against her mouth as she sagged back against the telephone booth, staring at the mess across the road. *I hated iving there, it was a horrible place*. But it had held all she'd had of eight years of her life. It had held her books and clothes and all her personal things.

Concentrate on something else, Sheryl thought. Count how many seconds it will take Tory to get here. But she didn't know where Tory lived. Had never asked her. Tory was a co-worker, and any overture at friendship had come from her not Sheryl. Sheryl had never asked her about her husband, about her life.

What an empty life she had lived the past few months. Come to think of it, the past few years. Jason had sucked everything out of her, had kept her from forming any kind of relationships.

The roar of a car engine made her look up. A small white vehicle screeched to a halt in front of her, and before it even rocked back, Tory was out and flying around the hood of the car.

"Sheryl, oh, you poor girl,"

Sheryl felt herself enfolded in arms that clung and hands that stroked. "You come and stay with us, girl. We have room. You come with me," Tory murmured over and over again.

And then Sheryl began to cry.

"Mr. Carlton's office, Sheryl speaking," Sheryl tucked the phone under one ear, typed the message on her computer screen and clicked Print, directing it to Dan's printer in his office. "Thank you, Mrs. Donalds. I'll see he gets the message right away."

She got approximately five characters typed when the phone rang again. A quick glance at the clock told her it was 5:10 and if she didn't watch it she would end up talking to another one of Dan's clients past suppertime.

It was Tory.

"How's it going, girl?" Tory asked, yelling into the phone.

In spite of Tory's raised voice, Sheryl could barely hear her over the background noise of the mechanic's shop. Compressors rumbled, pneumatic drills sang, and someone was clanging on a piece of metal.

Shortly after Sheryl had left for Sweet Creek, Tory's husband, Mike, purchased the shop where he worked, and Tory gladly had left her job at Dave's bar to help.

"Just fine," Sheryl said, raising her own voice. "I'm getting the hang of things."

"Great. I'm so glad Mike kept that lawyer's business card. I knew it would come in handy. Hey, before I left for the garage I got a call from someone named Elise. She just phoned to say hello and asked me to give you the message. Is this one of the Sweet Creek folk?"

Sheryl paused, her heart beginning an errant rhythm. "Did she say what she wanted?" Sheryl asked.

"No. Just phoned to chat." Tory spoke to someone, then she said, "Hey, I got to run. I'll be working late, but I put a casserole in the oven. You'll be okay?"

"I'll be fine, Tory."

"Good. See you later, eh?" Tory clicked off, and Sheryl hung up the phone feeling slightly dazed.

She had phoned Elise the day after she'd moved in with Tory and Mike, to give her the number just in case something happened with Ed. Nate had answered the phone. The next day Sheryl went for a job interview and the day after started this job. Then she had called again to give them her work number. That time she got the answering machine.

"Sheryl, it's past quitting time."

Sheryl looked up into the grinning face of one of the law students, Jordan Calder.

"I've just got this letter to finish, then I'll go."

"Sheryl, has anyone ever told you that you work too hard?" Jordan laid her arms across the smoked glass partition that separated Sheryl's desk from the hallway and rested her chin on them, her brown eyes narrowed. "If you're not working late, it's evening courses at the university. You put in more hours than I do, and I'm supposed to be almost-a-lawyer. Is relaxation not in your vocabulary?"

Sheryl said nothing, only continued typing. "I just want to do a good job," she murmured, frowning at Dan's scribbled note across a letter.

"Dan's been practically drooling since you came. You could ask for double what you earn now and he'd give it to you." Jordan finger combed her short hair, the dark strands falling perfectly into place.

"I'm making enough." Sheryl ignored her comment and turned the letter to Jordan. "You've read enough of Dan's scribbles, what do you suppose that says?"

Jordan took the paper from her, squinting as she turned it first this way then that. "It's getting clearer. It says, 'Go home.'"

"I doubt that." Sheryl laughed reaching for the paper.

"I'll hand it over tomorrow." Jordan held the paper out of reach and, bending around, switched Sheryl's monitor off, ignoring her polite protest. "The way you type, you can have it done in a couple of minutes on Monday. Now put the cover on the computer. The weekend is calling."

Accepting defeat, Sheryl stood, slipped on her sweater and closed the file on her desk.

"Someday you'll thank me for this," Jordan said, waiting as Sheryl walked past her. "Believe me, work isn't everything."

Sheryl smiled as they walked down the now-empty hall toward the reception area. Jordan Calder was not a typical student. She worked as much as she thought she should and didn't have the same hunger that usually typified student lawyers. And once she was off work, Jordan was fun and good for a few laughs.

Living with Jason had not given her much chance for social interaction. He had tended to discourage any relationship she might have had with anyone but himself. Since coming back from Sweet Creek she'd been given the time and space to rediscover relationships both with other people and with God. She was finding out who Sheryl really was.

"You're lucky Dan was out today, otherwise I'm sure I'd have to help you finagle your way out of yet another request for a date," Jordan said, punching the ground floor number as they stepped into the elevator. "I've never seen him so stuck on anyone before."

Sheryl let the comment pass. "He's a good boss."

"Of course he is, Sheryl," Jordan reassured her, tying the belt of her long, black trench coat. "I'm not trying to cast aspersions on his sterling character. It's just that he can't keep his eyes off you."

"I'm sure."

Jordan rolled her eyes. "Goodness, girl, I've never met anyone so obviously unaware of her own good looks. If you dropped that cool and composed act you'd have guys hanging all over you."

"I'll keep it then. That's the last thing I need."

"Oh, don't tell me someone as gorgeous as you is a man hater?" Jordan wailed. "I hate it when that happens."

"I'm not a man hater."

"'I just don't want that complication.' As if guys are some kind of problem to figure out. I tell you, girl, this nineties garbage is really starting to get on my nerves." The elevator stopped, and the doors swished open. Jordan flung her purse over her shoulder and picked up her briefcase as they stepped out, their footsteps echoing on the marble floor of the foyer. "Now me, I've had to claw my way to the bottom of this little law firm. I'm allowed to be disillusioned and cynical. You're not."

"Men aren't a complication, Jordan. It's just that they want so much and give so little," Sheryl said as she paused to button up her coat.

Jordan narrowed her eyes at Sheryl. "You're basing your

judgment on a narrow experience. There're lots of generous, good-hearted guys out there.''

Jason wasn't, thought Sheryl, shoving her hands in her coat pockets. Ed wasn't, Nate wasn't...

Her thoughts quit as a gust of wind swirled through the foyer. The doors were shoved open and a tall figure strode into the entrance. Long brown hair hung on his shoulders, his jean jacket sat easily on broad shoulders, his long legs easily covered the distance between them.

Sheryl's heart leaped to her throat. Her purse slipped out of numb fingers spilling on the floor as she took a step toward him.

''Sheryl, what's wrong?'' Jordan stopped, glanced at Sheryl's eager face, then at the man she stared at hungrily.

He paused, pulled a handkerchief from his pocket and as he wiped his nose he glanced around.

It wasn't Mark.

''Are you okay?''

''Yeah.'' Sheryl's shoulders sagged. Feeling slightly dazed she looked around, then, at her purse lying on the floor.

''You know that man?''

Sheryl bent over to pick up her purse, hiding her burning cheeks. ''I thought he was an old friend.''

Jordan slanted a skeptical look at Sheryl, retrieved a brush from the floor and handed it to her. ''One of your 'give so little' friends?''

Sheryl drew in a deep breath as she straightened and shook her head at her lapse.

''I thought for a minute you were going to throw yourself at him...''

''Please stop, Jordan,'' Sheryl pleaded, feeling bereft and close to tears. She clutched her purse close to her, biting her lip.

Jordan laid her hand on Sheryl's shoulder. ''I'm sorry. It's just that you're normally so cool and collected.'' She squeezed, then let go. "Anyhow, what are you doing this weekend? I've got tickets for a concert on Sunday."

"I don't think so." Sheryl flashed her an apologetic grin, pulling herself together. "I want to head to church on Sunday." She had been attending for a couple of weeks, finding peace and comfort there that she wouldn't at a concert.

"Probably a better idea," Jordan shrugged. "Well if you change your mind you know my number." She patted her shoulder once more, then turned and left.

Sheryl walked in the opposite direction to her bus stop, still feeling shaky. Mark was on her mind so much any little thing would bring back the memories—jeans on long legs, cowboy boots, a pickup truck on the city streets. One of the boys stocking shelves in the local grocery store was almost as tall as Mark and wore his hair just as long. Sheryl stopped going there because every time she saw him her heart stopped.

Living with Tory and Mike eased some of the emptiness that pervaded her life since she left Sweet Creek, but not totally eradicated it. Each time Tory said goodbye to Mike their leave-taking was reluctant, and Sheryl took painful pleasure in watching them, even though it was such an aching reminder of her own lack.

Loneliness was nothing new to her. But the angry loneliness of coming home to an empty apartment when she'd lived with Jason, or the sad loneliness that was her constant companion after the accident had never been as unmitigated, as heart-wrenching as the emptiness she felt when she'd arrived in Edmonton.

It frustrated her. Tory and Mike treated her almost like a daughter. She finally had a decent job that paid her enough so that she could attend evening courses at the University of Alberta.

But it wasn't enough. The courses left her feeling flat, the job was exciting but she felt stifled sitting inside day after day. The city was starting to get on her nerves with its busyness, its impersonal attitude.

The city bus sighed to a halt in front of her, and Sheryl climbed in, forcing herself past the people packed in the front of the bus to the back where there was usually a little more room.

She clung to a pole, staring out of the window as the buildings flashed past, her mind traveling with ease to a place surrounded by purple mountains, broken by creeks and rivers.

They would be baling again, she mused, thinking of Mark driving a tractor, a bandana around his head holding his long hair out of his face. It made her smile.

She wondered how he was doing. Now that Elise had called, maybe she would return the call. She could casually mention Mark's name, and she knew Elise would take off from there.

If she dared.

Two quick jabs of Mark's jackknife cut the last of the twine on the large, round hay bale suspended in front of him. With stiff fingers, he picked up all the ends, and in one jerk he pulled the twine loose. Backing up, he motioned to Nate, in the cab of the tractor, to drop the bale into the feeder.

The cows were milling about, bawling, trying to get past Mark to get at the hay. The crazy things were going to get run over with the tractor if they didn't watch it.

A bone-chilling gust of wind caught the strings and pulled a couple out of his hand, blowing them across the yard. Mark rolled up the remaining twine as he hunched his shoulders against the cold and chose to ignore the others. Later, later, later.

He and Nate had too much to do right now, and pieces of twine didn't concern him.

Another icy blast of wind pierced the cocoon of coveralls, sweaters and shirt, chilling him to the bone. The coldest day of the coldest October on record, and already that morning he'd fixed the well and taken their new bull in to the vet. Then he'd come home to a tractor that wouldn't start and a waterer that Nate had forgotten to put a heat tape down.

Mark's mood was as foul as the weather.

Nate picked up another bale, and it tipped precariously on the bale forks. Mark waved to him to stop but Nate was looking over his shoulder. The bale tipped past the center of gravity and fell off the forks to the ground.

Mark ground his teeth in frustration. Nate got out of the tractor to see how bad the damage was.

"Didn't you see that the bale wasn't on the forks?" Mark yelled.

"So I'll pick it up again." Nate yelled back.

"It didn't need to end up on the ground if you had done it right the first time."

The two of them faced off, glaring at each other as a plume of exhaust from the tractor swept between them. Nate turned, walked over to the offending bale, poked it with the toe of his boot and climbed back into the tractor without a second look at Mark.

Mark turned and got into the truck. He knew he was miserable, but he was also unable to stop himself. Nate could feed that last bale on his own. He had to get to the house to make a phone call anyhow.

With a sigh he put the truck into gear, hesitated a moment, then released the clutch and drove away. Elise had invited him to have lunch at their place, and he could apologize to Nate then. Maybe the drive from his place to Nate's would settle his temper.

Shivering, he turned the heat up full and stared at the gray clouds drifting over the mountains heading toward them. Snow for sure.

He'd been edgy the past couple of months, and no one

knew it better than he did. He couldn't settle down, and lately he'd found any kind of excuse to go running around the country.

After finding out it would be cheaper to rent a truck and haul the hay himself, he had done so. Four trips to Langley had done little to improve his temper. If anything, driving a semi down the Coquihalla then the Trans-Canada had almost given him a nervous breakdown.

On his return, the third cut of hay had been ready to be baled. He'd run one tractor, Rob another and in a couple of days they'd had their feed for the winter rolled up in large round bales.

Then he'd saddled up his horse, packed up a second and ridden up into the mountains. He had spent a week longer in the hills than he'd needed to, rounding up strays and herding them back home.

It wasn't necessary that he personally take care of needling all the animals but with the help of a halogen lamp and a few all-nighters, he'd gotten it done.

Nate had helped with the baling, but after the second trip to Langley he'd told Mark he wasn't going to try to keep up. Mark had sensed Nate had his own problems to deal with, but wasn't going to drive himself into the ground doing it like Mark was.

Last week Mark had snapped at his mother when she'd asked him if he was ever going to slow down and take some time out to be with his family.

The truck fishtailed, Mark pulled his foot off the accelerator, glanced at the speedometer and then at the hay trailer.

With a sigh he braked, slowing the truck down, pushing his hat further up his head, leaning back against the seat.

For a moment he let his thoughts drift where they did far too often, as he remembered long blond hair, green eyes lit up with laughter, delicate features.

Sheryl.

When he'd come back from the pack trip, two and a half months ago, to find out that she had left already, he'd felt lost, empty and even more alone than when Tanya had mailed his ring to him here at Sweet Creek.

Tanya was a good woman, prettier than Sheryl, more refined. Tanya was friendly, open and fun to be around. She had no major hang-ups and gladly accompanied him to church. But he had never felt the same feeling of absolute rightness with her that he felt with Sheryl.

Or that feeling of emptiness when she'd left.

He tried to see that it was all for the good. Each day he struggled with the same loneliness, the same sense of happiness, elusive, just out of his grasp. If he stopped to analyze his own actions, they didn't make much sense. Sheryl had only spent two weeks here. She had been gone nine.

In theory he should have forgotten her after the first two. So why had he spent the past couple of months wondering what she was doing? Why did he constantly remember exactly how the light caught her hair when it hung loose, flowing to her waist? Why could he still feel the slenderness of her in his arms?

Theories only worked on paper, not in life.

And the worst of it was his own fear. It had been difficult getting over Tanya. And she was pretty straightforward about her reasons for breaking up with him.

There was nothing straightforward about Sheryl. She confused him, puzzled him and scared him.

He knew Jason had abused her. She had said as much, and Nate had confirmed it only a month ago, telling him about her scars. Even now the thought made him clench his fists around the steering wheel, wishing it were Jason's neck. But knowing that had also created a distance. Did she hate men? Was she scared of him? He had bared his heart to her, given her as much as he could.

She had never called, never written. But then he wondered if he could expect her to. Given what she had lived with, would she make the first move to him? But also, given what she had lived with, could he expect to be welcomed?

He was torn between wanting to run to Edmonton and letting go and letting God take care of it all.

He sighed and slowed to make the turn into Nate's place. It had been a few days since he'd seen his sister and Ed. Initially he'd turned down the invitation to lunch, preferring to keep himself busy with nothing. But his loneliness became too much even for him and finally he accepted.

A few flakes of snow hit his cheeks as he stepped out of the truck, and he squinted up at the gray sky. It was going to be a full-blown storm by the time evening came. Feeling even more depressed, he pulled his coat closer around him and trudged around to the back of the house.

The porch was almost as cold as the outside, and Mark quickly shucked his coat, coveralls and boots. He stepped into the kitchen, and a wave of warmth, heavenly aromas and the sound of the coffeepot burbling on the stove wrapped around him. This was what a home should smell like, feel like, he thought, inhaling the smell, letting the warmth seep into his cold body.

"Hello, Mark," Ed greeted him, looking up from where he sat at the kitchen table. He slowly reached with his good hand and shoved a piece of paper across the table toward him. "A message from…Calgary. Confirm…reservation for the Stockgrowers Convention."

Mark picked up the paper and glanced at it before shoving it in his pocket.

"And Marla…is coloring…a picture…"

Marla was bent over her coloring book, her nose inches away from the paper, tongue between her teeth. "It's a present," she said not looking up.

"Could you color one for me?" Mark asked, hooking a chair with his stockinged foot and dropping on it across the table from his little niece. "I'd like a picture to hang up in my kitchen."

She pursed her lips at that, tilting her head to study the picture she worked on. "When I'm finished this one," she replied, flashing him a mischievous grin.

"Got the...cows fed?" Ed spoke up.

Mark nodded, picking up Marla's crayon box. "Nate and I just finished doing the ones at the other corrals. He'll be by in twenty minutes or so." He turned back to Marla. "Which color do you want now?"

"The gray one." She handed him the pink crayon, its paper peeled off.

"Shouldn't you make the sun yellow?" he asked, leaning closer to Marla's picture.

"No. This is a sun in Edmonton. Auntie Sheryl told Grandpa that the days are gray where she lives." Marla finished coloring the sun a dull gray as Mark sat back, his heart hammering in his chest. The mere mention of her name, coming so close on the heels of his own thoughts, filled him with sudden longing. "Grandpa talked to her on the phone," Marla continued, tilting her head to look at the picture. "I talked to her, too. Mommy's talking to Auntie Sheryl now, and if you ask, maybe you can." She looked up at him and flashed him another grin.

Right then Elise stepped into the kitchen, the cordless phone tucked under her ear, a loaf of bread in her free hand. "It's not been great weather here, either, like Ed told you," she was saying. "Yes, Lainie had a baby girl and she's adorable. Nate's foot is just fine.... No, he's out feeding cows with Mark. I can give him the message." She looked up and just about dropped the phone when she saw Mark. "Sorry, what were you saying?" she asked, dropping the frozen bread on the counter.

Mark listened to the one-sided conversation, straining his ears for even the faintest sound coming out of the headset, almost hungry for even the slightest connection with her.

"Well..." Elise leaned her elbows on the counter, staring down at it as if afraid to look at Mark. "To tell you the truth, Mark's miserable."

Mark felt his breath leave him as he realized what Sheryl was asking.

"He's been running around all over the country trying to keep busy. He looks exhausted half of the time. I don't think he's very happy, Sheryl."

Mark glared at Elise, but she kept her eyes glued to the countertop.

"I think he's missing you.... Don't start that again, it's the truth." Elise bit her lip as she clutched the headset. "I think he's still in love with—"

A few angry strides brought Mark around the table and across from his sister. He held out his hand, and without even looking up, Elise handed him the phone.

Mark held it a moment, his breath coming in short gasps as if he had just run ten miles instead walked ten feet. He blinked, swallowed and then, drawing a steadying breath, he put the phone to his ear.

"Elise are you still there?" Sheryl's soft voice still held a hint of pain, he thought, his anger melting at the sound of it.

"Hi, Sheryl." It was all he could say. Nine cold empty weeks and he could barely say her name.

"Mark?" Silence, then, "Where's Elise?"

That hurt more than it should. "If you want to find out how I am, why don't you ask me yourself?"

"Please don't do this, Mark," her voice pleaded. "I can't take this."

"Take? That doesn't seem to be something you do." Mark couldn't seem to keep the angry hurt out of his voice.

She said nothing.

Way to go, Mark, he thought, wishing he had held his tongue. You're tearing me apart, girl, he thought, wishing he could voice his inner feelings, wishing she would give him any kind of encouragement, any kind of reason.

"Sheryl—" his voice became pleading "—why did you leave?" Mark leaned back against the counter, rubbing his forehead, eyes closed, silently pleading. "Are you afraid of me?"

"Ye-es," she said, her voice breaking. Mark clutched the phone, her single word hitting him and hurting beyond understanding.

"Why? You know I would never hurt you...."

A sudden click in his ear told him that she had hung up. Mark lowered the phone, staring morosely at it. She hadn't even given him a chance to tell her that he loved her.

Chapter Fourteen

Sheryl lifted her hymn book, flipped it open to the page and, as the organ began playing, felt a lift of her heart. The songs, the music, all seemed to come together to fill empty spaces in her life.

Since leaving Sweet Creek she'd felt a deep desire to attend. Tory and Mike lived a few blocks from a small community church, and Sheryl saw this as a clear indication of what she should do.

Sheryl drifted back to the service she had attended in Sweet Creek. A light smile lifted one corner of her mouth as she remembered the emotions that had spun through her mind, tangling up her thoughts.

Much had happened since then. She had relaxed her guard, but not without a struggle. It had meant soul searching and required confession. Since her visit with Ed, they had written, and in each letter he repeatedly apologized, repeatedly offered her his love. It became easier and easier. She found the less she fought, the more she received.

Love was a peculiar emotion. Ed's love had been misguided, Nate's confused. She wondered if Jason had loved her or just needed someone to dominate.

And Mark…

Sheryl closed the book and dropped it in its holder with a "thunk." She didn't know what to do about Mark. It was easier to feel unworthy of God's love. He was perfect.

Mark was a man. A man she was attracted to with a depth that frightened her. If she were to give in to him and to find that once he really knew her he didn't want her…

It would break her, and she had no reserves to draw on. So she ran away from it.

Leaving Sweet Creek without seeing Mark had been a wise thing to do. It had been three months since she'd left and still she couldn't forget him. The power of her caring frightened her.

During that time he had never called her, and she knew she had saved herself from a heartbreak that would be deeper than any that Jason, Ed or Nate had inflicted on her.

The chords of the closing song broke into her thoughts, and with a sigh, she got up. She let the words of the song wash over her, soothing and comforting. God was faithful, his love perfect and sacrificial—that she was reassured of each Sunday. People were sinful and frail and disappointed, but each time she came to church she became more convinced of God's love.

She stopped a moment to chat with fellow churchgoers, turning down an offer for lunch. Tory was expecting her, and she hadn't seen much of her and Mike the past couple of weeks.

The walk home chilled her, and when she let herself into the apartment it was with a thankful sigh as the heat rolled over her.

"Is that you, Sheryl?" Tory called out as she hung up her coat. "Lunch is on the table."

"Be there as soon as I wash up," she replied with a smile. Every time she stepped in the door from church, lunch was on the table. She knew Tory kept an eye out, and as soon as she saw her coming down the sidewalk, went into action.

She spent an enjoyable hour with Tory and Mike. After three months of living together they had found a comfortable rhythm. They had been good for her, and they were part of the reason that Sheryl hadn't gone actively seeking an apartment on her own.

Mike excused himself for his usual Sunday afternoon nap, and the women lingered over the remnants.

"So I see you got another letter from Ed," Tory said, pushing her plate away. She took a slow sip of her coffee, savoring it.

"Yes. He's been writing quite a bit lately."

"I thought he had a stroke?"

"Elise writes his letters. She always adds a little on the end."

Tory nodded, pursing her lips. "And...does she say anything about Mark?"

Sheryl shrugged, hoping her disappointment wouldn't show. "Sometimes. He seems to be doing well."

"You don't sound happy about that."

"Of course I am. Mark, well, he's..."

"He's a good-looking guy. And I told you to hang on to him, remember? You didn't take my advice. You shouldn't complain that he's carrying on with his life."

"I'm not." Sheryl frowned, pulling Tory's plant toward her.

"Leave that poor thing alone," grumbled Tory, pulling it back. "You always leave the dead leaves lying around."

"They make the plant look ugly."

"It's all part of the life-and-death cycle." Tory grinned back. "Anyhow, the least you could do is throw them away or stuff them back into the dirt."

Sheryl plucked one off and with exaggerated motions, did as Tory suggested. "Anyhow," she mused, "I don't have time for anyone right now, and I'm not sure Mark is interested in me anymore.''

''You don't have time because you don't make time. You mope around and pretend you want to be an independent woman and get a career, when I know you'd just as soon be living at home and having babies.'' Tory pulled a leaf off the plant, looking at it.

''I'm not moping around…''

''Oh, c'mon,'' Tory chided gently. ''I knew you before you went to Sweet Creek and I know you now. Something happened there, something that made you a little softer, a little less reserved, a little more lovable. Only you still like to pretend you're the same person.''

''It was because Ed and I had a chance to straighten out a few things.''

''That might be part of it. But making up with a stepfather doesn't put a dreamy look on a girl's face, doesn't make her stop what she's doing to stare off into space, like I've seen you, when you're supposed to be studying.'' Tory plucked off another leaf, inspecting it as if weighing her next words. ''And since you've come back, I've heard you crying. And not just once or twice.''

Sheryl swallowed. ''I've had a lot of pain that I've hidden, Tory, you know that.'' She stopped, then sighed. ''I hadn't had a chance to cry since I got married. Maybe it's like pulling out these dead leaves. Maybe I'm just getting rid of tears I held back all that time.''

Tory smiled a sad smile, reaching across the table to clasp Sheryl's hand. ''Interesting comparison. But I think some of those tears are new.''

Sheryl blinked, then looked away, out the window to the gray day outside. She knew that Tory was right, but she didn't know what to do about it. It had been three months since she'd left Sweet Creek. Mark had never contacted her.

''Have you tried calling him, writing him?'' Tory asked quietly.

"I can't do that, Tory. I can't go running after him. Not after all the humiliation that Jason dished out. I just can't." Sheryl bit back a sigh, her confusion mocking her resolve. "Besides, I'm sure he's forgotten about me by now."

"You're not that forgettable." Tory squeezed her hand. "Do you love him?"

Sheryl laid her chin on her other hand, still looking out the window. "I don't even know. I thought love was supposed to be so easy, just a straightforward emotion, but it isn't. I thought I hated Ed, but I don't. He said he loved me but didn't know how to show it. Nate said he loved me, and he hurt me so badly and yet, lately I find I can't dislike him as I should. I'm starting to feel sorry for him and bad for not paying more attention to him when I was younger." She laughed, a soft laugh, free from its usual bitter sound. "I'm finding out that love is a complicated, frustrating business." She risked a glance at Tory, who smiled in understanding. Sheryl rubbed Tory's wedding ring with her finger, sighing deeply. "I still miss Mark."

"Well that's a good sign," Tory replied.

"Maybe. I'm afraid of him, too."

Tory clucked. "That's not."

She was about to speak again when the phone rang, making both of them jump. Tory got up and Sheryl looked back outside.

December in the city was a dismal affair. The snow piled along the streets was streaked with gray and black, and everyone, including the cars, looked like they'd sooner be someplace else. The Christmas lights strung along buildings and houses provided the only cheerful note.

"Sheryl." Tory stood beside her, holding on to the handset. Sheryl looked up, surprised to see pain on her face.

"What's the matter?"

"It's for you. It's Elise."

Sheryl's heart tripped, then raced. Ed. It had to be Ed. Sheryl grabbed the phone. "Hello, Elise?"

"Hi." Elise paused, her voice strained. "I'm phoning to tell you that Ed passed away."

Sheryl sagged back against her chair, her hand covering her eyes. "When?"

"Last night."

"I guess it wasn't so unexpected, was it?"

"No." Sheryl could almost hear Elise swallow her tears. "But it's still hard."

Sheryl only nodded, a knot of sorrow building in her throat. "When's the funeral?" she managed to whisper.

"Thursday. Can you come?"

"Of course. I'll take the bus." Sheryl pressed her hand tight against her eyes. "Tell Nate I'm sorry for him."

"I'll do that. Are you going to be okay?"

In spite of her sorrow, Sheryl felt a rush of love for this considerate and caring person. "I'll be okay. How about you?"

"My mom's here and Mark's coming later." Elise drew in a shaky breath, audible to Sheryl. "I know I shouldn't be sad. He was waiting for the end. I should tell you that he told me, just before he died, that he was so glad you came and very thankful for your letters. He…he wanted me to tell you that he loved you."

Sheryl bit her lip, wishing she could say goodbye and retreat to her bedroom. "Thanks."

Tory knelt beside her, her arm around her as she handed her a tissue. Sheryl smiled weakly at her and wiped a tear that drifted down her nose.

"I'll let you go, Sheryl. We'll see you on Thursday then?"

"I'll be there. Bye." Sheryl waited until Elise hung up, then pushed the button ending the connection. For a moment she stared at the phone, a heavy sorrow dropping down on her.

Without a word Tory gathered her in her arms. Sheryl dropped her head on her shoulder and wept.

* * *

Mark hooked his finger between his tie and his collar, stretching his neck. He disliked wearing the thing. And he disliked funerals. The music was always so dreary, so hushed.

We really should be rejoicing, he thought. Ed has gone to the place he's wanted to be for the past four months. Instead the church was hushed, the music sombre. No one spoke.

Quite a few people had come out on this cold December day, and Mark was glad for Nate's sake. Here and there he heard a sniffle, saw someone wipe away a surreptitious tear.

But Mark couldn't summon tears. He had spent enough time the past few weeks with Ed to know that he yearned to die. He had made his peace with Sheryl, and she had forgiven him fully.

Mark turned his head ever so slightly, looking for her. She was sitting behind Nate and Elise, beside a sister of Ed's Mark hadn't even known he had. Sheryl's head was bent, her hair loose, and Mark felt again the weight of longing press against his heart.

Three months had made no difference.

His only contact with her had been that intercepted phone call and the little bits of her life she wrote in her letters to Ed that he would read when he found one lying around Elise's place. As usual she gave him nothing. As usual he wondered why he still cared about her.

He shifted his weight, trying to catch a glimpse of her face, trying to make some kind of connection. They had shared so much. He knew what she had to live with, and he didn't know how to make a connection with her.

He didn't even know if she would want it.

He caught his mother's puzzled look, and he looked ahead again. He should feel guilty for thinking only of Sheryl when he should be contemplating Ed's life, but he couldn't dredge up the proper emotions.

The minister announced the final song, and as they stood,

the funeral director motioned for the pallbearers to carry the casket out of the church.

Mark shook out the leg of his pants, straightened his suit jacket, borrowed from Nate, and turned. For a brief moment his gaze locked with Sheryl's. Awareness arced between them, tangible, real, powerful.

Mark almost stumbled, then drew in a shaky breath and, looking toward the doorway at the end of the church, walked out.

Because of the cold weather, the graveside ceremony was mercifully brief. When it was over, Nate, Elise and the children lingered a moment. Sheryl stood to one side, as if unsure of her place. Her lips were pressed together as she reached out and plucked a flower from the top of the casket. Holding it close to her she turned.

Mark watched her go. He wasn't going to run after her again. He wasn't going to go where he wasn't wanted.

Then she paused a moment at the headstone beside Ed's grave. It belonged to her mother, Blythe.

She stared at the inscription, her hand pressed to her mouth, tears coursing down her face. Mark remembered her crying in his arms, remembered her pain, and he couldn't stop himself.

A few steps was all it took and he was beside her, silent, waiting.

She glanced furtively at him, reaching into her pocket, and when she pulled out an old handkerchief of his, Mark felt as if he'd been hit.

He swallowed and, without stopping to think about his actions, took it from her, tipped her chin up and gently wiped the tears from her face.

He tried to be clinical about it, but his hands were shaking, and his insides were churning. When her soft green eyes, bright with tears connected with his, his restraint fell away. Slowly he drew her toward him. Fear flickered in her eyes, and she pressed her hands against him.

"Please don't, Mark."

Mark dropped his hands, heat rising in his face. The same words she had whispered over the phone just a couple of weeks ago. What was he? Some kind of ogre? What could he possibly have done to her that she felt she had to beg him to leave her alone.

He wanted to shake her, to give her a reason to be afraid of him. He wanted…to kiss her.

"Are you coming, Sheryl?" Nate had come up beside them. "We're going to have lunch at the house."

Sheryl nodded, avoiding Mark's eyes, her relief obvious.

Mark turned, staring at his brother-in-law, feeling betrayed. Three months ago he had rescued Sheryl from the uncomfortable situation of being with Nate and now, it seemed, the roles were reversed.

"Are you coming, Mark?" Nate asked.

He tried to affect a light tone, glancing back at Sheryl. "For a little while." He paused a moment, hoping for what, he didn't know. Some kind of sign, some kind of recognition.

When she looked down, he turned and stalked off, berating himself for being such a sucker.

All the way to Nate's place he wondered why he was so stuck on her.

Why he couldn't get her out of his mind. He had defended her to Nate, to Ed. Had argued for fair treatment for her. And now he had to live with the consequences.

The house was full. The scent of coffee permeated every corner, the subdued chatter of people drifted about. Mark and Nate set out chairs, talked to people. Elise sat in one corner beside Sheryl, while other ladies of the church served the coffee.

Mark made small talk, consoled some of the older folk, talked ranching with a few men, kept the kids from eating all the food and tried not to look at his watch. Ed hadn't planned his own death, but the funeral couldn't have come at a worse time. The Stockgrowers Convention in Calgary had been set up months ago. He had tried to find someone else to take his place as director, but no one could. The longest he could stay was another two hours.

One hundred and twenty minutes to find a chance to talk to Sheryl.

He picked up a few dirty coffee cups and with a quick glance to make sure Sheryl still sat in the corner, he walked into the kitchen to wash the cups.

Elise had a sinkfull of water running, and when he came close, she handed him a tea towel.

"You shouldn't be doing this, sis," he said, stroking her hair.

"I need to keep busy," she replied with a faint smile. "I'm sure it will all hit me once everyone is gone, but for now I feel better pretending this is just another family get-together." She dropped a cup on the drainboard and glanced sidelong at Mark.

"Have you had a chance to talk to Sheryl?" she asked. "You don't have a lot of time before you have to leave."

He shook his head, picking up the cup and inspecting the soap suds that ran down the sides. "One hundred and eighteen minutes, to be precise." He wiped the bubbles with an angry swipe. "What am I going to say?"

"How about, 'I love you, I'm crazy about you,'" Elise replied softly.

"And how would that look with what Nate has to tell her?"

"Hey it was your idea to talk to Ed about his will."

"I know," he replied irritably. "I just didn't think it would jeopardize my own position with her. Besides she's scared of me."

"What do you mean by that?" Elise frowned at him.

The door to the porch opened and Lainie Jesperson came in, carrying a bundle of blankets, her husband right behind ner, carrying a diaper bag and car seat. The baby, Mark guessed, putting down his towel to go and help her, ignoring Elise's question.

He took the bundle from Lainie as she took her coat off and dropped it on the pile on the table. Mark shifted the bundle around and the blankets slipped open. Tiny unfocused eyes stared up at him. Soft black hair stuck up from a head no larger than the palm of his hand. It wriggled, its mouth opening up in a miniature yawn.

He couldn't help the smile that curved his mouth.

"I didn't know if I should bring her along," whispered Lainie. "But I wanted to come, to see Sheryl." She turned to her husband. "Anthony can you take Deidre from Mark?"

"That's okay," said Mark to Lainie's husband. "I don't mind holding her for a while." Anthony shrugged, took a cup of coffee that Elise had poured for him. After offering her his condolences he went in search of Nate.

The baby lay lightly in the crook of his arm, and Mark couldn't keep his eyes away. Kids always brought out his mushy side, babies even more so.

"I'll finish up in here, Mark. Can you take these around?" Elise pushed a plate of squares across the counter at him. He settled the baby more securely, picked the plate and carried on with his duties.

He worked his way around the living room, avoiding the corner where Lainie now sat beside Sheryl.

Mark watched as Lainie stroked Sheryl's shoulders. She looked up at him as the baby squirmed in his arms and let out a gentle cry.

Their gazes locked, and all else fell away. Gray eyes held green for what seemed like forever till the baby in Mark's arms cried again. Sheryl broke the connection, looked at the bundle Mark held, her expression wistful.

"Here, I'll take her from you." Anthony came up beside him. Mark awkwardly shifted the red-faced baby into An-

thony's arms, desperately afraid that he would drop it. But
she settled against her father, and Mark couldn't resist
touching the downy hair nestled against Anthony's shirt.

"She's beautiful," he said softly, a smile curving his
mouth. He touched the creamy soft skin of her cheek, then
turned.

Sheryl's mouth curved up in a smile directed to him. Just
then Crystal tugged on Sheryl's arm. Sheryl reached down
and hugged her. Benjamin toddled up to both of them,
yanking on Sheryl's shirt. Sheryl grimaced and swung Benjamin up in her arms.

"You don't smell good, little man," Mark heard her say
with a lilt in her voice. She dropped him on her hip, caught
Crystal's hand in hers and worked her way through the
crowd up the stairs.

Mark paused, tempted to follow up on the hesitant smile
Sheryl had directed at him. It was the first acknowledgment
she had made of his presence.

"Mark," an older lady stood beside him, tugging on his
shirt. "My car won't start. I left the lights on."

Mark glanced at Sheryl's retreating back.

"Probably just needs a boost, Mrs. Newkiski," he said.
"Just let me get my jacket and I'll be right out."

He still had time to catch Sheryl before he had to leave,
he reassured himself.

Sheryl pressed Benjamin to her as she made her way up
the stairs, and, undaunted by the smell of his dirty diaper,
kissed him soundly on one sticky cheek.

"How can you kiss him, Auntie Sheryl, he smells so
bad," Crystal complained, holding her nose primly with her
thumb and finger.

"It's not bad, not for him." Sheryl gave him another
squeeze at the top of the stairs and turned into his bedroom.
She paused a moment in the doorway, looking at the
changes made since she had slept here.

A wallpaper border decorated with rabbits ran around the room, halfway up. Elise had painted the room a pale green below the border and white above. Marla's bed had a pale pink quilt with rabbit appliqués and a green-and-white striped bedskirt. Benjamin's crib quilt matched Marla's except his was green. A rocking chair sat in one corner of the room. It looked cozy and inviting.

"What did this room look like when you slept in it?" Crystal asked, standing beside Sheryl as she looked it over.

"It was just plain white," Sheryl replied, walking to the far wall and plopping Benjamin on his change table. "I didn't spend a lot of time here. Mostly I was in the cabin."

Crystal handed her a clean diaper. "Are you sad about Grandpa?" she asked, leaning on the change table, her clear blue eyes gazing up at Sheryl.

"In a way," Sheryl replied, unsnapping Benjamin's pants, smiling at the difference between him and Lainie's baby. "I think he's happier now."

Crystal sighed, wiping away a stray tear with her thumb. "I wish I could be."

Sheryl paused, then bent over to press a kiss on Crystal's head. "You'll miss him a lot."

"Do you miss him?"

Sheryl smiled down at Crystal, her sweet face blurred by unexpected tears. "Yes," she said softly. "Yes I miss him."

A light tap on the door made them both jump. Nate stood, almost hesitantly, framed by the doorway. "Crystal, do you mind to go find Mommy. I would like to talk to Auntie Sheryl for a minute."

Crystal shrugged, then left. Nate watched her go, his expression melancholy. He closed the door quietly behind him, then walked over to his son.

Sheryl sensed a change in him. Anger and antagonism didn't surround him, as it had when she'd left. Since she'd

come back, his overtures to her were of a tentative nature
as if unsure of how to proceed.

In his own gruff way he had been solicitous and caring
Sheryl had begun to see the side of Nate that Elise mus
have become attracted to.

"How are you feeling, Nate?" she asked, pinning u]
Benjamin's clean diaper. She didn't look at him as sh
pulled up the plastic pants and snapped his coveralls again

"I'm okay." Nate bent over and kissed his son, lettin;
Sheryl pick him up. He looked up at her, and Sheryl wa
surprised at his expression. Pain had pulled his feature
down, sadness tinged the deep blue of his eyes. "Hov
about you?"

"It's hard. I'm just glad I could see him before—'
Sheryl stopped, remembering. "I'm glad we could mak
some kind of amends before he died."

Nate blew out his breath in a sigh, tapping his finger
nervously against his leg. "Sheryl, I really need to talk t
you. I know now isn't exactly the right time…" he let th
sentence hang as if giving her an out.

Sheryl sat down on the rocking chair behind her, holdin;
her nephew on her lap. Benjamin nuzzled into her, hi
thumb in his mouth. "It doesn't matter, Nate." She trie
not to feel afraid, wondering what seemed to weigh s
heavily on his mind that he'd followed her up here whil
his community and family congregated below. Outside :
car started. People were beginning to leave. He should b
saying goodbye. Instead he'd come up here.

Nate lowered himself to Marla's bed, across from Sheryl
He plunged his hands through his hair, holding his head :
moment, looking down at the floor.

"I don't know where to start, what to say." He rubbe(
his face, then shrugged. "I've been thinking about you s(
much since you left. After what you showed me." He swal
lowed, loosening his tie. "I feel terrible about this, but,'
he looked up at her, his eyes seeming to plead for under

standing. "About a month ago I went to your cabin. I knew you had a box of papers in it and—" he hesitated "—I read your diaries. I needed to know more about you." He pushed himself off the bed, walking over to the window, looking out of it, his voice softening. "I found out a lot about you, your mother. I got to see me and Dad through the eyes of a little scared girl who was trying to become part of a family that didn't know what to do with a little girl. Some of what you thought was happening was wrong, but I couldn't discredit your reaction. My own feelings weren't exactly without prejudice." He turned to her. "I guess I'm trying to say that Dad and I tried. We made mistakes and we pushed you too hard."

"Please, Nate," Sheryl whispered, overcome with emotion.

"No, I really need to tell you." He rubbed the back of his neck, looking down. "I wish I could go back. I wish I could take what I've learned from my wife, my children, and use it. I know better how a family works." He sighed and walked over to Sheryl, hunkering down beside her. He toyed with Benjamin's hand. Sheryl felt a wave of sorrow and regret, remembering happier times with Nate, allowing those recollections to brush away the last memory she had of him, sitting in the bus depot, telling her about the letter he sent back.

"Once I thought I loved you. I read in your books how that looked to you…"

"Nate," she whispered, "I'm sorry."

"Don't be sorry about the truth," he said bitterly.

He took her hand, and Sheryl had to stop herself from pulling back, like she always did.

Nate must have felt her reaction, because his lips twisted. "When you showed me your scars, Sheryl…" He paused, biting his lip. "It hurt me to see that. I had disliked—" he laughed bitterly at that "—no, almost hated you for so long. I heard that love and hate are two sides of the same coin, and when you showed me what Jason had done to you, it was like the coin flipped again,'' He stroked her hand lightly then dropped it. ''I'm so sorry, Sheryl.'' His voice broke and he turned away.

Sheryl sat, stunned. She didn't know what words to use, what to say. The last time she had seen Nate his animosity was like a shield. Some sense of change had come through in Ed's letters, but this? This was a complete reversal of everything she had dreaded coming back to face.

''I'm asking you to forgive me, like you forgave Dad,'' he continued. ''I don't deserve it...''

''Please don't say that, Nate.'' Sheryl hugged her now-sleeping nephew closer. ''None of us *deserve* the forgiveness we've been given, either by people or by God. I have to forgive you.''

Her stepbrother nodded. ''Thanks,'' he whispered. ''I wish I could take away everything that happened to you, I wish I could take it on myself...''

''Nate,'' Sheryl said, stopping him. ''No one forced me to leave with Jason. No one pushed me out of the house. I left on my own.''

Nate nodded, turning to her. ''We could have made it easier for you.'' He smiled wanly. ''I'd like to say we tried, but after reading your books, I can see that we failed, badly.'' He hesitated, as if he had more to say. ''Mark read your books, too. In fact, he was the one who told me I should look them over.''

Sheryl felt her heart skip at that, trying to picture Mark delving into her past. Why would he do that if he wasn't interested in her?

Nate pursed his lips, staring down at his shoes, unable to meet her eyes. ''I don't know if I should be the one telling you this, but he was heartbroken after you left. He would spend hours in your cabin, sitting on the bed, reading your papers.''

Sheryl closed her eyes, imagining his large form on her bed, delving into her past, creating yet another intimacy.

Nate was quiet a moment, as if giving her time to understand what he had said.

"There's more I need to tell you." He slipped his hands in his pockets, leaning back against the wall behind him. "I don't know if you're going to stick around for the reading of the will, but you'll find out one way or the other. Dad willed half of his share of the ranch to you."

Chapter Fifteen

"What?" Sheryl stared at Nate, trying to absorb what he said.

"I have to confess, it wasn't my idea."

"How did that happen?"

Nate sighed, lifting one shoulder up. "After you left, Mark came down from the mountains. He went straight to Dad and talked to him about you and the treatment you've received."

Sheryl frowned, trying to understand. "Why would he do that?"

Nate bit his lip, glancing over his shoulder as if making sure they were alone. "He wanted to make sure that you got what you deserved. But more than that, he did it because he loves you."

"I don't understand." Sheryl chose to ignore the last part of what Nate had said. It seemed too wonderful. "What am I supposed to do with a share in the ranch?"

"Well you would either get some income a month from us, or Mark was talking about giving you a lump sum."

Sheryl got up, agitated, afraid to probe too deeply the implications of what Mark had done. If she took a lump-

m payment she could get her degree in three years instead
six, the way she was doing it now.

But was that what she wanted? Tory's words came back
her. "You pretend you want to get a career when I know
ou'd just as soon be living at home and having babies."
heryl shook her head, holding the now-sleeping Benjamin
oser. But babies required a husband and a husband re-
uired...everything.

"If I wanted a lump-sum payment," she asked, her voice
uffled as she laid her head against Benjamin. "What
ould that mean for the ranch? I thought you guys were
rapped."

Nate sighed behind her. "We are. I would be lying if I
aid different."

"So..."

"Mark was going to go back to work for a few years, at
east until the river-bottom land was paid off."

Sheryl kissed Benjamin's warm head, staring off into the
iddle distance, trying to imagine Mark living in the city.
ictures of him flashed through her mind—Mark on the
ack of a horse, driving his pickup truck too fast, balancing
n a stuker, pitching bales. She pulled herself to the present,
lancing at Nate. "He doesn't want to, does he?"

Nate walked slowly around to the other side of the crib,
is eyes on his son. "No, he doesn't. But he's willing to
o it for you, because he loves you."

Sacrifice. Mark would sacrifice what he loved for her.

"Why didn't he call?" Sheryl asked, confused. "If he
oves me like you say he did, like he says he does, why
id he never call me?" She laid Benjamin carefully in his
rib, arranging the quilt around him, her heart beginning an
rratic rhythm.

"He was afraid to." Nate pulled the quilt around his
on's face, stroking his cheek. He sighed and looked up at
heryl. "I've had to work with him the past three months.
le's been miserable, torn between wanting to chase you

down and afraid that once you found out about the wi
you'd mistrust his motives. He knows you don't have
high trust level of our sex." Nate reached over and touche
Sheryl's hand. "Mark's usually very even tempered b
you've got him tied up in knots. Whenever we'd talk abo
Jason, he'd get furious. I told him about what Jason ha
done to you." Nate shook his head. "He grabbed me an
asked me why we let you go. I thought he was going
deck me. I've never seen him like this. He knows what yo
went through with Jason. He thinks you're afraid of him.

Sheryl clung to the top rail of the crib, the wood pressin
into her hands, the implications of what Nate was tellin
her beginning to fall into place. "But I'm not. Not the wa
he thinks…" She looked up at Nate. "What should I do?

He straightened, tapping the crib lightly with his finger
"Like I said before, Mark loves you. I don't deserve yo
forgiveness, but I'm thankful for it. And as for the rest, I'
leaving it in your hands, Sheryl. I don't think you've ha
a lot of choices in the past." He bent over, gave his son
kiss, nodded to Sheryl and left the room.

Sheryl hugged herself, restless. She walked to the wi
dow, staring out at the snow-covered yard, now full of v
hicles. She easily found Mark's silver pickup and she re
membered sitting in it, sharing her life while he listened.

He loved her. She knew that now. His words, his action
all made that very clear to her. So what should she do abo
it? Could she accept what he was giving her?

Sheryl touched the cold window, tracing her initials o
it, just as she used to when she was younger. Sighin
lightly, she let herself drift back, remembering her life wit
Ed and Nate, trying to fit everything in with what happene

Somehow everything seemed to come back to Mar
Mark and Elise. They had influenced this family in so man
ways, had shown them God's love in a different way. Mar
had shown her a different kind of man, a different kind c
love.

A tap sounded at the door. Sheryl jumped and without turning around, knew it was Mark. With an air of resignation, she turned to face him. He wore a jacket and hat as if dressed to go outside. His cheeks were red, and as he walked toward her, Sheryl could smell the clean outdoors on him. His eyes met hers as he came closer, and Sheryl felt her breath leave her in anticipation. Her heart sped up, her limbs felt weak, and when he stopped in front of her she had to clench her fist to keep herself from reaching out to him.

His unselfish act, which clearly showed her his love, also hindered her. How would he read her reaction to it?

"Sheryl…" His voice faltered, and he cleared his throat. "Sheryl, I've come to say goodbye."

"No." The word flew out of her, protesting, afraid. "No, don't say that."

Slowly he lifted his hand and caressed the fine line of her jaw with his knuckles. Sheryl's eyes drifted shut as she swayed toward him, her hand grasping his hard wrist, keeping his fingers on her face. She turned her mouth toward his cold hand, touching her warm lips to his palm. She couldn't stop herself, couldn't keep herself from connecting to him.

With a sigh as light as a snowflake, he carefully drew her against him, his other hand sliding along her jawline to her neck, his fingers tangling in her hair.

"I'm leaving for Calgary." His deep voice was a soft rumble beneath her hands. "I'll be back in a week." He said nothing more, as if waiting for her response.

She tilted her head, reaching up to cup his jaw, feeling its smoothness. "What do you want me to do?" she whispered, losing herself in the soft gray of his eyes. "I don't know what to do."

Mark looked at her, his expression sorrowful. Then he bent his head and found her lips with his own. Sheryl slid one hand around his neck, the other around his back, cling-

ing to him as their mouths met, explored, tasted. He held
her tighter, his fingers caressing her head, holding it, while
his lips moved from hers, lingering on her cheek, touching
her eyes then returning to her mouth.

She felt a hunger growing, even while his caresses created an emptiness within her, a need for more. She inhaled
the scent of him, soap and cold air, reveled in the strength
of his arms, the comfort and security she knew she would
find there.

Mark straightened, his hand still entangled in her hair,
his arm still around her.

"So, Sheryl," he lifted one corner of his mouth in a
careful smile. "Now what?"

"I don't know," she replied her voice subdued.

"Neither do I." He let his hand drop from her back. But
his other slipped through her hair then lifted it to his mouth,
brushing it softly. "I love you, I care for you, I want to
marry you." He let her hair drop then stepped back. "But
I can't make you feel the same."

Sheryl was surprised she could still stand. To hear him
open himself up to her, to make himself so weak in front
of her, showed her more clearly than anything, his strength.
She couldn't speak, didn't trust herself to say anything.

A rustling in the crib made them both turn. Benjamin
stood at the rail, rubbing his eyes, his mouth pulled down
in a pout.

Mark was the closest and he picked him up, swinging
him into his arms. He turned to face Sheryl, Benjamin sitting easily in his arms.

He would make a wonderful father, she thought. And an
even more wonderful husband.

"I have to leave, Sheryl. I've got a long drive ahead of
me." He kissed Benjamin on his forehead and handed him
to Sheryl, bending over to pick up the briefcase she didn't
even know he had brought into the room. He turned to

leave, hesitated and looked back at her. "I won't forget you, and I pray you find what you've been looking for."

He left, closing the door quietly behind him, sending an ache spinning deep within her.

Holding Benjamin close, she walked to the window.

He loved her. He loved her so much he was willing to give up his own work on the ranch, work that he loved, to ensure that she would have enough money to make her independent.

She laid her hot forehead against the window, listening to the sound of the snow ticking against it. The wind, drifting down through the valley, was picking up. It was going to storm.

She felt as tossed about as the small flakes. Since her father died she had been seeking, trying to find home, trying to find a place she belonged.

And now Mark had offered her a chance to do something on her own, with no outside influences. He had just given her power over him, she realized. By telling Ed to change his will, he had sabotaged his own life. If she decided she wanted her share of the will at once, he would have to go back to working in the city and away from the ranch she knew he loved. It would be her gain, but the sacrifice would be his.

She watched his tall figure, huddled in a bulky jacket, as he strode between the parked cars to his truck. As he opened the door he paused, looking up.

"Oh, Mark," she breathed, her heart winging toward him, her hand reaching out, stopping at the cold window.

He flipped her a wave as he stepped into his truck. He closed the door. A cloud of exhaust swirled around it, and in one motion he spun the truck in a turn and drove away.

Sheryl felt as if he had pulled part of her with him.

You belong with him, you love him. You need him more than he needs you. Still holding Benjamin, she ran out the door, down the stairs, past a group of startled people and out the front door.

But all she saw of his truck was a swirl of snow that disappeared over the hill and was gone. Weak with reaction, she hugged Benjamin closer and leaned against the verandah post, tears slipping unheeded down her cheeks. She had just discovered so much. She had just been shown unselfish, giving love.

The door opened behind her, and Elise came up, slipping an arm over her shoulders.

"I should have told him," she whispered. "I couldn't talk, I couldn't think." She turned to Elise. "What should I do now?"

"He loves you, Sheryl, that's all I can tell you."

"He gave up his own happiness for me," Sheryl said, looking up. She had been so afraid to make herself vulnerable, and Mark did it so easily.

"Love is not selfish." The quote from the Bible wove through her confusion, melding her thoughts, weaving them into a coherence. She knew she loved him. Loved him with a depth that frightened her.

"When is Mark supposed to come back?" she asked, shivering as another gust of wind blew across the verandah.

"A week from now."

Sheryl bit her lip, thinking, planning. She knew what she had to do.

"I'm sorry, Dan. I can't give you any more notice than this." Sheryl clasped her hands in front of her, keeping her eyes on the desk that sat between her and her boss.

Dan blew out his breath in a sigh, rubbing the bridge of his nose. "I guess there's not much I can do about it, is there?"

Sheryl shook her head slowly.

"Your mind is made up?" Dan stared over his hand at her.

She nodded. "Yes. I enjoyed working with you, but there's something I have to do that's more important."

"Are you going to finish your schooling?"

"No." Sheryl hesitated, then with a smile said, "I'm going to get married, live on a ranch and have babies." The words sounded so confident, and Sheryl didn't even want to examine her own doubts. She clung to what Mark had told her, and even more, what Mark had done. All for love of her.

"That's a waste," Dan snorted, getting up. "You have a lot going for you."

A discreet knock on the door intruded into what was becoming a hostile atmosphere. Jordan Calder opened it and walked in.

"Here's that brief you wanted on the Gerhard trial." She winked at Sheryl and laid it carefully on Dan's desk.

"Calder, I want you to help me out here." Dan gestured toward Sheryl as if she was some exhibit that he didn't know what to do with. "This girl here is going to quit this job, quit school and move out to some isolated part of British Columbia and...and—" he waved his hand as if what he was about to say was too preposterous to even voice "—get married."

Jordan pursed her lips, tilted her head to one side as if weighing evidence. "Good idea," she replied succinctly.

"What?" roared Dan. "Are you out of your mind? You of all people?"

"No temporary insanity here, Dan." Jordan smiled. "I think Sheryl made the right choice. No need for you to act like a jealous suitor." Dan glared at Jordan, who merely held her ground. "I think marriage is a much-maligned institution," she continued.

"You should know, you've handled enough of my divorce cases," he growled.

Jordan ignored him and turned to Sheryl with a grin. "So when's the big day?"

"I don't know. I have to ask him yet." Sheryl grinned, feeling suddenly free and confident.

"You're a real woman of the nineties, aren't you," Jordan said with a laugh, reaching over to give her a hug. "I wish you a lot of happiness. Call me and let me know when I can start shopping for pasta makers."

"How about diapers," grumped Dan from the corner of the office.

"That comes later, Dan." Jordan clucked disapprovingly at him, then turned back to Sheryl. "I'll take you out for supper tonight, and you can tell me the details of the entire romance."

"I'll do that." Sheryl smiled as Jordan gave her a thumbs-up.

The office was quiet a moment. Sheryl smoothed out a nonexistent wrinkle from her wool skirt, waiting for Dan's next sardonic comment. Instead he only sighed and walked around the desk, parking himself across from her, his arms clasped over his chest.

"You're sure about this?" he asked in his most stern lawyer voice.

Sheryl felt a momentary flare of panic. Then she remembered the notation on the copy of the will she had received. It was a verse from the Bible. The same verse she had read in her Bible on the way back from Sweet Creek: "When I am weak then I am strong."

"Yes, I'm sure," she replied quietly.

"Well then, I can only add my congratulations to Jordan's. I'll miss you, in more ways than one." Dan shook his head. "Hope your future husband likes babies."

Sheryl laughed. Then, surprising even herself, she reached over and gave Dan a quick hug. "Thanks for everything, boss."

In an elegant room of the Palliser Hotel in Calgary, Mark Andrews threw his briefcase on the bed and pulled the cupboard door open. With a complete disregard for the ironing Elise had done on his suit pants and shirts, he threw them on the bed, followed by his brand-new cowboy boots, bought especially for this conference.

By rights he was supposed to be sitting in on a banquet with a keynote speaker Dr. Something-or-other speaking on the potential of trade with Zambootyland, or some such place. He had forgotten. He stuffed the clothes in his suitcase, threw papers in his briefcase and snapped them both shut with a disdainful "click."

Come to think of it he had forgotten much of what he was supposed to be reporting back to his zone of the Stockgrowers' Association.

Three minutes ago he had called Elise to see how she and Nate were doing. Two minutes ago Elise had told him what Sheryl had done about the will. One minute ago he had hung up on her.

And for sixty seconds he had wondered if he was brave enough to risk running to Edmonton to find out for himself.

What if Sheryl had signed over her rights to him for Nate's sake? What if she felt she didn't deserve it, plain and simple.

What if she didn't want him?

But Elise's words rang in his mind, pushing him off the bed. "She loves you, big brother. She told me, then she laughed and said it again. I've never heard her so happy."

He glanced once more around the restrained elegance of the room, making sure he had everything, and left.

A quick punch on the elevator button, and Thank you, Lord, the doors glided open. He caught a glimpse of himself in the mirror on the side of the car on the slow descent. His hair hung in his eyes, and in the back it was tucked in the collar of his denim shirt. He quickly finger combed it into some semblance of order and pulled his shirt straight, tucking it better into his jeans. He could stop halfway to Edmonton to get prettied up.

He glanced at his watch. Five-thirty. It would take him three and a half hours to get to Edmonton, three if he could avoid any Mounties along the way. He would phone Sheryl's apartment when he stopped for gas.

The elevator stopped. Mark took a deep breath and stepped out. Leaving his suitcases parked by the elevator, he dug into his pocket for his room key and strode over to the desk, slapping it on the marble top with a clunk.

"I'm checking out," he said to the smiling clerk. "There'll be a few long-distance calls on my bill, as well." He reached behind him for his wallet and pulled out his charge card.

"Name?" Another hundred-watt smile.

"Mark Andrews."

The girl nodded, then leaned back as if looking for someone. "A lady has been asking for you," she said to Mark. "She's waiting by the stairs to the mezzanine."

Mark frowned as he dropped his card on the desk. He didn't know anyone in Calgary. He didn't feel like talking to anyone he didn't know. He was in a hurry.

"Thanks," he said, resisting the urge to drum his fingers on the marble top of the desk. He tapped his toes, shifted his weight and stifled a sigh.

"I'm sorry this is taking so long, Mr. Andrews. Are you in a hurry?"

"Yes, and I'm sorry to be so impatient."

"Well, I don't blame you. She's very beautiful." The clerk flashed him a discreet smile and ripped the receipt out of the computer. "Just sign here and you'll be on your way."

Mark pulled a pen out of his pocket, scrawled his signature on the bottom and waited as she ripped his portion off and slipped it into the wine red envelope with the hotel's name scripted in gold on the front. All very elegant and tasteful, right down to taking your money, thought Mark, slipping the envelope into his pocket.

"She's right around the corner, Mr. Andrews." Another coy smile. "And I hope you have a nice weekend."

Mark heaved a sigh, shoved his wallet in his back pocket and walked around the corner to get this visit with this mysterious woman out of his way. He was a man with a mission.

He paused, scanning the length of the room. Only one person sat on a couch near the steps. Her blond head gave him a start, but when its owner raised her head, he frowned and took a step closer. Her hair was feathered in layers that framed her face and drifted to the shoulders of her bronze and gold sweater. She stood slowly, her hand on her chest, and when their eyes met, Mark's heart stopped, turned slowly over, then began to race.

It was Sheryl.

For a long moment neither said anything as they merely stared at each other, each fearful, each excited, each hurting.

Mark made the first move, his empty arms aching to hold her, his hands itching to touch her soft hair.

"Sheryl," was all he said as he bent over her, wrapping one arm around her slender waist, his other hand tangling in the soft silk of her hair, clutching her head.

"Oh, Sheryl, babe," he whispered brokenly, hardly daring to believe he had her in his arms so soon.

Mark buried his face in her hair, his warm breath flowing over her neck. Her arms clung to him, her face pressed against his chest as she murmured his name over and over again.

Reality pierced the haven they had created, and he straightened, ignoring the surprised looks of the other guests and hotel staff. His eyes traveled hungrily over her face, his fingers tracing her beloved features. She was here. She was real.

"You cut your hair," he whispered stupidly, brushing a wisp from her face.

"And you didn't," she replied, her voice breaking as she reached up to touch his hair, his cheek, his chin. "I was scared I would miss you."

"Well, I was on my way to Edmonton." He looked down at her, a fullness and richness welling up in him. Thank you, Lord, he prayed. This is too much to take in. "I called Elise. She told me you signed away your share of the ranch." He looked up, suddenly aware of an audience. With a wry grin he tucked a strand of hair behind her ear. "My bags are waiting by the elevator. Let's go to my truck. We need to talk."

Sheryl bent over to pick up her purse, but when she straightened, her cheeks were flushed, her eyes bright.

"Oh, sweetheart," he murmured, drawing her against him. "Please don't cry. You'll break my heart."

"Sorry." She sniffed, swiping a palm across her eyes. "It's been a long five days."

He gave her a reassuring hug and led her across the lobby. His bags lay exactly where he'd left them. An elevator waited, its doors open, and as they entered, Mark pushed the Down button and they slid shut.

Mark turned to Sheryl, his eyes drifted lovingly over her face, his mouth curved up in a wry grin. Not satisfied with merely looking, he reached out and pulled her toward him, lowering his head. She lifted hers, meeting him halfway. Their lips met, a hungry tasting, a sealing of what they both had been seeking.

When the elevator stopped, Mark pulled away, regret tingeing his smile. "This is our stop," he whispered.

"Okay," she whispered back, smiling carefully.

He laughed and, picking up his cases, strode down the carpeted hallway to the car park at the end.

His booted feet echoed in the cement parkade as he led her to the truck. Dropping his suitcase, he stretched up and fished his keys out of his front pants pocket. Mark opened the passenger door and gave her a hand in. He hung on the door, watching her buckle up, feeling like it was his right, his privilege.

He slammed the door, the noise echoing hollowly. Sheryl sat back, inhaling the familiar smell of his truck. He unlocked the door and in one easy step, got in. She drank in the familiar sight of him adjusting the mirror, settling in, shrugging forward to turn the key in the ignition. Then he sat up, draped his arm casually across the back of the seat as he looked almost disinterestedly over his shoulder and backed the truck up.

He flashed her a grin, pushed the truck into gear and they left the parkade with a roar. Soon downtown was behind them, then the suburbs and finally they were on the highway heading out of the city, the gleaming white fields stretching like a blanket toward the mountains.

The ride was made in silence, neither quite knowing what to say, how to say it.

After half an hour Mark slowed the truck and pulled over. He stretched his hands in front of him, almost popping the seams of his jacket. He laid his head against the back window, his eyes drifting shut. Sheryl half turned, watching him, indulging in the luxury of just looking. He looked vulnerable with his eyes closed, the long dark lashes lying like two small shadows. Lines etched around his finely shaped mouth, stubble shaded the sweep of his jaw. His hair hung in disarray over his coat collar. He needed it cut, she thought, reaching out to brush a lock out of his eyes. He scared her, made her feel unsettled and vulnerable. She loved him.

Mark turned his head to her and caught her hand, curling his fingers around hers, his thumb lightly stroking the side of her hand. Then her breath caught in her throat as he gently pressed it to his rough cheek. He turned his head ever so slightly, and warm lips grazed soft, cool skin.

"Sheryl," he whispered, his eyes still closed.

Trembling, her fingers spread out, touching his soft lips,

exploring the shape of them, moving over his jaw, fluttering up to his sculpted cheekbones, tracing his eyelashes.

He opened his eyes, catching her hands. "Tell me why you signed over your share of the ranch to me?"

"Nothing like getting to the point, is there?" She laughed, feeling as if they had come to an epiphany. She took his hand and gently traced the calluses on it. Even after four days of city life, grit still lined the cracks in his knuckles, the lines in the palm of his hand. The hand of a worker, a rancher. "I did it because I couldn't see you working in the city, couldn't see you giving up what you love just for me."

"And," he coaxed.

Sheryl looked up into his soft gray eyes. "I did it because I love you."

Mark relaxed, as if he had been holding his breath.

"I didn't think this could happen," he whispered, his expression bemused. "I thought you were afraid of me."

Sheryl smiled tremulously. "I was."

Mark shook his head, his eyes following his fingers as they drifted over her face, tangled in her hair. "I'm sorry," he whispered, leaning forward to kiss her forehead. "I'll never hurt you. You have to believe me."

"No—" she straightened, catching his hand, holding it close to her cheek "—you don't know what I mean. I was scared of how much you mean to me. I was afraid you would break my heart."

"I wouldn't do that, either. I love you too much."

Sheryl pressed her lips against his hand and brought it down to her lap. "You know, I thought I didn't know how to love, I thought I wouldn't be able to forgive." She ran her finger across his palm. "I learned a lot about letting go and looking in the right places, the past few months. Once I forgave Ed, many things became easier." She looked up at him. "You gave me so much, you helped me deal with something that was eating me from the inside out," she said softly, her voice breaking. "I thought I was going to crack. I think God knew I needed to be around family, so He sent me to Sweet Creek. I've discovered how much love God has to give us, and once I let Him love me, it became easier to love others."

"I'm so glad, Sheryl," he squeezed her hand tightly. Then he sat up, brushing her hair from her face. "So is this where I can ask you to marry me?"

"Actually, I was going to ask you."

"Just what I thought. An independent woman." He smiled at her. Then, with a rueful shake of his head, he caught her and pressed her close to him, burying his face in her hair. "I promise you, with God's strength, I will love you and cherish you as long as I live."

Sheryl squeezed her eyes shut, her hands cradling his head, reveling in his strength, the safety he gave her.

"Are you crying?" he murmured against her neck, his breath warm.

"No," she said in a choked voice, trying not to. "Well, maybe a little."

"It's okay, you know," he said, pulling his head back, wiping her tears away with his thumb. He gently kissed the others away. "Crying is as important as laughing. I hope we can do a lot together."

He stifled a yawn.

"Are you tired?" Sheryl asked.

"Didn't get a whole lot of sleep the past few nights." He angled a mischievous glance at her. "Been thinking about you."

"Do you want me to drive?"

"That sounds great." He scooted over and lifted her past him, then helped her adjust the seat. "Just keep it around the speed limit, okay?" he said with a laugh.

He watched as she put the truck in gear, checked over her shoulder and pulled into the traffic. Sheryl tried not to feel nervous with him watching her and glanced over at him.

"I think I'm going to like this," he said.

Then, to her surprise, he stretched out and laid his head on her lap, staring up at her. "I think we'll do okay," he whispered, his eyes drifting shut, his head growing heavy and warm on her lap as he relaxed.

Sheryl glanced down at his beloved face, so close to her and let a full-bodied sigh drift out of her.

She stepped on the accelerator, looking down the highway to the hills as they graduated to the Rockies. They were the mountains of her youth, and beyond them was home.

She had come full circle. She and her mother had left Alberta seeking a home and now she had found it. She had found it not by becoming strong, but by becoming weak.

She glanced down at Mark's face, relaxed now as he drifted off to sleep. A wave of pure love washed over her, and she sent a belated prayer of thanks to Heaven.

In weakness is strength, she thought. I sought strength and found weakness. I sought independence and found a home.

Home. Next to *love*, the most beautiful word in the English language.

Epilogue

~

"The glasses are in the cupboard," Sheryl chided Mark as she dropped the bag of groceries and the mail on the counter of their kitchen.

Mark shrugged as he backhanded his mouth and shoved the milk carton back in the fridge. "Old habits, my dear wife," he drawled as he walked to her side. He leaned one hip against the counter and dropped a kiss on the top of her head. "How was the trip to town?"

"They didn't have the filters you wanted. They're still on order."

Mark grimaced and leaned back, crossing his arms across his chest. "So that means the tractor won't get an oil change until next week." He dismissed the problem with a shrug. He turned to her and slipped an arm around her waist. "And what did the doctor say? Everything okay?"

Sheryl leaned against him and nodded, relishing the feel of his solid body. She rubbed her cheek against his shirt and then leaned back. "There is one small complication though." She reached up and rubbed the frown off his forehead with a forefinger slanting him a mischievous grin. "It's not serious. Yet."

He gave her a gentle shake. "Don't do this to me, Sheryl. What do you mean?"

She smiled up at him, her love for him warming her to the tips of her toes. "Two," she said succinctly, holding up two fingers.

"Two?" He stared, not comprehending and Sheryl laughed.

"Twins. Two little tiny babies," she said.

Mark blinked, looked away, then back at her, an incredulous expression on his face. "Twins," he repeated. "Two babies."

"I think we've covered that." She leaned back, her arm still clasped around his waist as she watched with joy the play of expressions on his handsome face.

Suddenly he reached down, caught her by the waist and swung her around. "Twins," he yelled. He stopped, realizing what he, in his exuberance, had done. "Oh, no. I'm sorry. Are you okay, honey?"

Sheryl just grinned. "I'm as healthy as a horse." She cupped his face in her hands and pulled him down for a kiss. "And I love you."

Mark wrapped his arms around her and held her tightly against him. "Praise the Lord," he said softly. He buried his face in her neck, rocking her carefully. "Thank you."

Sheryl laid her head on his chest, silently echoing his prayers. Her own arms held her beloved husband close, his belt buckle pressed against her still-flat stomach. Hard to believe that two lives were growing and changing within her.

Outside the trees were tinged with the soft green of new growth. Life flowed from season to season, promises were made and kept.

She closed her eyes. God was good. He had taken her through trials and had brought her safely here. To a husband. A family.

A home.

* * * * *

Dear Reader,

Family is important to me. My husband and I have been blessed with brothers and sisters who share our faith and parents who have nurtured it from the very beginning. Through our family and relationships with siblings and nieces and nephews, our faith is strengthened. We are reminded of what God needs and requires of us.

What I wanted to do with *Homecoming* is to portray the consequences of ignoring the needs of family members. Sheryl had wanted to be a part of the Kyle family, but they didn't understand where she came from. By the time her stepfather realizes what he has done, Sheryl has become a person who mistrusts and wants to be strong on her own, thinking that leaning on God or family is a sign of weakness.

Mark, with his faith in God and his own loving family, shows her that, like an arch, leaning on each other creates strength. Through Mark, Sheryl learns to forgive and to lean on family and trust in God instead of trying to be strong on her own.

By writing this story, I found I had to reach back into our own families and search for the things that frustrate and yet strengthen. I like to think our families are a small reflection of the community of Christ. None of us are perfect, but we are united by one goal. We must always be forgiving and asking for forgiveness as we stumble along with our eyes on the One who is the epitome of love and forgiveness, Jesus Christ.

Carolyne Aarsen

Welcome to *Love Inspired*™

A brand-new series of contemporary inspirational love stories.

Join men and women as they learn valuable lessons about facing the challenges of today's world and about life, love and faith.

**Look for the following May 1998
Love Inspired™ titles:**

A FAMILY TO CALL HER OWN
by Irene Hannon

LOGAN'S CHILD
by Lenora Worth

THERE COMES A SEASON
by Carol Steward

Available in retail outlets in April 1998.

LIFT YOUR SPIRITS AND GLADDEN YOUR HEART
with *Love Inspired!*™

Steeple
Hill™

IS98

Available in May from

Love Inspired...

LOGAN'S CHILD

by

Lenora Worth

Trixie Dunaway couldn't deny that her heart still
belonged to her true love, Logan. Or that she felt a
powerful connection to his young son, Caleb, who
reminded her of her own lost boy. But when she
learned the stunning truth about Logan's child, an
overwhelmed Trixie turned to the Lord to help her
confront an uncertain future....

**Watch for LOGAN'S CHILD in May
from Love Inspired.**

Love Inspired™